LOVE
and
HOT
CHICKEN

LOVE
and
HOT
CHICKEN

a delicious southern novel

MARY LIZA HARTONG

WM

WILLIAM MORROW

An Imprint of HarperCollins*Publishers*

LOVE AND HOT CHICKEN. Copyright © 2024 by Mary Elizabeth Hartong. All rights reserved. Printed in the United States of America. No part of this book may be used or reproduced in any manner whatsoever without written permission except in the case of brief quotations embodied in critical articles and reviews. For information, address HarperCollins Publishers, 195 Broadway, New York, NY 10007.

HarperCollins books may be purchased for educational, business, or sales promotional use. For information, please email the Special Markets Department at SPsales@harpercollins.com.

FIRST EDITION

Designed by Bonni Leon-Berman

Library of Congress Cataloging-in-Publication Data has been applied for.

ISBN 978-0-06-330479-6

23 24 25 26 27 LBC 5 4 3 2 1

To Mom for the grit and the grits
To Dad for the joy and the joyrides

LOVE
and
HOT
CHICKEN

PROLOGUE

It's December in Pennywhistle, the time of year we shake down the Boy Scouts for a decent Douglas fir and dole out tins of fudge to both our elderly and our ne'er-do-wells. Season of giving and all that. The Christmas lights never do come off our roofs—who's got the time or the ladder?—but December means we can finally turn those suckers back on again. Sometimes, if we're real lucky, we'll even get snow. For a few days the cars will remain in the driveways, the children will travel by sled, and the gossip will screech to a halt.

I may be twenty-six and far from home, but, shoot, sometimes I still wish the power would go out. Mamma and Daddy and I would make shoebox igloos in the backyard. She'd heat up a can of beans in the fireplace and Daddy and I would walk through the woods in search of kindling and unscratched lottery tickets. Catching sight of raccoon tracks, we'd go deeper and deeper into the trees. In the winter, our hair's the same color, that once-blond, now dusty hue shared by fawns and squirrels. Our glasses fog up like old friends. Our coats sag, heavy with library books. From him I learned never to dog-ear and always to return. Pausing to watch a cardinal, he'd say, "Did I ever tell you how Tennessee got its name?" and I'd pretend he hadn't, just so he could tell it again.

At this point I'd listen to Daddy recite the dictionary. Instead, I find myself driving across this long, skinny state in seventy-degree weather. The sky shows no sign of snow. The power's doing just fine. The books in Daddy's jacket will soon be overdue.

ONCE I MAKE it off the highway, Pennywhistle's mainstays emerge from the trees: the Piggly Wiggly, the church, the adult store. Peep and

Nina wave as they lock up. In fact, everybody waves. Nothing like moving away to make you feel like a celebrity. Or maybe it's just they know where I'm headed, past the friendly blow-up dolls and two-for-one loaves of Bunny Bread and toward the one store you hope never to visit, not if you can help it.

"I came as fast as I could," I explain.

White ruffled nightgowns hang on one wall. A buffet of caskets lines the other. If we wanted Halloween decorations we'd scour the Quarterflute Walmart, I remind the human goatee behind the counter. He claims the cheapest urn here at the Half-Off Pass Away Depot is fifty dollars, firm. Can you believe that? In a town where you can get a pedicure for five bucks and a smile, fifty dollars amounts to a king's ransom. Ain't even cute, either. God-awful pink thing, buffed and shined like it's something fancy, when everybody knows an urn's just a hop, skip, and a jump from an ashtray. And certainly unfit to house our dearly beloved.

"Fifty dollars?" Mamma scoffs. "Come on, honey. How 'bout twenty?"

"What do you think *firm* means?"

"Twenty-five."

"Fifty, *firm*."

"Thirty."

"Dottie, please."

"Thirty-one."

"Mamma."

She holds tight to her purse handle the way a child does with a blankie or a grown man does with a Skoal can. Poor thing. Took me almost four hours with traffic to get home from Nashville, come to find her haggling over the price of a faux marble sandbox like it's redneck *Antiques Roadshow*.

"Can't you see we's grievin'?" she says.

"Everybody who comes to the Half-Off Pass Away Depot is grieving. I can't be making exceptions just 'cause Earl fished my hand out of a garbage disposal that one time."

"He coulda left you."

"I'm sorry, Mrs. Spoon."

Mamma's lip starts to quiver faster than a hand trapped in a garbage disposal. The town's taken care of just about everything. The flowers, the music, even the obituary. All we have to do is get Daddy to the church before the Elvis impersonator arrives. What with Mamma indisposed, I guess this leg of the journey depends on me.

"Fine. Just the baggie, then."

"What?"

"The Ziploc, please."

"I'm afraid I don't understand—"

"Can we get him to go?"

MAMMA SITS QUIETLY in the front seat of my Jeep, the bag of Daddy on her lap. I remind her to put on her seat belt and think, Damn, a little snow would be more than welcome at this point. The heat's making everything feel too summery, too cheerful, like we might be on our way to a Kenny Chesney concert. Instead the Nativity scenes sweat and swell, Jesus threatens to melt altogether, and I roll down the window in defeat.

"Your hair's got long," Mamma observes.

"I guess so."

"And school's going fine?"

"Same old, same old."

"Stand by Your Man" comes on the radio. *Et tu,* Tammy Wynette?

"They ain't gonna kick you out for missing class, right? I don't want you to get in trouble."

"I worked it out with my professors."

"It's just, you know, at Easter you said you couldn't miss—"

"It's fine, Mamma."

We pull into the driveway, where a gaggle of garden gnomes smile like it's just another day. I don't suppose Cracker Barrel makes mourning gnomes. Mamma wipes her eyes.

"Just let me freshen up and we'll scoot."

The back of her hand is black. I never realized Mamma wore mascara until just now, when, without the ink, her little red eyelashes poke out like crooked birthday candles from her sparkly blue lids. The sight of it catches me off guard. I'm used to the version of Mamma that chops wood for the winter and harangues the cable company until they start looking for Jesus in the fine print. When she returns from the bathroom, her lashes are black again.

"You ready?" I ask.

"No," she admits, "but I heard Peewee Dupree's bringing a fifteen-layer dip. So at least there's that."

"I thought it was seven layers?"

"Apparently the other eight were about to expire."

Driving to the church, we talk only of finger foods. Delilah Fisher-Trapper's pimento-cheese bites, Trumpet Williams's pot stickers. Sometimes it's easier to discuss the pig in the blanket than the elephant in the room.

The Ziploc shrugs and sags in Mamma's arms as we walk inside. Across the street, sniffing for snow, a raccoon makes his way into the forest.

THE EULOGIES RUN long. Damn near everybody in Critter County has waxed poetic about Daddy's bravery, his affinity for pork rinds, and the weird mole on the back of his neck, but there are still a few toothless stragglers who want their turn at the podium. Pageant of rascals, they talk until well after midnight.

Mamma and I are fast asleep when Mrs. Heller, the mildewing librarian, jostles us awake with *An Illustrated History of the Volunteer State*.

"I thought y'all oughta have this," she offers.

The blue of her glasses picks up the blue of her hair. Pink lipstick cracks along her lips. And is that a brooch or a belt buckle pinned to her sweater? Despite being somewhere north of ninety, Mrs. Heller still does puppet shows every Wednesday with the local kindergarteners, especially the rowdy ones who are determined not to learn to read. She ladles the book into my hands.

"Earl used to check this out every Friday afternoon. Then, like clock-work, he'd return it Monday morning. I told him, Earl, I said, you read it so much you oughta keep it, but he told me he didn't mind sharing it with the rest of Pennywhistle. Said it was better that way."

"Sounds like Daddy."

"I hear you're quite the historian yourself, young lady."

"Getting her PhD up at Vanderbilt," Mamma gushes.

"Oh, how wonderful."

"I'm surprised Mamma hadn't told you yet, Mrs. Heller. Didn't you get the postcard and the T-shirt like everybody else?"

"Darling, I can't hardly see anymore. I probably threw it away on accident."

I wonder how many jury duties and phone bills she's missed. Then again, Mamma's probably sweet-talked some Boy Scout or ex-con into sorting Mrs. Heller's mail for her. She takes care of things like that. Conjures up school supplies, airdrops casseroles. Even managed to get the old roller rink registered as a historical landmark last summer. It's strange to see her looking so small tonight. Like she can barely tie her shoes, much less water an entire town.

Mrs. Heller plants a soft pat on my shoulder.

"Your daddy must have been so proud."

"He is," Mamma says.

We let the present tense hang there like a bookmark.

THE NEXT MORNING Mamma makes us breakfast. She thinks I don't notice the way she starts off with three eggs, then quietly places the third back in the carton. That's one egg in thousands she'll have to put back. See, Mamma and Daddy were one of those couples that prac-tically shared underwear. None of that constant bickering you see with some folks, just two people who woke up every morning excited as hell to brush their teeth together.

The small house brims with flowers and fruitcakes. We almost had to duct tape the freezer shut. For now it's full, but I know when the lasagnas dwindle and the carnations wilt the place will start to echo.

As Mamma cooks, I look over my calendar.

"Everything all right?" she asks.

"Yeah, I'm just checking on some assignments."

December bursts with brightly colored to-dos, rainbow reminders of my life down the road.

"Shoo-ee! Look at all that. Don't let 'em work you too hard now."

"It's not all school. I've got a Secret Santa going with my study group on the twenty-first and I'm doing some extra research for the department the week after Christmas."

"What about the green ones?"

"Shoot, that's a symposium I need to finish my application for. I can probably knock it out in a few days with enough coffee. Don't let me forget."

By the look on her face, Mamma's holding back tears, a fart, or both. The eggs jostle as she sets the plates on the table. I put my laptop away.

"You gonna be okay?"

"Oh, don't worry about me, sugar." She clucks. "I've got my needle-pointing. And the Hog Club. We's real close to getting that tampon tax repealed, so I'll be up to my elbows in work, don't you know. Busy, busy. But enough about me! What's new in Music City? I heard Faith Hill and Tim McGraw just bought a new house. Think you could sneak over there and snap a picture for me? Bet it's real fancy."

Despite the smile, the red of her eyelashes pokes through the mascara again. Mamma and I don't look much alike—my hair stayed red for only a little while and my curves outran hers in the seventh grade—but what we do have are the same eye sockets. Deep as Mammoth Cave, Daddy used to say. Good for holding water. Last thing I want to do is fill the well again. So, no, I don't tell her that Nashville is sensational. That there are pretty girls and Pride parades and coffee with frothy milk on top. I leave Vandy's library out of it completely. Nor do I mention my book club or my perfect little apartment right off Centennial Park, where my neighbors, who always seem one song away from famous, play guitar late into the night when I'm trying to sleep.

Instead, when Mamma goes to wash the plates, I circle an ad in the Pennywhistle classifieds.

Fry cook. Chickie Shak. It ain't glamorous, but it's something to do.

THE CHICKIE SHAK

The Chickie Shak is something of a historical landmark. Red clapboard walls, a thriving wasp population, yard toilets resplendent with sunflowers. Tornadoes do not wither it. Instead, the building settles into the hill like a cat does a lap, time and tragedy be damned, and continues to purr.

My best friend, Lee Ray, and I used to go there after our softball games. Cleats caked with victory, pockets lined with Hubba Bubba wrappers. We'd mosey up the dirt road and snag a picnic table while our mammas ordered the home-team special. The line snaked around the building far as you could see, a real parade of diversity. White ass cheeks hanging out of jean shorts. Red necks poking out from mullets. The grimiest bunch of Jessies, Pearls, and Scooters you ever did behold, hobnobbing in the parking lot from noon until night.

"Well, well, well," the preacher would say as he approached our table, "if it isn't the finest first baseman and pitcher this side of the Mississippi."

"I don't know about *finest*," I'd say, shrugging.

"But certainly the best," Lee Ray would clarify.

At eleven, we were both still wiry. Me with great big glasses, him with feet that spoke of growth spurts but couldn't say when they were coming. You never saw two kids better loved than us.

"How 'bout that last out you two pulled off?" the preacher would nudge. "Don't get too humble on me, now."

"Okay," I'd admit. "We might be the finest."

"Amen."

Right on cue, our mammas would return with a tray of wonders. Hot chicken, pillowy biscuits, honey mustard so sweet it ran down our hands and fed the trail of ants that seemed to have followed us all the way from the dugout. The preacher doled out napkins communion-style.

"You kids are gonna do big things," he'd promise.

Wiping a spool of honey mustard from my chin, I wondered what they'd be.

"PJ?" LINDA CALLS from the register.

Somewhere underneath the memory, a wing starts to burn.

"PJ, wake up! I need three thighs, a burger, and a Baby Mamma. Extra secret sauce. No pickles."

"Sorry," I murmur. "I'm on it."

At first, working at the Chickie Shak wasn't all that different from going to school. I made note cards, memorized lists. *Ingredients for hot chicken: brown sugar, Texas Pete, eggs, flour, oil.* Every order a pop quiz, every clean plate an A. Someday I'd tell my book club about my stint with glittery orange poultry and they'd say, *I can't believe you really did that.*

"Order up!"

Now that I've been here awhile, it feels strange I ever did school. Was that really me biking across campus? Me snagging a seat in the front row?

Sometimes when a grease bubble pops on my forearm or a jumbo tub of mayo threatens to take my wristwatch, I start to get wistful for my classes. Then, with a pang that even the grease can't reach, I remember how much those classes used to feel like Jenga blocks. A little too wobbly, a little too easy to topple. Not here in the kitchen, though. Here I get everything right.

Truth is, you can't fail at something as small as this.

I CHECK MY phone between orders to find two new voicemails. The first is from my gynecologist—time for the annual honk and swab—and the second plays before I can stop it.

"PJ, it's Dean Jackson here. Just calling to check in about the fall semester. Professor Wynette's teaching a new course on the epistemology of Southern hospitality. She tends to spit when she lectures, but aside from that it should be a fantastic seminar. Oh, and there's a new donut shop on Elliston Place I've been meaning to try. Did I mention that in my last message? Word is they've got a maple bacon donut that'll knock your socks off. Anyhow, I hate to put on my dean cap, but we do need to talk about your plans to return. If you could give me a call back it's six fifteen . . ."

I bury the voicemail with the rest of its kind. A graveyard of expectations I'd rather not dig up just now, especially not with the second leg of the lunch rush heading in. These folks need their chicken. Who am I to deny them?

"Got a Jumbo Trucker's Plate and an Ankle Biter Meal walkin' in."

"Roger that."

Trumpet Williams always gets a Jumbo Trucker's Plate and his granddaughter, Deedoo, always gets an Ankle Biter Meal. Easy stuff. Truth is, most people around here order the same thing until the day somebody throws their ashes off a roller coaster at Dollywood. They don't even realize it, either. Plenty of our regulars still pick up the menu like it's a whole new world, but when it comes down to it, they go with the usual.

"Let's do an Ankle Biter Meal and, uh . . ."—Trumpet ponders—"a Jumbo Trucker's Plate. How's that sound?"

"Sounds about right," Linda says.

As she clears off table four, the waitress, Boof, spots Deedoo's birthday crown. We're way too busy to serenade anybody today. Nevertheless, Boof pokes her head through the kitchen door.

"Throw in some cheese nuggets and a Dippy Whip. My treat." She winks.

"You got it," I say.

I crank up the Dippy Whip machine, plugging my ears against the roar of its indigestion, while Trumpet collects his receipt. Boof crouches down to examine Deedoo's plastic tiara.

"How old are we turning today?" she asks.

"Ten."

"Double digits!" she exclaims. "That's a big one."

"Am I too old for the Ankle Biter Meal now? Says kids under ten."

Boof pretends to consider this, then pulls Deedoo in for a conspiratorial whisper.

"As long as you keep biting ankles I'd say we're in the clear."

With a wink and a smile, she moves on to table two, where a group of rowdy taxidermists beg for ketchup. Softhearted little thing that she is, Boof knows just when to ask a table if they're all done. Not aggressive-like. Nobody leaves a fry in the basket in this town. No, she says it in a way that makes people feel noticed. *You all set, Bud? How's that kidney stone, by the way? Let me clear that away so y'all can get the tarot cards out.*

"Don't you start with me," Linda advises an out-of-towner with an attitude.

We don't get many of those around here. The ones we do get either respect the Chickie Shak as the holy temple it is or die trying.

"I'm just asking if anything on the menu is vegetarian."

"You're gonna need a veterinarian after I'm through with you. Pick something or get lost."

In this case, the fella decides to get lost. Sure, Linda can be a little testy, but I reckon most Lindas are. Every now and then she'll call somebody sweetheart in a way that makes you want to piss yourself and die. I don't catch the *sweethearts* very often. Back in the kitchen, I've got the handy excuse of being busy and the useful armor of being good at my job. If I just take the yellow order slips and follow them, no shit can hit my fan.

Linda's first day occurred sometime before the advent of cell phones, but Boof's I remember. I'd been working at the Chickie Shak for approximately two months when the old waitress, Daphne Smutt, skipped town to star in a State Farm commercial without so much as an *au revoir*. Boof showed up the next day with a disposition so sunny it called for SPF. Bright red ringlets, little white apron. She kept a pencil behind one ear and a stack of bracelets on her arm that chirped like birds when she walked. She even wore a skirt. I remember how it clung to her like a promise. Point is, I thought she was cute, and part of me even considered asking her out, but a larger constituency of brain cells voted *no siree bob*. Not when Mamma was just getting back to work and Daddy's bait of the month subscription was still arriving in the mail.

"I've got a real name," she told me, "but everybody calls me Boof."

"Roger that, Boof."

"Linda says you're from around here. Is that right?"

"Born and raised."

The way she leaned against the kitchen door, all warm and familiar, scared me.

"Sounds like you're exactly the girl I'm looking for. I just moved down here last week."

"Whereabouts from?"

"Nashville."

My heart picked up faster than Swiffer on skates. I wanted so badly to say *Me too! Ain't it wonderful? Did you ever take a boat around the Cumberland River when the sun was setting and hear the hopes and dreams of every would-be Reba pour from the honky-tonks like a country-fried symphony? Did you ever walk the Civil War trails or eat at the Donut Den or complain about the potholes on I-440?*

"How about a drink?" she said.

"What?"

"You can tell me where to find a dentist and a good cup of coffee around here."

"Bobby Jennifer's Stain and Restore."

"Is that the dentist or the coffee shop?"

"Both. First they get your teeth nice and yellow and then they fix 'em up. I think that's what the bigwigs would call vertical integration."

"Genius." She laughed. "So, what do you say?"

If my poor heart had any power to say yes, it was trapped somewhere deep down next to my breakfast, my guts, and my grief. So I lied.

"I've got a big lasagna thawing. Better get on home and check on it."

"Oh, okay. Rain check?"

"Sure," I said, but every time she asked again, I made sure it was still raining.

NOTHING WRONG WITH keeping things professional. Truth be told, when it's packed, me, Boof, and Linda don't talk hardly at all. We've got a system. I cook, Boof serves, and Linda takes orders. In the busy times there ain't no nooks and crannies for conversation, so we just move things along and refill the salt and pepper like we're supposed to. Linda took off work in March to serve out her jury duty on some high-profile murder trial, and even then, all we got was a gruff harrumph upon her return. Had to learn the rest from the *Pennywhistle Psst*.

"Incoming," Linda calls. "Fancy 12 and a Lady Whistlestop."

Boof grabs the steaming plates.

"I'll be back in two for those fries."

Trumpet Wilson ushers Deedoo toward the register.

"Tell Miss Boof and Miss Linda and Miss PJ thank you."

"Thank you for my birthday treats."

"You're welcome," Boof says.

"Mm-hmm," Linda contributes.

I tip my hat.

"You ladies make a great team, don'tcha?"

I suppose he's right, other than the fact that teammates tend to know a little more about one another than we do. At the end of the day we don't chew the bit or shoot the shit; we simply pack our things and go.

Linda gets in her truck.

Boof walks to the bus stop.

And I ride my bike.

None of us has any idea where the other ones live or what we do once we're there. No talk of children, dogs, or lovers. No sickness, no health. We deal in processed meat exclusively.

"Wouldn't kill you to invite them over one of these days," Mamma likes to say.

Mamma likes to invite people over, show off her porcelain pigs and her aboveground pool.

"Don't see much point in getting to know one another," I tell her. "It's not like I'm gonna be here forever."

And maybe that was true at first. When I came back down here all I brought was a duffel bag and a black dress. Even got the dress dry-cleaned. I remember the way the bag flapped in the wind all the way down from Nashville, like it was trying to get out of the car and go back. A week went by. Then two. I missed my favorite socks, the sweater with the white flecks. But, as the days got colder, the car got harder and harder to start. If I leave, I thought, Daddy will really be dead. Not sleeping, not somewhere in the woods. Just gone.

I biked to the thrift store and bought a stack of sweaters.

"PJ, IT'S DEAN Jackson. Sorry to double call you like this. I forgot to mention Professor Wynette's class has a cooking component. Hospitality in practice, something like that. Really wonderful stuff she's got cooking up, pun intended. Give me a ring when you get the chance. We, uh, we miss you up here."

I wipe the grime from my hands and wonder what such a class would even be like.

"History of Biscuits," I muse. "Fried Chicken Praxis."

Linda and Boof have gone for the night. It's just me and the grill I swore I'd third-day Jesus by the end of the week. In other words: resurrect. With every scrape of the spatula it begins to gleam, which should make me happy. I want the burgers to stop looking like chimney sweeps, but the clatter of the spatula over and over again makes me want something else, too. I set it by the sink and, sneaking a grease-mottled notebook from behind the mustard, scribble my food notes down.

Dissertation, says the earnest cursive.

Pipe dream, says the mustard.

A few hundred miles away, my old neighbors pen their dreams willy-nilly. I used to listen through the wall. Some of the songs they wrote were pure hell—"Runny Tattoo Blues," for example—but every now and then they'd surprise me.

> *Don't let your aspirations take the back seat*
> *Don't let your common sense have all the fun*
> *Keep reaching for the keys*
> *Or at the very least*
> *Make sure your dreams are always calling shotgun.*

I haven't phoned to ask how the music biz is treating apartment 3B, but I do keep the radio tuned to the country station, just in case. Maybe they'll spend the rest of their lives plucking for nothing. Maybe they'll go to law school instead. Maybe one day when I'm frying an extra-hot tender, they'll come through.

A chunk of black char breaks free from the grill.

"There." I grin with delight.

The feeling's short-lived. *You could be in Nashville*, the notebook reminds me. *Should be in Nashville.*

I wedge it behind the condiments before it can utter another word.

PRIVATE LIVES,
PUBLIC RECORDS

The wheels on my little blue bike bald a bit more with every trip to the library. Back and forth, back and forth I go, like somebody who didn't use to catch concerts on a whim and meet friends for beers in places where the music's too loud. Instead, I'm the first bike in the rack, starting my Saturday morning with a pile of returns and a new pair of glasses for Mrs. Heller.

"Mamma ordered these special for you. Let's try not to lose them, alrighty?"

She wags a finger at my dubious expression.

"Don't you look at me like that, PJ Spoon. It's the puppets to blame. They ran off with my last pair, the scoundrels."

The puppets slumber in the children's section, innocent as can be. War-torn Elmo, threadbare Peter Rabbit. Even little Robin Hood comes up clean. Meanwhile, the last four pairs of Mrs. Heller's glasses pile and crunch under the wheels of her desk chair, a mosaic of failing vision. She smiles.

"Just so happens I've got a treat for you, too."

"Oh?" I say, eyeing the disco-era bowl of hard candies. I'm polite, but I'm not emergency-dental-visit polite. Mrs. Heller shakes her head.

"Not the butterscotch. I thought you might want the new Emmens Clementine."

"I thought it wasn't coming out until July."

"Advanced copy. Saved it just for you."

She pulls the book from a drawer the way a drowsy magician might reach for a rabbit. As in, slow-motion magic. I can't help but hug the thing. *The Raccoon King of Lake Tomorrow*. Purple cover, turtlenecked author photo. When I was a kid, we'd wait all night for the latest installment to come out. Faces painted, crowns polished, we'd line up at the bookstore and hobnob until the stroke of twelve, when, high on Fun Dip and Sprite, we'd read furiously until morning. Most kids outgrew the magic of Emmens Clementine around ninth grade, but I never stopped following him. Come hell or high water, there will always be another book.

"There goes my weekend," I gush. "Thank you, thank you, thank you."

"You're welcome, sugar."

"You know, *The Tennessean*'s calling it his best one yet. Took long enough, too. Three years I've waited. Three!"

"Genius takes time," Mrs. Heller tuts.

"He wrote *The Raccoon King of Fiery Gizzard* in four months."

"And it showed. The plot had more holes than a beggar's shoe. Now, you take that home before somebody else catches sight of it and let's both us pray Emmens did his homework this time. Go on, get."

As I turn, a smile still plastered on my face, someone taps me on the shoulder. Someone with bales of red hair and a smile that says *try me*.

"Fancy meeting you here."

The Raccoon King of Lake Tomorrow clatters to the ground.

"Oh, hi, Boof."

"Don't worry," she says. "I'm not gonna ask you to hang out."

"I would, but I'm . . ."

"Making another one of those all-day lasagnas?"

I blush into my shoes.

"Sorry."

"It's okay. I was just gonna ask where the public records section is. I get the feeling you know your way around an almanac."

Something about the way she says this makes me stare. Boof's always moonlighted as a psychic—any waitress worth her salt does—but I never imagined she might be reading my palm, too. I don't talk about books at work. I talk about grease, mustard, the urine mural in the fellas' room. If Boof and I have nothing more in common than the grime under our fingernails, nothing all that awful can happen. I'm not so sure about almanacs.

"Over by the local interest section." I point. "First left."

Her face falls only slightly, like good plastic surgery in a riptide.

"Roger that," she says. "And, hey, bon appétit."

"Thanks."

As she walks away, I resist the urge to run back and show her all my favorite maps. Does she like puppets? I wonder. How about raccoon monarchs? Girls with long, once-blond hair who fall asleep with the reading lamp on?

Mrs. Heller peers up through her new peepers.

"What?"

"At least your daddy knew how to flirt."

"Recessive gene," I explain, hugging the book to my chest. "I'll have this treasure back to you in a few days."

As Mrs. Heller crunches over her old glasses, Boof hauls a stack of records onto a desk with a loud *thwack*. I wonder what she's looking for. Or, rather, who. Those records are full of names, but that doesn't mean they're still around. Feels like I oughta warn her. *People stick to paper a lot better than they stick to the earth, Boof, regardless of love's adhesive properties.*

"See you Monday," she calls from the almanacs.

With no good words in my pockets, best I can do is wave goodbye. One-eyed Elmo, who must know buckets about love and loss from his dramatic readings of *Hop on Pop*, shakes his head.

Sorry, Elmo. Maybe next time.

As I bike home, I notice Linda's truck parked by the river trails. I can just make her out as she begins her hike. Something runs ahead of her in a blur. A child? A dog? Can't imagine who'd want to follow old Linda into the woods if they weren't hog-tied and blindfolded, but from the sound of her laugh it must be love. The longer I stop and look, the more the pages rustle. Even the trees shiver with the sudden breeze.

For a summer day, it sure feels like it could snow.

HAPPY PRIDE MONTH, Lee Ray texts me. *How are we celebrating?*

If it were last year, I'd be sweating glitter and sipping too-sweet Solo-cup cocktails while rainbow-clad dachshunds were wheeled past in red wagons. Hell, I'd be flirting. Alas, I text Lee Ray back from Mamma's kitchen where this year's parade consists of nothing more than a family-size Stouffer's mac and cheese turning idly in the microwave.

I'm watching C-SPAN.

Oh?

Pigeon County's tampon tax referendum. Rescue me?

I would, but I'm stuck at work. Say hello to Dottie.

Will do.

And let me know if they nix the tax.

I roll my eyes.

How you manage to stay interested in the tampon tirade is beyond me.

The family-size feast turns in the microwave. What's family-size anyway? Surely not two. Surely not us. Maybe we should have gotten two individual dinners or a pizza, easily left for tomorrow, wrapped up, taken to work. The family-size box only makes plain what we used to be.

Mamma scoots behind me to grab the forks.

"Whatcha reading these days?"

"The new Emmens Clementine."

"He's kind of a heavy one, right?"

Mamma gets most of her books from Peep and Nina's little free library, smutty nothings you'd be embarrassed to read even on a beach, hence the Clementine looking like Tolstoy.

I stir the still-icy macaroni and pop it back in the microwave.

"I mean, sure. It's about four hundred pages."

She fetches the paper towels.

"Well, when you're done with Harry Potter I've got a real juicy book I think you'd like. Sit tight. Let me just see where I put it."

"I just started this one."

"I think it's on my nightstand."

"Mamma, I said I'm not interested."

The microwave beeps. Settling into opposite sides of the couch, we watch Pigeon County hang on to its tampon tax for dear life. As expected, the family-size mac and cheese proves too big for us.

I SPEND MOST of my Sunday with the Raccoon King and convince myself the snowy breeze I felt on Saturday was just a whiff of rain, one of those made-you-look moments that oughta inspire a raincoat purchase, not a spiritual revolution. Indeed, when I return to work on Monday things are just as I left them. Boof rolls silverware, Linda fusses with the cash drawer, and I do my best not to lose an eye to the deep fryer. And yet . . . something tugs on the sleeve of my brain. Boof with the almanacs, Boof with the archives. Boof with those cute little puppy dog ears.

"Did you find what you were looking for?"

"Not yet," she says, a knowing smile spreading hammock-like across her face. "But I'm getting somewhere."

I lean forward in spite of myself.

"Where?"

Before she can answer, the clang of the cowbell announces somebody at the front door. The sound of fate, you might call it. For out the clear blue butthole of destiny, in walks Rosco T. Puddin, founder and CEO of Chickie Shak Enterprises.

In a purple pinstripe suit.

Botoxed to high hell.

Followed by a TV crew.

Thereby changing our lives forever.

AND THEN
THEY'S THREE

The closest we have ever come to meeting Mr. Puddin is the framed headshot in the ladies' bathroom. Why there is not a second picture hung in the fellas' bathroom, I could not say. All I know is, every dump I ever took at work involved his face.

Age does not wither him. Nor do the plastic eyelids or the artificial cheekbones that hold up his skin as a pole does a tent.

"Howdy," he says to the camera. "We're here at the flagship Chickie Shak with some of our MVCs—Most Valuable Chickies. Come on out, ladies. Don't be shy. Yes, you. Come out, come out, wherever you are."

Linda closes the cash drawer on the register. *Cling.* Lord, this might be serious, because Linda never stops long enough to close that thing all the way. Usually it just floats back and forth between customers, a buoy in the sea of Chickie Shak prosperity. But now, *cling.* Resigned, I click off the burners and make my way around to the counter. Boof pours sweet tea for table four. The pitcher's still in her hand by the time she reaches us, like this whole ordeal might be quick. A dream, or a joke, or a front for Evangelicals. I tell you what, ain't none of us got time to learn about Jesus Christ today.

Mr. Puddin scrutinizes our name tags.

"America, meet Linda, PJ, and . . . Boof."

It's supposed to sound like *poof* with a *b*, but in his beak, it comes out more like the French word for *beef*. *Beuf*.

"Beuf, is that your Christian name?"

"I'm Jewish," she says.

"How brave!" He beams.

"Thanks?"

"And PJ, I see we're really taking that hairnet seriously."

"I cook the food."

"Some like it hot." He laughs. "And how about Linda, here. You can't buy skin like that."

The hair on her beauty mark glistens.

"Your point, sweetheart?"

Mr. Puddin looks around the restaurant for a cue card or a life raft.

"It seems somebody didn't get our company-wide email."

I vaguely recall unsubscribing after the newsletter started quoting the disciples.

Unflappable, Mr. Puddin continues. "We're here on the Chickie Shak Hot Chicken Beauty Tour. This summer Chickie Shak employees from across the South—and the New Jersey branch—will compete for the Chickie Shak Hot Chicken Crown."

"Pass," Linda mutters under her breath.

"Look to your left. Now look to your right. These are your first opponents."

Mr. Puddin attempts to drum up some *oohs* and *ahs* from the lunch crowd to no avail. Most people are still trying to figure out what the hell he's wearing.

"Opponents?" Boof asks.

"We've got fifty-five branches, but each Chickie Shak branch will send only *one* employee to the national competition."

Like a shoulder-bound toddler on the Fourth of July, Mr. Puddin waits for fireworks. Still nothing. According to Lee Ray's favorite show, *Judge Judy*, by now there should be at least gasps, if not a full-on slap fight.

"Ladies, I feel like we're not listening. This is a chance to show off not only your womanly figures, but also your devotion to the Chickie Shak. The best of both worlds!"

"Golly gee, do we get to wear a bathing suit, too?"

"Very cheeky, Beuf!" Mr. Puddin says. "Yes, we'll get to that portion along with talent, elocution—"

"I left mine at my cousin's house. I'd have to call her and she doesn't pick up calls between ten and twelve because of the twins."

"We wouldn't want to wake the children."

"No, it's her boobs. They're mighty sensitive to noise and this time of day if I ring her up, well, I'm not gonna hear the end of it."

I swear she cuts me a wink, but I'm too startled to be certain.

"I'm sure we can find something for you to wear, dear. Now, as I was saying—"

"To be clear, the male employees are required to slap on a bikini, too. Right?"

"Heavens, no, PJ. That would be absurd."

"Oh, *that* would be absurd?"

"Yes, the male employees are there to scrape the grills and fix the toilets and look handsome fixing the toilets."

"Mr. Puddin, with all due respect . . . ," Linda starts.

"I'm not feeling very respected at the moment." He pouts.

"Yeah, well me neither." She huffs. "As far as I'm concerned, you can take your pony show elsewhere. We got work to do. Turn them cameras off."

"Howard, do not turn them cameras off."

Despite his silicone forehead, I can tell Mr. Puddin is genuinely shocked by our reluctance. It's more than vanity on the line, only I'm not sure what.

"Sir, what could possibly be in this for us?" I ask.

"I don't get it," he says to the crowd. "The Quarterflute branch was ecstatic. And they're not half as cute as you three. They have skin tags. One of them just had a baby. Truly!"

"What's the prize?"

"This is why we read our emails, honey!" Mr. Puddin smooths his lapel. "As was detailed to you two months ago in not one but *four* messages, you have the chance to win one million dollars and—even better—free Chickie Shak for life!"

Trumpet Williams drops his burger. If I had my spatula I'd drop that, too. Hell, I hope nobody's holding their baby because life just got pretty damn slippery. None of Lee Ray's shows have prepared me for this. In place of a slap fight, Boof, Linda, and I just look at one another. The standard of beauty at any given Chickie Shak is low, which normally doesn't matter. We make your tenders, your burgers, and your Biggie Shakes, and you don't whistle when we walk by. Kind of an unspoken customer-employee agreement. All of a sudden, we're adding bathing suits to the mix?

"Thought that might *beak* your interest." Mr. Puddin chuckles.

Linda runs her hands through her bangs. Shoot, I couldn't have told you her hair color before today. This was all supposed to be temporary. A few days turned into a few weeks turned into a few months. Then again, it's like they say. Sometimes when you ask for hairspray God gives you a perm instead.

"What do we gotta do?" Linda asks.

"Check your emails and gussy up, ladies. Competition starts now."

"AND, CUT!" MR. Puddin says with a flourish of his white snakeskin boot. "Now, for this next shot I want cinematic. I want sleek. Pan the patrons and then zoom in on the dramatic exit on my cue."

Due to the lunch rush, it takes a while for Mr. Puddin to make said dramatic exit.

"Excuse me. Pardon me. Hands to ourselves, please. Are you rolling?"

I can tell he's used to scurrying to and fro, but with Gunner Fisher-Trapper's triplets hanging off table three like acrobats and mean old Trudy Brown's can taking up half the line, any attempt to scuttle gets turned to mustard in this crowd. For all his tarped-up flaws, I'll give Mr. Puddin one thing: he knows how to make the most of a bad situation.

"Clearly, the mothership is doing well!" he calls to the register.

The three of us stand and watch.

"I hope they don't eat me!"

Dainty little paws lifted to the heavens, he shimmies through the sea of sweaty elbows and wobbly jowls.

"Almost there!"

Strange to think this latex-jawed hooligan started it all. Rumor has it he founded the Chickie Shak back in 1974 with only five dollars and a chicken breast. Now half the county lunches here.

"Competition starts in two weeks. I expect to see the three of you waxed, tanned, and lubed."

I muster a sarcastic double thumbs-up.

"Think to yourselves, 'Should hair grow out of this appendage?' and then think, 'No!'"

"Roger that, boss."

"Soap is a great place to start, but the sky's the limit when it comes to womanly care." He winks. "There I go, rigging things. You'll figure it out!"

Mr. Puddin finally manages to exit, and like a freshly waxed upper lip, we're free of the nuisance.

"Well, that was special," I say to Boof and Linda.

"Damn fool," Boof says quietly. "Acting like we've never seen the right side of a hairbrush. Gussy up, my ass."

"Back to work." Linda huffs.

We both turn. This huff is a huff we ain't never heard before.

"I said get!"

Linda's beauty mark shakes with unprecedented fervor. We scoot. Every customer is *sweetheart* for the rest of the day.

WHEN WE CLOSE up shop, Linda does not say goodbye. The dust from her truck shoots back at us like a pungent fanny cloud. Linda doesn't take shit, but she usually doesn't give a shit, either. Maybe it was what Mr. Puddin said about hair. Or the thing about her skin. Did I mention Linda's the oldest among us? Not by too much, but she's at least two Dolly Parton albums our senior. Old enough to be standing on the edge of something, the line of missing out. I wouldn't have thought she worried about things like beauty queening. Then again, I'm not solid on her favorite color or her home phone number, so what do I know? All I can say is, this behavior makes me feel one-third more alone than usual and it's no tasty feeling.

As I wash my hands all the way up to my damn elbows, I consider what would happen if our flock of three became one wolf and a flock of two. Or worse, a flock of me and a pack of wolves. What am I say-ing? Boof's about as wolfy as Scooby-Doo. Thank the Lord. I don't know much about her, either, just the food we make that she eats and the food we make that she doesn't. Does she get cavities? Does she be-lieve in ghosts? As we turn off the lights, it suddenly seems important to know.

Normally she and I head in separate directions, but tonight I feel like talking. She locks the back door and gives it one safety pull while I wait on the step below. We smell so much like grease we don't know what grease smells like anymore. Not until it runs down the drain at the end of the shower and we're human again. Not many people get that, but Boof does.

"Heading to the bus?"

"You know it," she says.

"Long day."

"You're telling me."

Boof takes off her red Chickie Shak baseball cap and shakes her hair out. I'm never around for this part of her day. Seeing her curls tumble out makes me want to be.

"Sunset's pretty nice tonight. Want me to walk with you?"

"Sure."

I walk my bike beside me, the spokes catching cigarette butts and dusty pacifiers.

"Walking in pairs wards off the perverts and the snakes," she says.

"Sounds like an old Patsy Cline number."

"Walking in pairs wards off the perverts and the snakes," she sings in mock Patsy. *"Don't be scared of the reptiles and the Jakes."*

"Damn, Boof! You can sing."

"Course I can. Before this I worked at the Grand Ole Opry."

"What the hell? Why didn't you say anything?"

She runs her hand through her curls and laughs. Another sound I haven't heard before.

"You've never asked me a single question that didn't involve ketchup, mustard, or mayonnaise. It stands to reason you ain't heard my back-story."

"Fair enough," I offer sheepishly. "Sorry."

"It's all right, I don't know yours, either. What's PJ stand for any-ways?"

"Pajama Jeans."

"No, it does not."

"It's far worse than that, actually. Keep hanging out with me and you just might find out."

We're quiet for a moment as we continue down the road. I don't want the sun to set and I don't want to reach the bus stop.

"Hey, you didn't tell me your real name yet. I want to say Belle?"

"It's a surprise. Speaking of, I have a feeling we're gonna be real sur-prised with Linda tomorrow."

"How's that?" I ask.

Boof points to the bus stop and waves goodbye.

"Let's just say she's gonna have hair on the right appendages."

AS THE SUN sinks below the magnolias and children take their last leaps through the water sprinkler, Mamma and I place tampons on the doorsteps of Pennywhistle's lawmakers.

"It's called making a statement," she says.

More like making a collage. She's dipped the tampons in red nail polish and glued them to various denominations of Monopoly money so as to illustrate just how ridiculous the tax is. Most of the men in Pennywhistle have probably never seen a tampon, the way a Canadian might never have seen a fried Twinkie. Frankly, they'd prefer to believe they don't exist. Too bad. Mamma's got a way of taking a broom to the cobwebs.

"How you feeling about everything?" she asks as she darkens a welcome mat with a bloody hundred.

"You mean this ridiculous pageant?"

"Well, sure. I was thinking about school and Daddy and—"

"I feel fine."

"You know you can talk to me, right?"

A stray tabby bats the tampon into the bushes.

"PJ?"

"I know."

Something about going door-to-door reminds me of the year Daddy was too sick to take me trick-or-treating. I practically wilted inside my papier-mâché pumpkin.

"Mamma can take you," Daddy said.

"No." I pouted. "I want you to take me."

I don't know who struck a sadder sight, me on the floor, bawling my pumpkin costume back down to its wet newspaper rinds, or Mamma in the doorway, wiping off the black cat whiskers she'd drawn on in the bathroom. We never did go out. I spent that Halloween watching Westerns under the crook of Daddy's arm while Mamma ferried bowls of soup and jugs of Gatorade to us. I can still see the smudge of a whisker etched on her cheek as she turned back to the kitchen. She probably started up a pie or called her sister. Whatever she did, the roar of cowboys drowned her out.

"Dottie Spoon, so help me God," a man says from behind his peep-hole. "Get that trash off my porch before I write you up for disorderly conduct."

"Only thing disorderly is taxing tampons like a damn luxury," she replies. "Think it over, Bocephus. And tell Jeanie I said hello."

"Roger that."

She flings a bouquet of blood stoppers over her shoulder as we make for the next house.

"For good measure."

Mamma wasn't kidding when she said she'd throw herself into the Hog Club. She and the other would-be activists been leaping onto soapboxes for months trying to get the tax repealed. That is, when they're not reading to seniors or building houses or distributing condoms at the Harley-Davidson rally. I can't help but stare as Mamma shimmies to the next little house, one foot in front of the other the way they tell you to do with grief. I stoop down to tie my shoe. Frayed laces, somebody's gum caked deep into the heel. Maybe I can blame my inertia on them.

"Come on, now, little miss beauty queen," Mamma hollers.

"I think I'm gonna head home."

"What for?"

"I want to catch up on my book."

She brightens.

"One of them textbooks for school?"

"No, the new Emmens Clementine."

"Oh," she murmurs. "Well, suit yourself. I'll be out here for another hour if you get bored."

"Good night, Mamma."

"Night."

Biking away, it occurs to me that I should have stayed. Who lets their mamma wander the poorly lit streets of Pennywhistle with no weapon but a tampon? Maybe I oughta stop skedaddling, but it's too late now, with a mile of dirt road between us and the moon blinking on like a good idea.

WHISKERS

The next morning when I go to brush my teeth, I notice a pair of old hoop earrings by the sink. Funny sight next to the sea spray of my spit, the lone ranger of my toothbrush. I cradle the loops in my palm. No bigger than macaroni. Modest you might say if you were polite, which none of us are in my family. The gold paint's wearing off the brass like a bad spray tan. All this to say, they are not mine. Mamma must have left them the last time she was here. Either took them out to fight with Aunt Wanda or left them like a prayer for me to find. I hate to admit it, but I think they're kinda pretty. Or purty, as Mamma would say.

"Oh, what the hell."

Glistening in my shitty brass earrings, I ride to work.

There's not much to Pennywhistle, but there's enough. You got your post office, your public library, your roller rink for special occasions. Your Piggly Wiggly, your Half-Off Pass Away Depot. We're twenty miles from Memphis, two steps from the Loosahatchie River, and within shouting distance of anything you really need in this life or the next. That is, unless you break your leg or long for a Frappuccino. Then you gotta get your ass to the city. Mostly we stay put, falling asleep to the sound of the train and waking up to the rusty water sprinklers going *skeet, skeet, skeet.*

My morning ride takes about six minutes, so I really get to take in the scenery. The main road through town is peppered with neighbors hollering at one another about garden gnomes and plastic deer. Little wishing wells clogged up with cigarettes. Big glass balls sitting proud on concrete pedestals. Dogs that belong to nobody in particular. A regular Walt Disney World, if I do say so.

Tennessee's long but she's also skinny, so from here to Nashville don't take but a few hours of cruising past XXX billboards and blown-out tires. Shoot, that's a pretty drive. Nothing but Jimmy Buffett and Jesus on the radio. Growing up, we'd go every summer to see Lee Ray's auntie June, a psychic ventriloquist with half a dozen boyfriends and a pet snake. Sweet old thing. Lee Ray's mamma lost her license due to some unpaid parking tickets, so Daddy would drive us. He made the whole thing historical, educational.

"Summer school starts right here, right now," he'd announce as we filled up the tank at the Snap Sak. We learned things like how to call a chickadee or which state parks you can't piss in. My favorite fact was and remains that our state animal is the raccoon. Daddy thought Tennessee looked a bit like a scrawny old raccoon. He'd point out all the cities on the map and say what part they represented.

"Lookee there. Memphis is the nose and we's the whiskers."

"What's so special 'bout that?" I'd ask. "Can't we flip it? Then we'd be the tail."

"What's so special? Don't you know what whiskers do?"

"No."

"What do they do?" Lee Ray'd press.

Daddy would take a dramatic pause, gazing off into the horizon in a way that assured us he knew everything there was to know about Tennessee and the world that had sprung up around it. The lines around his eyes boasted adventures. The knots in his hands, secrets. Just when we couldn't wait any longer, he'd spit his tobacco out the window with a flourish and tell us what whiskers did.

"Well, whiskers, they feel things."

Daddy was an expert at feeling things, the same way other daddies were experts at corn and pumpkins. He didn't shy away from a good cry. Always leapt at the chance to toast a long-lost friend or weep his way through a karaoke rendition of "Travelin' Soldier." I can still see him now, up on the stage with a voice so creaky it put the wooden floors to shame, singing about that soldier who wasn't coming home. He waved me up in case I wanted to make it a duet—back then I was the kind of girl who participated in duets—and we sure made those Chicks proud, crooning and aching and singing our hearts out. Even did a couple of encores. Somewhere between "Goodbye Earl" and "Wide Open Spaces" Mamma snapped a picture I can't bear to look at.

"Why not?" she asked when she saw the frame facedown on the mantel.

What could I tell her? I ain't so wide open anymore.

I ROUND THE corner to see that despite Mr. Puddin's grand arrival, the Chickie Shak itself remains unchanged. Same red clapboard, same toilet full of sunflowers out front. Phew! Another day in paradise.

Boof walks up as I'm chaining my bike to the hose rack, the closest thing we have to a bike rack. Enough to give the impression that if you wanna steal my bike you're gonna have to take the whole Chickie Shak with you.

"Boof Elizabeth . . . Last Name, are those French braids I see?"

She flips them around all pageant-like.

"Best foot forward, baby."

How some people pull off *baby* like it's a regular vocabulary word, well, that's beyond me.

"PJ, how come you know my middle name but not my last name?" she asks.

"You're what, twenty-five, twenty-six?"

"Maybe."

"Damn near everybody our age's middle name is either Anne or Elizabeth. Fifty-fifty shot."

"It's Kidston, by the way. My last name."

"Blank Elizabeth Kidston," I muse. "Now all I need's your real first name and I'll have the whole set. Brooklyn? Bridget?"

"Why do you assume it starts with a *B*?"

"Don't make me search the whole alphabet, girl."

We laugh and linger by the hose rack. Despite yesterday's walk, talking anything but small is still new for us. Especially now that I've realized how darn cute she is. I pray she'll keep talking so I won't have to.

"What do we have here?" She hoots. "Somebody's wearing earrings for the first time in her life."

She reaches out to inspect them. Nobody touches your ears in regular life, I tell you what. I can see why dogs like it so much.

"Only the best for Mr. Puddin," I say.

Too bad she lets go.

"Well, I reckon now that we're a couple of hot tickets we're bound to win this thing."

I survey the premises as I turn the key in the back door.

"We ain't seen Linda yet."

FOR THE FIRST time in our hen history, Linda is late to work. Not so late that she misses the first customer, but late enough for Boof and me to Rock Paper Scissors about who's gonna take Mr. Tucker's lunch order. His spit talking's legendary round these parts and what with that nasty canker sore outbreak this summer, we ain't taking chances. Boof throws paper to my scissors.

"Damn it!"

She hovers over the register like it's a blender full of gravy. One wrong move and you're ruined.

"Hey," Linda calls as she unlocks the front door. "Paws off."

"We were just trying to get set up before Mr. Tucker comes in," I explain.

The first thing I notice is the rhinestones. Not on her jean jacket—we call that formal wear in Pennywhistle—but hanging off her nails on little silver chains. And by nails, I mean long acrylic things that make me wonder how in the hell she wiped her butt this morning. Underneath her yellow Chickie Shak polo she's sporting what Mamma would call a hussy upper. To put it plainly, her girls are pushed up so far they're practically parallel parked with her chin. Lordy. At least the polos only have three buttons. Otherwise we might have to see what kind of rollercoaster contraption's keeping everything above sea level.

Linda, sporting shoes that look straight off the Jessica Simpson shelf at Dillard's, walks toward us, her gait aggressive but unsure. And sweet Jesus on Easter, is that a *purse*? No bigger than a pencil pouch, but instead of that bright blue Crayola material it's made out of what can only be described as faux-dillo. Somebody's been to Pigeon Forge and back by the looks of it.

Now, listen. I'm surprised, but I'm not an idiot. I know better than to make a big fuss about Linda's transformation, because the last time I so much as pointed out a ketchup stain on her apron she scrunched up her face and said something about with eyes as beady as mine it's a wonder I can even see past my nose.

I pretend to check the inventory list while Boof rolls forks and knives into napkins.

"Don't touch my register again. You hear?"

"Got it," I say.

As Linda types in her passcode, the chains on the ends of her nails jump like fleas on a cat. Close up, I notice they've got little palm tree charms on the ends of them. How very exotic. This from a woman who frequents the Bait and Shoot.

"You do something different with your hair, honey?" Boof asks.

"No."

"Huh, I always thought you'd look nice as a blonde."

Linda considers this. Hard to be ugly to Boof, especially in those two braids. She gives off the kind of goodness that melts meanness like a Ding Dong on a dashboard.

"Thank you," Linda mumbles. "Now, back to work, y'all. First hour's always a bitch."

WHEN I SLIDE open the walk-up window, Boof meets me there.

"Are we alone?"

I glance up. Linda's got her pinky palm tree stuck in the shift key, so like a state fair port-a-john, she'll be occupied for a while. I nod.

"You were right," I whisper. "I think she even plucked the mole."

"This is only the beginning," she whispers back.

"What's next?"

"Hair, makeup, probably some sort of god-awful diet."

"Jesus." I arrange the condiments in a neat line. "If she starts the one where you eat like a caveman, I'm gonna lose it."

Boof pats my hand. Picnic! Lightning!

"At least we have each other."

She fans out the red-and-white plastic tablecloths while I start the fries. Each table gets a little vase and a plastic daisy, which turns into a little vase and an American flag on the Fourth of July. Little vase and a skeleton hand on Halloween. Little vase and condoms on Valentine's Day. We're no Cheesecake Factory, but we still got some class.

Right on time, a car full of regulars parks beside Linda's truck. Boof gives them a wave.

"Does this mean we're friends now?" I ask, heart still cartwheeling from her touch.

"Girl, I've been trying to crack you for months."

"Am I tough to crack?"

"Practically hard-boiled."

She swats a family of flies off a mustard stain and heads for the screen door. It occurs to me that she's been fanning out tablecloths and I've been fonduing curly fries every day for four months. Four months of hellos and goodbyes with nothing in between. All because I wouldn't recommend a dentist. One time Boof tried to invite me somewhere and

I didn't even let her finish before claiming to be in the middle of an extensive papier-mâché replica of the state capitol. Truth be told, I was, but I could have put that on hold for one night to go see some music with her in Horse Creek. Hard-boiled? When did that happen?

"I'm tasty on the inside," I blurt out.

Boof raises an eyebrow.

"What's that, now?"

I used to be smooth, dammit! Now I'm just a fool with a deep fryer.

"Shut up! I didn't mean it like that."

She breaks into a grin so bright it could turn margarine to butter.

"I just mean I've got a tough exterior but I'm . . . shit, you know what I'm trying to say. Go on, get."

No earrings, gold or otherwise, can save me now. Boof savors the moment, smoothing a tablecloth to red-and-white-checkered perfection.

"Don't worry, PJ," she assures me. "I always suspected you'd be right delicious."

HEART PUMPING AND wheels giddy, I ferry the latest gossip to Lee Ray's house. Well, *house* is a strong word. He lives in his mamma's basement, a tornado shelter turned chic loft by his careful efforts. The walls bloom with costumes and fishing reels, *Playbills* and champion bass. He's endlessly proud of his headboard, built from an abandoned—or possibly stolen—canoe we found on the banks of the Loosahatchie. Not that anyone's shaken said headboard recently. Poor thing, his spell's been dry for a while.

"You're up to something," he says at the sight of my earrings. "Come in, come in."

Lee Ray and I have been best friends ever since the fourth grade, when he quit baseball and joined the softball team instead. Now, I know what you're thinking. Usually it's the little girl who says, *I'm plum tired of the Girl Scouts! I'm gonna play baseball!* But in this case, it was Lee Ray.

I still remember him walking up the hill to practice one Sunday afternoon in March, perfectly natural, explaining that all the boys on the
baseball team wanted to do was chew Hubba Bubba and pull out their
ding-a-lings to pee the word *damn* in the sand. He was through with
'em. The whole lot.

"Ain'tcha worried about what they're gonna say?" one of the mammas asked.

"Don't you know the boys is stronger?" said another.

Lee Ray shook his head.

"Ma'am, they may bruise one another up, but not a one of them can
swing a bat. I watched the Bee Stings play last week. You girls take
things seriously. I'd like to be on a team where somebody gives a damn
instead of just pissing it."

The other mammas seemed uneasy. All their lives they'd prayed
for little girls they could gussy up. Whose long hair they could fiddle
with, festoon. By the time they got to be mammas things had already
changed. This was a time people started suggesting that girls could
do anything boys could do. Cereal commercials and pediatricians and
bumper stickers on cars coming down from places like New Jersey.
Even those damn American Girl dolls had big dreams. So, mammas had
to start teaching hunting and buying socks without pom-poms on the
end. They even started the Bee Stings. All in the name of being taken
seriously. And here was this wiry, determined little fella who believed
more than any one of them that they deserved to be.

Mamma stepped through the throng of Patsy Lynns and patted Lee
Ray on the shoulder.

"You're in."

Lee Ray led the Bee Stings to victory three straight years in a row.
He wasn't a showboat about it, either, like you might expect the biggest,
strongest player to be. No, he seemed to be most cheerful just working
behind the scenes, playing the spots the rest of us didn't want. When
Terri Judith Anne McDaniels got her period in front of everyone at the
Battle Creek game and refused to play first base for a month, Lee Ray

stepped in. When Denita Robertson started getting psychic visions, he covered the whole outfield. Sure, he got lip from a few ne'er-do-wells at the gas station and the occasional balding umpire, but save for those asswipes, Lee Ray was universally adored.

Mamma said he spoke like a Victorian, by which she meant historian. Truth be told, he was just about the only boy in the county who could recite the Constitution but couldn't fart the ABCs. He liked to stand on the bench in the dugout and give us pep talks before the games, speeches that might have garnered votes or Tonys if they'd been heard by the right set of ears. Lee Ray worked hard to prove himself in all arenas, not just scoring home runs but also sewing the mascot costume, a bulky bee suit that Tamara Dupree's baby brother wore as he ran the bases between innings, shouting, "Buzz, buzz, buzz. Ouch, ouch, ouch! We'll sting you so hard you'll fall on the couch." Still, Lee Ray refused to accept the MVP trophy year after year.

"I'm startin' to think he don't believe he's valuable," Mamma said once.

How could that be? I remember thinking. In both life and softball, Lee Ray was pretty darn valuable to me.

Turns out, the Bee Stings would be out of luck before we had a chance to foist the title on Lee Ray again. Come seventh grade, the daddies in town got worried that so much time with the girls would lead him to getting one of us pregnant. True, Lee Ray's voice had dropped down so low it just about reached the Gulf of Mexico. His shoulders had stopped looking like a coat hanger. He even got hair on his chinny chin chin. That fall, the Billys and the Bucks of Pennywhistle pulled him aside to talk about the birds and the bees. If you know what I mean. Like me, Lee Ray was a bona fide homosexual, unlikely to get anybody pregnant without a Bethlehem variety miracle. Nevertheless, he left the team to pursue his other passions: sewing, fishing, dancing, composing, and building canoes for the Elderly Fishermen of Pennywhistle, who he convinced to change their name to the Elderly Fisher*people* of Pennywhistle.

"You remember Boof from work?" I ask as he pulls a pair of Coors Lights from the mini fridge.

"Redhead? Dimple? Huge crush on you?"

"What?"

The Coors Light cap ricochets into a tackle box full of earrings.

"PJ, I've eaten my fair share of Dippy Whips in the last four months. Trust me, your last name is all over her diary."

"She said she'd been wanting to be friends for a while but I was tough to crack. Emphasis on *friends*."

"Emphasis on *wanting*."

I roll my eyes and take a long drag of my beer. Sometimes I wonder how my enormous best friend fits under this ceiling. Not just his height but his dreams. Lee Ray's drawers are bursting with sequins. Mine, with doubt. A freshly painted poster is drying on the coffee table.

"What's this?"

"Summer Paddle Adventure. Just a little something I'm cooking up for the EFPs."

"I like the glitter. Draws the eye."

"Thank you. Most of them have cataracts, so I have to be strategic."

He applies a dollop of glue to a patchy section on the letter *A*.

"You really think she likes me?" I ask.

"Shhh, I'm working."

As he sprinkles a fresh layer of glitter, I survey the framed posters that crowd the walls of the basement. Every show he's ever written, every spirited flyer he's ever produced for the EFPs. Maybe he'll never show up in the *New York Times*, but he sure dazzles the *Pennywhistle Psst*.

"Of course Boof likes you. What remains to be seen is what you'll do about it."

"What would you do?"

"Easy," he says, admiring his work. "I'd start writing her name next to mine, too. If you need supplies, you know where to find them."

He blows a gust of silver in my direction.

"Don't get me all glittery."

"Check your smile. You're already glittery."

"Am not."

"Are too."

"Maybe it's just the advanced copy of *The Raccoon King of Lake Tomorrow* I happen to have in my bag."

"The *what?*"

"Mm-hmm."

He tears through my backpack like a hot Cheeto does a colon.

"Where in Critter County did you get this?"

"Mrs. Heller."

"I should have known. Forget Boof. Drop everything and speed-read this so I can have it next."

Lee Ray scans the inside cover with a loving eye. We both know that by the time we're through with it, the spine will be cracked in three places: the first kiss, the big fight, and the part where they smooch and make up. Lee Ray's a far better softball player than I ever was, and I make a meaner corn dog, but we're equal in our love for love stories. The sappier the better. Animal or human. Matter fact, when we were kids, we watched *Lady and the Tramp* so many times the VHS heaved a sigh and spilled its film, as if to say, *Enough with the meatballs, already.*

"What happens if she doesn't like me?"

"Nothing," he says. "You'll be back where you started."

I think of cocker spaniels, spaghetti. How much longer can I spend my Friday nights between the pages of a book?

"I'm not sure I wanna go back to where I started."

"See." Lee Ray grins. "Glittery."

THE PINK NAIL
OF DOOM

Linda's pinky palm tree slows Chickie Shak operations down all week. With each order, it gets stuck in some key or other, and instead of asking one of us for help, she slams the void key and has to start all over again. As the orders pile up, a lagoon of sweat collects in her cleavage.

"Next!" she hollers.

I wish she'd pry the nails off and go back to normal. A middle finger doesn't look any better in bubblegum pink, but after a few orders that's what I get. Linda bursts through the swinging kitchen door with a fresh order and a soiled attitude.

"What the hell am I lookin' at, PJ?"

"Number six with extra coleslaw?"

She grabs the yellow slip. Her writing is all mangled up by the nails. Grinch writing. I think I even see a drop of blood in one corner.

"Does this look like coleslaw to you?"

She outlines the words with her claw.

"Uh, yes?"

"Corn dog. It says corn dog. Number six with a corn dog." She slams down the slip. "Make it again. Correct-like."

"Look, Linda, it was an honest mistake. I just couldn't read your writing."

"Six months and all a sudden you can't read?"

"I think it's the nails," I mutter.

"Are you blamin' my nails for your lunch order?"

Boof, precious angel of checkered tablecloths, pokes her head in through the swinging door.

"Everything okay in here?"

"Somebody's envious of my manicure and is using it as an excuse to screw with me."

"*Envious* ain't the word I'd use."

"Not with that limited vocabulary, I reckon."

"Hey, hey, girls," Boof says. "No need for all this. We're all friends here."

"Friends?" Linda scoffs.

"We work well together. We run a tight ship."

Linda flips her hair and adjusts her hussy upper.

"That don't mean I give a lick about you two or you give a lick about me."

I wonder if this conversation is playing out at every Chickie Shak across the South right this very moment. If Mr. Puddin's publicity stunt might just lead to the destruction of an ecosystem built on bored women in small towns.

"Honey—" Boof tries.

"Don't honey me. That million dollars is my ticket outta all this and I'm not gonna sit around and play nice with you two just so you can sabotage me. Starting yesterday we ain't friends."

"Fine, if we're not friends, at least we're still coworkers," I offer.

"Neither. We's competition. Now make that order again and this time"—she raises her voice—"act like you know how to read."

THE FRYER'S LOUD and the steam's thick. If somebody leans through the window looking for extra grease on their chicken or a fifth hot dog, I can blame my dewy eyes on the onion rings.

Lucky for me, most people mind their business when they're hungry. They sprawl out over the parking lot and into the beds of their trucks, happy as can be. Sometimes I envy the *out there* folks. The *out there* folks don't always think about the *in here* folks. Easy to forget who touches your fries if there ain't no hairs in 'em. Mamma says I oughta be where the people are, a line she lifted right off *The Little Mermaid* soundtrack, but for better or for worse, I'm mostly on my own in here. Right now, that's a relief.

Never-the-damn-less, the door creaks open. Now? When I'm fresh out of patience and paper towels?

"Onions got me again," I mumble, back turned.

"It's me."

Shit. I stay turned.

"Let me just get these in the fryer. One second."

I mop at my eyes with my sleeves, hoping Boof will chalk the ocular precipitation up to sweat.

"At first it was funny, but now it's just stupid," she whispers angrily.

Funny to hear her pretty little voice all worked up. Like seeing a porcelain doll in overalls.

"What do you mean?"

"The register! The whole system. Regulars are frustrated. New folks are walking right out. And our tips have gone to hell in a handbasket."

"Pinky nail?"

"Pinky nail! I'm about to rip the whole thing off, so help me God."

"I'm with you." I sigh.

"I swear, that walking mole's gonna drive me to up and quit."

"You can't quit!"

I swivel to face her. The moment Boof catches sight of my splotchy red tomato face she stops talking. Doesn't comment, just grabs a glass and pours me a water. Even waits for the ice machine to work so she can make it a nice cold one. I never wait for that old ice machine. She hands the glass over.

"Hey, hey, I'm just talking big."

"I sure hope so." I sniffle.

"You don't think I'd quit this place? Things just started getting interesting."

"The pageant, you mean?"

"Sure, the pageant."

She winks. I look right into her green eyes. We stay put. Or maybe we inch closer. The kitchen's all a sudden very small and very quiet.

Ding! That's the void button, meaning like a diaper in a bouncy castle, shit's about to break loose.

"Damn it," I mutter. "Better get back to it."

"What if I don't want to?" She groans.

"You'll feel the wrath of a once-hairy chin as it chews your ass out."

"A fate worse than death."

Boof tucks a rogue curl back into her hat.

"Thanks for the water."

"Course."

"Boof!" Linda calls.

"Coming!"

Parting really is a sugary sorrow. Boof looks back at me just before she reaches the door.

"Hey, PJ?"

"Yes?"

"How about you walk me to the bus again tonight and we'll come up with some new songs for that Patsy Cline album? I think we got a few more number ones up our sleeves."

BOOF AND I work on our discography every evening until Friday, when I find Deedoo waiting by the back door like a kitten, hoping for a spot of ice cream and some company. As the last few customers make their way to their cars, a little old lady furrows her brow at the stray ten-year-old.

"Young lady, it's nearly dark. Does your mamma know where you're at?"

"Grandpa says if anybody asks, Mamma's running errands."

Deedoo's mamma has been gone for five years and change. Skipped town with one of those fast-talking Bible men who claim the good lord just needs a few thousand bucks to rustle up a miracle. Then again, somebody brushes Deedoo's hair. Somebody insists on summer reading and flu shots. Her shoes never get too small, her nose too runny. She laps at her Dippy Whip like somebody who's loved.

"Who gave you that pretty French braid, Deedoo?"

"Miss Linda."

"Linda?" I balk.

"She comes over and does my hair every morning. Grandma and Grandpa try, but they're not very good."

"Every morning?"

"Oh, yes," Deedoo assures me. "She can do all kinds of hairdos. Two braids, fishtail. She told me when I'm older she can do me a perm or even make me blond if I want. But I have to wait awhile."

"Huh."

Deedoo licks the drips from the soggy cone. I instinctively pass the napkins, but she waves them away.

"Miss Linda could do your hair, too, if you want," she says.

"Can't say she's ever offered before."

"Well, you've already got a mamma."

"That I do."

"So, you should probably let her do your hair. It's looking a little messy."

"Hey."

"I know a lot about hair," she assures me, grabbing a handful of my brownish-blondish, will-they-won't-they locks with her still-sticky hands. "Yours is type two, the wavy kind."

"You don't say."

"You probably wanna brush it in the shower, not when it's dry. But you have to brush it sometime or else it'll end up like this. Tangled, I mean. Like a rat's nest."

"I get the picture."

Linda lives by the river; Deedoo, by the fire station. It's not too far, but in the winter it's awful dark. Does she saddle up the truck and pray the heat works? Does she travel by dogsled? Hard to imagine her chapped hands weaving Deedoo's long hair into something as pretty as this.

"Do you know if Linda has any kids of her own?"

Deedoo frowns.

"Grandpa says to mind your own business."

"Alrighty then."

"But one time she told me I reminded her of a little girl."

"Who?"

"Said it was somebody she'd never met."

Before I can work out the logic on that one, Trumpet calls up the hill. His shouting voice sounds a lot like his name. Startles the both of us into good posture.

"Gotta go. Bye, PJ."

"Bye, Deedoo."

The tail of her braid yips happily at her back as she makes her way down the hill. When she gets close to the bottom, she lies down and rolls the rest of the way. Oh, to be buoyant, I think. To wake up with not just grass in your hair but somebody to comb it out.

DOTTIE SPOON,
PEARL OF
PENNYWHISTLE

Well, shoot," Mamma says, slapping the kitchen counter.
"Linda Carter Creel, puttin' on the Ritz."

I biked over as soon as I could, knowing that Mamma laps
up drama. In a town this small, I reckon it's every mamma's favorite
nectar. They gather at night, lean up against their mailboxes to talk
smack, just praying somebody'll turn up drunk, pregnant, rich, or
dead. It's been two years since Pennywhistle's post office was featured
on *Ghost Hunters: Y'all Scared?* so they've been real starved for content
lately.

"I don't think Linda's quite reached the Ritz yet," I say. "At least not
with today's ensemble."

Mamma considers this.

"Puttin' on the Denny's?"

"Slightly better than that."

"Puttin' on the Red Lobster?"

"Yes, she's just about puttin' on the Red Lobster."

Mamma heaves a sigh.

"Man alive, I wish that place hadn'ta burned down."

"I'm happy for the lobsters," I concede, "but I miss the food."

"Me too, baby girl. 'Member my birthday dinner there? 'Bout three, four years ago, before they closed the butter bar? I haven't had a lick of decent seafood since."

"Not even the frozen crap?"

"You know I just don't cotton to that Gorton's fisherman."

"Never trust a man in yellow."

"Correct. Back to Linda, though. Linda, Linda. Don't that mean *pretty* in Spanish?"

"I think so."

"Ain't gonna be too pretty when she's pissin' in your pillowcase."

Mamma always did have a way with words. While regularly honored as Pennywhistle's Citizen of the Year, she has also been banned from every Kmart in the tristate area for the use of foul language in the presence of minors.

"Oh, the pissing has already begun," I lament. "Today she threatened to dock my paycheck for adding an extra scoop of ground beef to my lunch fries. I mean!"

"You don't mean!"

"Sure enough."

"Shoot."

Mamma's making pies today. Making pies for half the county, I should say. A few times a year, she barges in on every great-uncle, second cousin, and randy stepsibling she can rustle up, saying, "Ding dong, it's me, your old lady. Here with a pie and a set of ears. Gathering up gossip and clothes to mend." Some call her Santa and some call her Satan. Same letters either way.

"Do I get one of these?"

"Depends," she says. "You gonna tell me why you're smiling so big when it sounds like Linda's plum ready to ruin your life?"

"I'm not smiling."

"And I'm not fightin' a yeast infection under my neck folds."

"Mamma!"

"Your daddy always said I could grow anything. Bless his heart."

She gazes up at the Mr. Potato Head full of Daddy's ashes on the mantel. Same mustache, same ears. Almost like he's still here.

"I'm not smiling, I'm just animated from my riveting tale of press-on nails and ground beef."

She shakes the rolling pin at me.

"Liar."

"Fine. I made a new friend."

"A friend, huh?"

"Yes."

This is the part where she gets all *Law & Order* on my ass. When something doesn't add up, she picks it apart like a TV detective. Comforting, really, in that if I ever do get murdered I'm more likely than most to be found, avenged, and laid to rest in a plastic potato.

"You's an introvert and you already got a friend," Mamma says. "Lee Ray."

"I can have more friends than just Lee Ray."

"Speakin' of, you better tell that boy to bring back my rhinestone gun."

"I will."

"You know how I feel about my rhinestone gun."

"I do."

"It's right there in the Second Amendment."

"I don't think the Founding Fathers were referring to the Kirstie Alley Sparkle 'n' Shine 3,000 when they wrote that clause."

"Look, I didn't make three easy payments of nineteen ninety-nine to have my rights taken away."

"I'll be sure to let Lee Ray know."

As she rolls the dough, I stir the filling. After all these years of pies, you just sorta jump into the assembly line. Today we're doing cherry. When Daddy died, Mamma should have been on the receiving end of pies, but she said it made her feel better to keep making them for other people. Went a little dodo, to be honest. Thought she could make a pie for everybody in the phone book including the boarded-up Blockbuster and the personal injury law firm. Eventually Peewee Dupree down at the Piggly Wiggly had to ask her to cool it.

"We gotta keep some flour in stock for everybody else, honey," Peewee said.

"Course you do." Mamma smiled.

To this day, that's one of the only times I've ever seen Mamma embarrassed. By the general manager of the Piggly Wiggly, no less. Still, after that she kept her distance from the baking aisle. Maybe she knew that Peewee Dupree, thrice widowed and two-time survivor of geese attacks, was onto something. Without the constant companionship of butter, flour, and sugar, she had to let grief into her kitchen instead. Even let it sit at the counter for a few months. Mamma treated grief like a long-lost uncle come to visit. Meaning, of course, she eventually kicked it out. After that, she built the aboveground pool, ran for president of the Hog Club, and, grief be damned, stocked up on flour again.

Lee Ray says I should get her on a dating app. Apparently there's one for every type of single you could be. Jewish single, farmer single, cheating-on-your-husband single. He thinks she'd be a hit on the one for folks over sixty on account of her "zest for life" and "nose for bullshit." He's probably right, but the idea of somebody else occupying Daddy's beanbag chair just don't sit well. Between you and me, grief's been ringing my doorbell for a while. Persistent little fella. I haven't peered out the peephole, much less offered it a cup of coffee. Keep hoping it'll get tired and bother somebody else, but so far, no luck.

"Now, let me ask you this about your new friend: What's bigger, her can or her rack?"

"Mamma!"

"Lee Ray and I were talking about this just a few weeks ago at the Piggly Wiggly. We's saying how you ain't had a girlfriend in a while and I said well, that's on account of nobody in Pennywhistle's got a nice enough can for PJ—you always go for the ones with a big ole can—and he was spittin' some nonsense that no, what you're really after is a nice rack. Plenty of nice racks in Pennywhistle, I says, but still no girlfriend. Anyhow, we got so caught up that's how I forgot to ask for my rhinestone gun back."

"I shoulda never let y'all become friends."

"He's my oxygen."

Defeated, I prepare my book-report-style spiel. I don't know what I'm afraid of. Mamma ain't one of them throw-you-out-type parents. More the "get your gay ass in here and set the table" type. When I came out to her all she said was something about how come I can't change a tire proper.

"Earl, get out here and teach her some skills or she won't be able to find no date for the prom."

Mamma learned most of her gay stereotypes from Subaru commercials and the dirty jokes her old boss used to lob at the ladies who wouldn't sleep with him. Always reminds me to keep my nails short and my oil changed "if you's planning on gettin' laid." Shoo-ee. Not exactly the kind of thing you want to hear from the woman who birthed you. However, much as it might embarrass me, I have to admit Mamma single-handedly brought Pride to Pennywhistle. One summer she passed out rainbow flags alongside a fleet of pies and that was that. Did the same thing when folks weren't sure what to make of gluten-free bread and climate change.

"Let's just talk about it, why don't we?"

"My new friend's name is Boof," I begin. "She works at the Chickie Shak with me. No, you don't know her mamma because she's not from here. Yes, I'll be careful. And once again, no, I will not tell you how it works between the sheets. Does that about cover it?" I breathe out, exhausted.

"No," she says.

"What?"

"You didn't answer my only real question. Rack or can?"

Mamma looks so eager to find out, I can't possibly deny her. Who could say no to those buggy blue eyes and yeast-ridden neck?

"Can. She's got a nice can."

"I knew it! Suck a duck, Lee Ray!"

As her laughter calms down to a rickety giggle, she turns and looks at me serious-like. I know just exactly what she's gonna ask next. Nothing about Boof's jean size or whether she's got any ASAPs—"Mamma, it's STDs"—but something else. Her favorite question. It's never more than a week since the last time she mentioned it. Holidays and birthdays especially. Sometimes she'll even knock on the bathroom door, poke her head in, and ask it.

"So, pumpkin, when you gonna finish your PhD?"

For a woman who calls the ob-gyn the Obi-Wan Kenobi, this is one acronym she always says right.

"Mamma." I sigh.

"What? I's just askin'."

Just askin' pummels my stomach harder than a short fella in a bar fight. *Just askin'* salts my pits with sweat. *Just askin'* leads to *just answerin'*, which is precisely what I haven't done for the past six months when Dean Jackson's called to say, I imagine, something like *You better get your tardy little butt back here, you hear?* Except much nicer, on account of his thick drawl and affinity for underdogs. It's probably more like *I'll thank you kindly for getting back to me at your leisure, Miss Spoon.* Can't be sure, though. I haven't deleted his voicemails, but I also haven't listened to most of them. They just sit there, wedged between my usuals. Lee Ray calling with a detailed account of his aunt's latest psychic vision or Mamma asking if I need anything at the store. Then there's the fella who's mighty enthusiastic about my car's extended warranty. Somehow his calls are easier to field than any of the ones concerning my future. Why is everybody so damn keen on knowing my plans anyways? The only person who truly believed they were possible sleeps in a plastic potato now.

Truth is, I ended up at Vanderbilt the way you end up most important places: by complete accident.

It was my senior fall at the University of Memphis, one of those Saturdays you wake up feeling game for just about anything, be it a tattoo or a turkey leg. As soon as my feet hit the carpeted floor and my roommate left to confront her boyfriend about his phone records, I decided that my hankering was not for ink or poultry, but for a Twinkie.

U of M lacks a Piggly Wiggly, but the stoners across the hall from me could usually be counted on for snacks. Look, not everybody at school was what you'd call a rocket scientist. The boys across the hall dealt in beanbags and Doritos. They played acoustic instruments. One of them fostered kittens. His Christian name was Rufus, but we called him Noah.

"Morning, Noah. Y'all got any Twinkies?"

"Of course we do. Come in, come in."

While I unsheathed a Twinkie and a little orange kitten settled into my lap, Noah tuned a fiddle. A stack of dusty textbooks propped up the corner of his bed. Freshman Biology, Intro to French. Every language you could learn if you bothered to take the plastic off the book.

"So, what are you doing next year, Noah?"

"Same thing I'm doing this year. Getting my PhD in tomfoolery."

"You don't even have a BA yet."

"Baby steps. How 'bout you?"

"I'm not sure," I admitted. "I'm supposed to meet with my advisor this afternoon with a, quote, *plan for my future*."

"Scary stuff." He nodded, though I doubted a man with a metric ton of marijuana could understand the weight of fear.

"What do you think I should do?"

"Well, when I get stuck on what to do I think about what I already like doing."

"Such as?"

"Smoking, for one. And I like little wet noses. And sleeping under the stars. What do you like?"

"Well, I like to read. Which is kind of the whole thing as a history major."

"What part of history?" he asked. "Dinosaurs or Pilgrims?"

"American history. Well, Southern especially. Hospitality, little forgotten stories. Stuff like that."

Noah's roommate, Brock, looked up from his cloud of smoke.

"She got that big award last year, remember? The Tennessee Williams one."

"I got that one freshman year. Last year I got the Jon Meacham Award and the Summit Grant."

"You're great at talking, too."

"You think?"

"Hell yeah! You're the reason I know what *LGBTQ* stands for. And how the Civil War turned out."

"Glad we cleared those up."

"I liked when you gave that talk at the student center," Brock added. "They had, like, ten types of donuts at the reception. Pretty cool."

Noah nodded in agreement.

"Is there somewhere you can go to keep reading and talking?"

"Well, like you said, I could get a PhD."

"I heard it's like college but they pay you."

"Something like that."

A calico emerged from a crack in the wall and joined its brother on my lap. I got the feeling that the longer I sat there, the more cats I'd accumulate. Bales and bales of them, warm and comforting. No wonder Noah didn't want to graduate. I, on the other hand, was suppressing a sneeze.

"Where should I go?" I asked, passing the cats back.

"My cousin just got kicked out of Vanderbilt, so I know they've got a spot."

"Thanks. I'll look into it."

"Glad I could be of service."

I bid Noah and his menagerie adieu. By the time I arrived in my advisor's office that afternoon I had a runny nose. And a plan.

"Enough about me," I tell Mamma. "What's new with the Hog Club?"

She shakes the rolling pin at my weak attempt to change the subject.

"This ain't over."

I'm content to wait it out.

"To tell you the truth, we's busy as all get out. Turns out most of the legislature assumed folks was getting periods out their cans not their, you know"—she gestures southward—"so now I've got to whip up an educational segment."

"Well, that's special."

"The whole thing's two heaps of stupid. You know in Critter County tampons is taxed the same as booze and cigarettes? A luxury tax. I mean!"

"You're preaching to the choir here, Mamma."

"I know. I know. We just ain't gonna stand for it no more, I tell you what."

She shepherds the first batch of pies out of the oven. Shoot if they don't smell like heaven on a Sunday.

"Correct me if I'm wrong, but didn't you go through menopause already? I seem to remember a whole summer you wore one of those fan key chains around your neck like a rosary to keep up with the hot flashes."

"Honey, just cause my tap's run dry doesn't mean I can't fight for yours." She gives my nose a honk. "And your girlfriend's."

"She's not my girlfriend!"

"Well, by the time she is you can both bleed free."

Founded in 1985, the Pennywhistle Hog Club meets wherever God can spare a chair. The church basement if it's raining, Mamma's backyard if it's sunny, and, if they're really in a pinch, the old tennis court that's half sucked into a sinkhole. No matter where they roam, they always find something to care deeply about. Dental hygiene, suicide prevention. I was about seven or eight when I asked Daddy how they decided on a cause.

"Well," he said, "I reckon they read the *Pennywhistle Psst* and start from there. Either that or they flip a coin."

"That seems silly."

"Sillier than not giving a rip? Life would be mighty boring if we was all too big for our britches to care."

I pawed at the floor, feeling as though I'd disappointed him.

"It's not like she's putting out fires or anything," I mumbled.

"What's that now?"

"She's not brave like you."

Other daddies might've slapped my rear with a wooden spoon or washed my mouth out with soap for talking ill about my mamma, but my daddy was more the teaching sort. A professor at heart with a high school education, he never did miss a learning opportunity. That day, as I watched Mamma set up chairs in the backyard, Daddy pulled out a scrapbook and explained.

"Your mamma fights things that are much harder to put out than a little old fire. That takes a special sort of bravery that even I don't got. Take a look-see."

The album was like a tiny stable in itself, so full of horses and smells that if you closed your eyes you'd swear you were right there in the barn. Pointing out this horse and that, Daddy told me about Mamma's days in the rodeo, when women didn't make near as much money as men for the same tricks. No matter that she was the best of the best, she still didn't have two nickels to rub together. So, one summer Mamma rode her horse from town to town and talked to other girls in the same boat. Some two hundred riders banded together for better contracts and bigger venues all because she decided to make it so. I gazed at a picture of her holding an "Equal Neigh, Equal Pay" banner at the Tennessee State Capitol. My mamma! And there, just a little ways back, my daddy, smiling with his thumbs up.

"You were in the rodeo, too, right?"

"Yes, ma'am. See that guy with the mullet?"

"Looks like the hairdresser forgot to finish cutting."

"You little stinker. It was the look back then."

I found this hard to believe. Something else nettled me, but I wasn't sure if I was allowed to say it. The other mammas and daddies in town worked different than mine. Like they were swapped. The mammas were gentle and sensitive, the daddies, charismatic and bossy. Though, come to think of it, Mayor Fisher-Trapper was like my mamma. Her husband arranged flowers for weddings and the Half-Off Pass Away Depot and she gave big, funny speeches on the steps of the courthouse in a hat the size of a tire swing. Mostly, the daddies in town seemed grumpy if the mammas ever did anything big all by themselves. I had to wonder if Daddy was secretly one of them.

"You musta got real jealous when Mamma got famous."

"Jealous?" He chuckled. "The only thing I ever got for your mamma was goose bumps and palpitations."

"So, you don't mind that she wears the boots in the family?"

"Where'd you pick that one up?"

"Nowhere."

Daddy rested a hand on my shoulder and looked out at Mamma. So much might in one little person. She weighed just one hundred pounds soaking wet and holding her purse, but suddenly I saw what Daddy saw. She was a giant. She had not only found the chairs, but also a group of women to fill them. Daddy waved.

"What? I'm working," she said.

"Just saying hi."

At this she sweetened.

"Hi, sugar."

Daddy turned back to me.

"The day I met your mamma I knew we was two of a kind. Redneck Archimedes."

"What do you mean?"

"We both had a mind to change the world, each in our own way."

The first of the club members started arriving, their arms full of meat loaves and brownies, their minds ready for the next challenge. Mayor Fisher-Trapper tipped her enormous yellow hat at us.

"Did you change the world yet?" I asked.

"Course we did." He smiled. "We made you."

JUST THIGHS

Gunner Fisher-Trapper, who just finally got his wisdom teeth out and can eat again, orders the Trixie Biscuit.

"Been a few weeks, but I've got a butter memory for this one."

Butter memory. This strikes me as awful poetic. Before I can forget it between wings and shakes I snatch the red notebook out of its hiding place and jot the phrase down. *Butter memory* makes me think of churning butter, which makes me wonder who invented butter in the first place. Who said let's beat milk with a stick? Who agreed to try? And who, oh who, reckoned it might taste good on a biscuit? You could probably draw a map of all the places butter'd been before it landed here on Gunner's plate. I wonder if the library has any farming records from way back when . . .

Linda clears her throat.

"Linda," I wheeze. "You scared the bejesus out of me."

"I hate to break it to you, Miss University, but they ain't paying us to wax poetic. I don't want to see any more scribbling in this kitchen. Period."

"I was about to go on break."

"Not in this kitchen you're not. You don't see me smoking at the register. Take it outside."

"Yes, ma'am."

"Don't yes, ma'am me," Linda spits, adjusting the hoops and springs of her hussy upper. "I'm practically your age."

I lower my voice.

"Whatever you say, *ma'am*."

"Now, that's it."

She snatches my notebook hawk-wise and dangles it over the deep fryer.

"Hey!"

"Let's not forget who's in charge here."

"I'm sorry, Linda. Just give it back."

"I will when you start showing me some respect."

She whips the notebook dangerously close to the grease, enough for a bubble to pop on the back cover, then tucks it smugly under her arm.

"A little light reading for my break. Or maybe something to line my hamster cage with. We gon' see."

"Linda!"

"Ta-ta."

I brace myself on the sink. Deep breaths. Deep, greasy breaths. Who cares if my notebook goes the way of our frozen tenders, really? Not like I'm gonna do anything with it. And yet, every time I reach for an order slip I check to see if it's still there. Boof catches my eye more than a few times, furrows her little red brow.

"What's wrong?" she mouths.

"Nothing," I lie.

When Linda goes out for her smoke break, she totes the notes with her. I pray to poultry and Jesus they don't emerge with singe marks—or, worse, footnotes—and try to stay busy enough to forget.

Lucky for me, she leaves without saying goodbye again. The second she's out the door I rush to the register, come to find my notebook still missing. Shit. I check the ladies' room just in case. The coatrack. No luck. Resigned, I make my way to the back door, mourning I don't know what.

"I take it this is yours?" Boof smiles, notebook in hand. "That or Linda's an even bigger mystery than I thought."

"No, she's really not. It's mine. Thank you."

Without thinking, I pull Boof in for a tight hug. I'm a good bit taller, so my hands land in the soft spot between her shoulder blades, right where the curls peter out. Her hands circle my waist. It's a slow dance, a time warp. A crepe paper, play us a ballad, don't let go until the teachers pry us apart kind of feeling. Are we swaying? I can't say. The moment I feel the urge to lean down and kiss her, it occurs to me that I haven't established if Boof even likes women, much less fry cooks. I jump back.

"You didn't, uh, read it or anything?"

"No."

"Oh, phew. But also, why not?"

"Because that would ruin all the fun of getting to know you."

"Right."

"Besides," she says, "I once read my dad's diary when I was a kid and it said something about how he really wanted a teapot. He'd just always wanted one. I thought that was so tender. For years I'd look for them at garage sales, but I realized I couldn't get him one or he'd know I'd read the diary. I'm still waiting for him to tell me he wants a teapot. I don't think it's gonna happen."

"I'll just come right out and say it, then. I would love a teapot."

"Good to know."

"I'll see you tomorrow?"

"Yes, ma'am."

We stand at the back door longer than two people should. The sunflowers rustle in their toilets. A whip-poor-will chirps good night.

"Thanks again for rescuing this," I say, mostly as an excuse to hug her again. As we embrace, she wraps her hand softly around my ponytail. Read my diary, I think. Ruin my sleep.

The bus rumbles up the road.

"I should catch that."

I nod solemnly.

"Don't want my lasagnas to burn," she says with a wink. "You understand."

"I do."

Sounds like a vow. Maybe it is.

A WEEK LATER, I'm out on the river in Lee Ray's boat, *Just Thighs,* when I spot what is either Boof or a very large red badger.

"I'm starved for information here, PJ. Starved."

"I'm sorry, I've been—"

"Busy? No, I've been busy. The EFPs think we can make it down the Mississippi for the Summer Paddle Adventure. We can barely make it down the lazy river at Wet Barf Water Park, much less what Mark Twain once referred to as the—"

"Shh! She's over there."

"Who?"

"Boof!"

He turns around. Boof spreads a checkered blanket over the riverbank. She's done up in the unofficial Pennywhistle summer uniform: jorts and a Kenny Chesney T-shirt.

"Well, I'll be! Dottie was right about you and cans."

"Hush. She'll hear you."

"Don't you hush me. You wouldn't even have a fighting chance with that girl if I hadn't twisted off that skin tag last week."

"And you know how much I appreciate your services."

"Then what? We can't say hi?"

"I've just got a few more emotional skin tags to get rid of before I can go around approaching her in public."

"You see her at work all the time."

"That just makes it even more, you know . . ."

Lee Ray considers this. He knows full well not to ask about the logistics of a workplace romance. The bridges to be burned, the wounds to be licked. He simply asks, "Are you drowning or am I drowning?"

Lee Ray and I have helped each other seduce many an unsuspecting vacationer via Pennywhistle's murky river. One of us falls headlong out of the canoe while the other one carries the waterlogged fool and *Just Thighs* safely back to shore, plopping both right down in front of the good-looking stranger, who is always terribly impressed by the heroism of whoever does the saving. It works about half the time. The other half we have to explain to the 911 operator that it's PJ and Lee Ray again and yes, we promise to start asking people out the old-fashioned way, sans deception.

"I may be past my drowning days." I sigh. "Least with this one."

"Intriguing."

"She just, I don't know. Makes me wanna tell the truth. Or some gooey garbage like that, you know?"

"How very meteoric. Reminds me of Lionel," he says. "What's New Orleans got that I haven't?"

Beads and bright colors and culture is what I don't say. Everything that's too big to fit beneath our stoplight.

"He's just a river away," I prod.

"A pretty big river."

"The EFPs would be delighted."

"Speaking of drowning."

We're getting closer now. Near enough that decisions must be made.

"I guess we could just say a quick hello."

"Look at that emotional growth!"

"Don't rub it in." I grin.

But just as I'm about to paddle us closer, another badger appears. Rather, a burly, redheaded fella sits down next to Boof, right close and touching like freckles on a cheek. They toast a pair of Coors Lights, the pinnacle of intimacy, if you ask me.

Lee Ray steers us away silently. Suddenly drowning don't seem so bad.

POSSUMS
IN A CREEK

Mamma always says, "When God closes a door it's cuz he needs to fart," which is her way of saying when things don't work out, it's probably for the best. Maybe she's right. Despite yesterday's romantic setback, it's still a regular Sunday night for me. I'm curled up on my couch reading about the Raccoon King's latest shenanigans. As he escapes the clutches of Sir William, the Dark Armadillo, I put on the kettle.

Times like these I'm glad I have my own place. After a few months of shrugging to fit back into my childhood bedroom, I started combing the lawns of Pennywhistle for To Rent signs. Nothing special, just a bathroom I didn't have to share with Mamma, who was still of the opinion that toothbrushes oughta be shared property. Saw a couple of carpeted basements, a souped-up dog house. Finally, Mrs. Heller's nephew went back to Memphis to meet his kids, meaning I lucked into a perfectly pint-size cottage by the river. Long as I mow the lawn and turn away any would-be spawn, the rent stays low.

Not to say I don't miss my place in Nashville. My coffee shop, my postman. But that's in the past. This place came furnished, so all my sweet little songwriting neighbors had to mail me back were my clothes, my banjo, and my books. I told Carlos and Rick they could go finders keepers on the ice cream and the spare change. They took their time mailing everything, like I might change my mind. Sorry, fellas, I wrote, I've got a job.

Truth be told, I've got a lot of nice things. It's a cozy night. My quilt covers my sock feet and my tea fogs up my glasses like when somebody sees a hot girl on TV. You know, *hubba, hubba*. Best of all, from my perch I can hear the sweet sounds of the neighborhood strays eating the evening slop I left out for them. Three cats, a dog, and the occasional goose make up my menagerie. They're chowing down as usual when the phone rings. Just a number. No name. Which don't make a lick of sense because damn near everybody in this town is already saved on my phone as who they are and how I know them. Julie-first-kiss. Good-for-nothing-Uncle-Elmer. Henry-who-fixed-the-toilet-after-the-Super-Bowl. Keeps my life organized, familiar. Then again, seems like everything's coming right out of the blue these days, so I might as well pick up.

"Hello?"

"Hi, PJ, this is Rosco Puddin. Yes, *the* Rosco Puddin."

He elongates the *hi* like we're best friends, but says the *the* like he's famous. Kind of conflicting messages, if you ask me.

"Hi, Mr. Puddin. What can I do for you?"

"PJ, dear, I'm so glad I reached you."

"Uh, me too. Is everything okay?"

"Heavens, yes! I'm calling each of our Chickie Shak Hot Chicken Beauty Tour contestants to remind you that the first heat of the competition will take place this Friday night at the Pennywhistle High Memorial Auditorium."

"Right. The fashion show round?"

"The *God's Brilliant Grace* category, yes."

"Okay."

"I'm really looking forward to your performance. It is, as you know, mandatory."

"I believe I saw that in the email."

"So, we're reading emails now! Splendid. It sounds like you're in the loop."

Ain't the purpose of emails that you don't have to pick up the phone? No talk, small or otherwise? I let my end of the line go quiet, which works on most people. Five seconds of awkward and they rush right off. Mr. Puddin clears his throat.

"I guess that's just about it, isn't it?"

"Reckon it is, Mr. Puddin."

"Well, PJ, before I sign off I just wanted to offer my personal thanks for your beauty. Both inner and outer."

Never thought about it, but I guess when it comes to beauty we're a lot like belly buttons: innies and outies.

"Thank you, sir. I'll see you on Friday."

Click. Only the goose remains at the back door, nibbling on pound cake and ham bones with the reckless abandon of a freshly minted divorcée. I'm reminded of Mr. Puddin's email, which advised us to "watch our weight" before Friday. *The trimmer the face the bigger the grace*. Or something like that. Lordy. I'm certainly not in this thing for the attention. Not the million dollars, either. To be quite honest, without the constant swirl of deadlines, lectures, and impromptu Maren Morris concerts, I've been a little bored. Only so many sock drawers to clean out, so many teeth to floss. If tarting around in a sparkly dress means I've got something to do on a Friday night, I might as well bite. Though, frankly, I'm not sure how much of God's Brilliant Grace I'll be able to muster. That's entirely up to the work of Mamma, Lee Ray, and the Kirstie Alley Sparkle 'n' Shine 3,000.

I fall asleep reading my book. As a consequence, I dream of the Raccoon King. He wears a Dolly Parton wig and strums a bejeweled banjo with his wee trash hands. It's just crazy enough it might work.

COME MORNING, I find another sneaky jewelry delivery on my soap dish. This time it's a little silver necklace. Either Mamma's meddling or Daddy's ghost escaped from that potato again. And don't you start with me on "ghosts ain't real." Daddy's ghost does all kinds of unruly things that only Daddy would do. Turns on QVC in the afternoons, takes a beer out of the fridge and forgets about it in the shower. On special occasions he'll lay out church dresses for me. Then, when I refuse to wear them, he just folds them right on back into the trunk where we keep the fishing gear. No fuss. No fight. He always said it was real important to let everybody row their own boat. The first time it happened, Lee Ray asked me if I was okay. I'm more than okay, I told him, holding up my Easter dress. Daddy's Caspering means he's still here. If I close my eyes I can pretend he's not dead, just busy, like every time he comes around I've just missed him by a hair. There's the screen door clattering, I tell myself. There's the coffee mug in the sink. The great beyond must not be very exciting, because Daddy spends an awful lot of time in Pennywhistle.

I wash my face and fix my hair, humming one of Boof's homespun country tunes all the while. This one's called "Possums in a Creek," a play on Dolly Parton and Kenny Rogers's song "Islands in the Stream."

Possums in a creek. That is what we are. Little pointy teeth leave an awful scar.

What would make Boof want to up and leave what I can only imagine was a promising career writing songs at the Grand Ole Opry? Then again, you might ask me why I went all the way to the big city to get my degree only to pedal my little red wagon back to Pennywhistle. I wonder when Boof and I will get to all this. The unspooling that leads to the kite. Answer: we won't.

Possums in a creek. That is what we are. Stop singing her songs, I tell myself. Mamma or Daddy—whoever it was who put the necklace out—be damned, I am not about to gussy up for a woman who doesn't want me. I mean, why bother with a necklace when Boof's more interested in Ball Park Franks than chicken breasts? To be fair, she could be into both Ball Park Franks and chicken breasts. Lots of people are into both Ball Park Franks and chicken breasts. Hell, some people are into the whole grocery store. Pardon my metaphors, but that's just how I put it to Mamma. And that's how she in turn put it to the Hog Club. *Now,*

Dede, that's just how they is. You stick to your hot dogs and Lee Ray'll stick to his. You hear? I guess what I really mean is something about that red-head on the riverbank makes me think Boof is not sweet on *my* chicken breasts. Which is too damn bad. Because I've always really liked Patsy Cline.

Maybe I'm still a little wounded from my first crush, Paola "Peppy" Hernandez. Her daddy was the director over at the Quarterflute Playhouse and would take us to see all the latest shows, the type of cultural event that's hard to come by this side of the Loosahatchie, not counting Circ de Moon and the county fair. It's Tennessee, y'all. We got plenty of singers, but the only actors around here are the kind of miscreants who call up the lawyer on the billboard and claim broken necks until the settlement pays for their new RV. Slim pickins. Still, Mr. Hernandez knew if you pull a net through enough podunk little towns you'll catch a few stars. He strung them together year after year, play after play, until the playhouse could afford things like curtains and non-stolen wigs.

Peppy and I liked the musicals best, especially *My Fair Lady.* I can still see us in the front row as Eliza—who'd been discovered after appearing in one of the personal injury lawyer's commercials—and Henry Higgins—who'd been culled from a stirring performance at jury duty—argued in song. Our knees touched as Freddy sang about the street where Eliza lived. The tips of Peppy's hair grazed my shoulder when she leaned over to tell me Henry's fly was unzipped. Later, as we belted the words to "I Could Have Danced All Night" at each other from opposing twin beds, it occurred to me that sleeping over at Peppy's house gave me the exact same feeling Eliza Doolittle was singing about. I didn't want to brush my teeth and settle down. I wanted to dance all night, dammit.

"You sure spend a lot of time over there," Mamma said of my weekly presence at the Hernandez house. "Next thing I know you're gonna be a child actor."

I remember blushing.

"I just like going to see the shows."

"All right, sugar. Just make sure you ain't bothering those nice folks."

Was I? I leapt at any excuse to putter over to Peppy's house. Not just opening night but dress rehearsals, auditions. Line by line, play after play, sleepover by sleepover, something was building up in me. Finally, when the song was over and Peppy exclaimed, "Again! Again!" I knew what the feeling was. Oh, I thought, I want to kiss her. It seemed important to ask, rather than jump right in, so I perked up my best Eliza accent and said, "Oi, Peppy! Can I kiss you?"

"What?"

"I said, can I kiss you?"

"No." She recoiled. "You're a girl."

"Girls can kiss girls."

"Says who?"

"I don't know. Maybe I made it up. But it sounds fun, right?"

She scratched her head.

"I guess some girls can kiss some girls, but I'm the kind of girl who wants to kiss boys, okay? Like Eliza and Henry."

"Okay," I said. "Do you want to keep singing?"

"No, I have a stomachache."

She assembled her pajamas into a harried pile and carried them to the bathroom to change. I tucked myself into bed. Peppy's family moved away a few years after that, and I can only assume wherever she is she still has that stomachache. Her father put on a dozen more plays before the move; she never invited me over again.

YEARS BEYOND THAT first rejection, I now consider the silver bicycle charm hanging down from my necklace. Heaving a sigh, I spin the wheels and watch the spokes whir. The basket's got little flowers in it. I swear it even has a kickstand. "You cain't forget to be loved," Mamma likes to say. Then she does something like this to make sure you don't. So, what if Boof's gone poof? There's other girls out there, girls who'll come right out and say *Howdy, I like you*, without beating around the deep fryer. So, I carry on. Brush my teeth and put on the necklace.

As I paw around the dresser for my keys I feel a breeze run through the house. Smells a bit like pork rinds and peaches. Distinct. And sure enough, when I turn around there on the bed lies my old Easter dress. Bright pink tulips, fat lace collar, sleeves big as all get out. Laid out next to a pair of saddle oxfords I haven't worn since I was twelve.

"Nice try, Daddy," I say, "but I think I'll just stick to the necklace."

AS I CAREEN into the Chickie Shak driveway, I can hear Boof walking up behind me. She's got a walk you can recognize. A jaunt. Only today I act like I don't hear it. Hell, I don't even bother to lock my bike to the hose rack. Instead, I head for the door like I used to. Back when we were just coworkers and I didn't know her up close. Ball Park Franks is all I can think of. Maybe that's what I'll call her lover: Frank.

"Hey, PJ, wait up."

"Oh, hi."

I fumble for the store key. Boof checks her watch and furrows her brow. We both know we have a good ten minutes before we really need to unlock.

"What's up?" she asks.

"Nothing."

"Hey, so I was thinking about our songs and I thought if you really like music you could get a little radio to attach to your bike."

"Maybe."

"Come on, why not?"

"Radio's pretty patchy in Pennywhistle. You can only get 96.5 if you go out past the fairgrounds. Otherwise it's static and polka."

"How 'bout I just sing into a walkie-talkie every morning for you."

Sweet, beautiful Boof. She turns me red and softens me up until I'm practically a clown nose.

"More on the perverts and the snakes?"

"Oh, I've got a whole discography of creep-themed ballads. Real gritty stuff."

"Such as?"

She glances around to see if any of our bona fide early-bird customers are within earshot. As far as the town of Pennywhistle knows, Boof's a cute little redhead who serves milkshakes with a smile, not a randy little songstress with a couple dozen swear words in her apron pocket. Luckily, the only customer in sight is Mrs. Heller walking up the drive at a mile-an-hour pace. She can't hear, either, so we're practically alone.

"This one's an original song based on a truly harrowing experience I had in the Piggly Wiggly last week. Think upbeat. Little bit of spunky banjo. Maybe a cowbell."

"Got it."

She clears her throat and grasps an imaginary microphone.

"Way down yonder at the Piggly Wiggly, where the meat is fine and the patrons are jiggly, I'm checking out when a man approaches me, says baby how's about you show me the goods, please."

"Oh, Lord."

"I said my name isn't baby, my answer's not maybe, my goods don't come out just because you said please. Don't call me a whore at the grocery store. This kitty you like has got rabies."

"That's amazing—"

"But wait, there's more. Here's where it picks up. Clap along."

I furrow my brow. Prepare a cautious clap.

"As he reaches down my torso close to my thighs that's the moment I discover my butt's the prize. I stand on my toes and look him straight in the eye. Say, step away from my rear or prepare to die."

"Oh, my God, that's terrible!" I laugh.

"I thought you'd enjoy it seeing as you're always staring at it."

"Staring at what?"

"My butt."

Now I know what they mean when they say *jaw drop*. Hard to get anything out of my mouth with my damn chin on the floor. Boof grins.

"Well?" she asks.

"In these parts we call that your *can*."

"So, you don't deny it?"

"Boof, I'm sorry if I, um, overstepped or anything . . ."

"Overstepped? Girl, don't you know I've been staring right back?"

If Lee Ray were here he'd start running the imaginary bases around the Chickie Shak while singing a new victory chant. *Two-four-six-eight! PJ found a girl to date!*

"But you have a boyfriend."

"Is that right?" she asks, hands on her hips.

"I saw you this weekend on the river. Not that I was stalking you or anything. I was out with my friend Lee Ray."

"Thought that was you. I like the boat, by the way."

"*Just Thighs* was my idea. He wanted to call it *Britney Oars*."

Boof nudges me with her elbow.

"Why didn't you come say hi? We had enough Coors Light to last 'til the resurrection."

"Well, I wasn't about to crash your date."

Why is she making me say it? I'm already having a hard time not talking directly to my sneakers. Spending all day on the fryer's looking pretty good compared to imagining how her romantic rendezvous turned out.

"Not my best date, to be honest. Seeing as he's my *twin*."

My head shoots right back up.

"Twin?"

"The red hair didn't tip you off?"

Now that I think of it, Pennywhistle has only two or three redheads, Mamma included.

"Right. I'm an idiot."

"In just so many ways," she says.

We stand around doing that not-quite-talking-but-not-yet-kissing thing. The time zone where everything goes quiet and still. Like right before the Big Bang or God's grand entrance or a powerful sneeze. We don't have time to create any universes right now, unfortunately, because Mrs. Heller has almost reached the Chickie Shak and will soon be asking for her usual: two sweet teas and a honey biscuit. Remind me why folks need to eat, again? Couldn't they just stay home and let a couple of star-crossed Hot Chicken contestants make out for once?

"I guess we better unlock." I groan, turning to the door.

"Wait!"

"What?"

She steps closer and twirls the wheels on my necklace.

"Now that we've established that you've been looking at my can and I've been looking at your can, what do you plan to do about it?"

I consider this as Linda's truck pulls into the parking lot. Boof takes one strategic step back but keeps her eyes locked on mine.

"I have an idea," I say, "but it's a little crazy."

"You've got exactly twenty seconds to tell me while she tries to undo her seat belt."

The pink claws make this task, like so many others, a nightmare for poor Linda. She fumbles with the buckle as I hurry to explain.

"How would you feel about teaming up for the God's Baby Angel category?"

"You mean God's Brilliant Grace?" she asks, rolling her eyes.

"Yes, that one."

"What did you have in mind?"

"I was thinking I'm pretty decent on the banjo, so maybe you could sing one of your original songs and I could play it. Or we could write something new together."

Linda finally manages to get the door open. Damn it.

"You know I would absolutely love that, PJ," Boof whispers. "But God's Brilliant Grace is the beauty portion. We don't get to talent until Gabriel's Shining Star next week."

"You mean I have to do beauty all on my own?"

"'Fraid so. But good to know you own a banjo."

"It's a long story."

Actually it's not. Lee Ray, Daddy, and I found the banjo one sum-mer on our journey to see Dollywood and Auntie June. We stayed with her for three nights, during which she told our fortunes and cooked us the saltiest collard greens you ever did eat. Practically turned our tongues to jerky, but it was worth it to get a sneak peek into the great beyond.

"Lee Ray, child, I see you in the water."

"Dead or alive?" he asked.

We'd recently watched *Cast Away* and had our doubts about the ocean.

"Alive and well. My, my. Looks like you're in charge of a whole lot of people."

He leaned in to search for her vision in the crisscross of his palm.

"Like a captain?"

"Something along those lines. Why don't you take that old canoe out your mamma's shed and start sanding it down."

"What canoe?"

"Exactly."

"What about me?" I asked.

She held my palm in her soft, knobby hands. They had a jitter to them, like an electric current ran straight down from the future into her fingers.

"Let's see. Oh, we got ourselves one smart cookie. I see big dreams. Earl, drive her through campus on your way out of town, would you?"

"You think she's gonna make it to college?"

"Not if she don't see the place."

"Roger that, Miss June."

She turned her gaze on him. Daddy didn't want his fortune told, but I'm sure she could see it anyway, the short stretch of years pooling in her milky left eye. Sometimes I wish she'd have warned us. Instead, she implored him to eat up.

"You look positively famished, Earl. Why don't you have another plate of collard greens?"

"We should probably start heading out, Miss June. The kids are itching to make it to Dollywood by sundown."

"Nonsense. There's at least three more servings left. Here, let me scoop some into a Tupperware for you."

She started to let go of my hand, but I guess as she rose from her chair she felt a new crease, a little river she hadn't detected before. A smile cracked across her face.

"What?" I asked.

"Oh, nothing," she said. "Just be sure to take a left on your way out."

After a few more spoonfuls of collard greens and a heap of hugs, we finally made it to the car. As promised, we took a left. Two houses over, somebody had left a box of sheet music and an old banjo next to the trash. I called dibs. The rest is history.

LINDA STRIDES TOWARD US.

"Morning, Linda," Boof tries.

"Get."

"Kitchen, noon," I whisper.

"Smoking break?"

"Smoking break."

While Linda puffs four cigarettes as fast as she can, I plan to make far better use of my mouth.

I BELIEVE IT'S
NOT CHEESE

I return home to find Lee Ray and Mamma sprawled over a pile of old jeans as high and wide as the Blue Ridge Mountains. The Kirstie Alley Sparkle 'n' Shine 3,000 sits patiently on the kitchen table along with a few feet of jump rope. What kind of backwoods seance am I walking into?

I set my keys down on the counter. Almost time to feed my strays and catch up on the Raccoon King. Sometimes Mamma calls me Patsy *DeCline* on account of my introverted tendencies. Aside from her and Lee Ray's company, I'm likely to say no to just about any other social invitation.

"I assume there's a perfectly normal explanation for this, so I'm gonna grab a beer and heat up my corn dog."

"Deal me in, baby," Mamma says.

"Lee Ray?"

"But, PJ, my figure!"

I make three, just like always.

As our dogs do-si-do in the microwave, Mamma cuts a clear line through the leg of some tired overalls. She's got straight pins hanging out of her mouth like buckteeth, which means we're well past stage one of this ensemble. I scan the living room. Somewhere, some vaguely human object is wearing her half-fangled creation. Anything will do.

Stuffed bear. Coatrack. Propane tank. As long as it sits still, she can build a dress around it that will somehow fit me, too. Ah, there she is! Today's stand-in PJ is Bruno, the CPR dummy from Lee Ray's water safety course.

I walk the dogs to my faithful stylists.

"Thank you," Lee Ray says. "We've been brainstorming all day and we finally have something."

"Oh?"

"Your mother is a visionary."

"A real Leonardo, if I do say so m'self."

She's referring to the Ninja Turtle, not da Vinci.

"Tell me more, little turtle."

"I've been racking my rack about what to do with your daddy's old jeans," she says. "See, at first I kept 'em just in case I started to put on some weight. They're good backup pants, you know? But turns out I'm an old fart who couldn't gain weight if I was screwin' Little Debbie herself."

Lee Ray interrupts this disturbing visual by placing his early-aughts scrapbook into my lap and opening to the pop culture section. Among his many hobbies, my bizarre, beloved best friend keeps detailed, museum-worthy records of his life via construction paper and *People* magazine. *Sell them when I'm famous!* he always says, though he's yet to decide what it is he wants to be famous for.

"Moving on. Page twenty-two. One recalls the iconic denim-on-denim look that Britney and Justin wore at the 2001 American Music Awards."

"I reckon one does."

"We thought, How can we take that raw denim magnetism and bring it to the next level? Rhinestones, obviously."

"Obviously," Mamma echoes.

"Dottie's got the gown, I'm on hair and makeup, and you'll be happy to hear that, much as I'd like to, we do not have time to festoon a pair of denim shoes, so you can wear your Friday boots."

Up there you got day-of-the-week undies. Down here we got day-of-the-week boots. That's how you know if somebody got lucky. Step one foot in town with the wrong day on, all the mammas'll be squawking from their kitchen windows, *Shoo-ee, look who's still wearing her Wednesday boots!* I curse my luck, that I, too, could be wearing the wrong day's boots tomorrow if it weren't for the crowd today.

Customers came clear out of Lucifer's pits to suck down chili dogs and gossip about the pageant. I mean everybody. Martha Turley from the state park. Senator Brill First. Even Jed Murdock, down at the motor pool. Folks who haven't come out of their hidey-holes since the Y2K barbecue suddenly wanted in on the town gab. As a rule, Pennywhistlers love to celebrate. We adore the Olympics, go hog wild about Halloween, and make any and every excuse to sing "Happy Birthday." By this logic, I should have expected the pageant to rustle up a hullabaloo. Still, the crowd and the volume have exceeded my wildest notions. They're proud. Hopeful, even. Much as I'm dreading shaving my legs, their excitement makes me want to try. With a million dollars, I could fix a few roofs, start a few scholarships. Or, at the very least, tuck a five-dollar bill and a chocolate orange into every mailbox as a thank-you for loving me so well.

Somewhere around two, the crowd turned into a picnic. Kinda sweet when you think about it. All those long-lost friends talking smack and taking bets over a plate of hot chicken. Most took one look at the three of us, threw their wagers like lassos, and spent the rest of lunch making amends for the drunken brawls and stolen coonhounds of yore. Did so much talking, we ran out of stanky fries halfway through lunch, and I had to bike out to the Piggly Wiggly just to restock the jalapeños.

When I came back, I caught sight of table four. Daddy's old firefighter buddies, Tommy Robertson, Jesse Dupree, and Horse Wilson. The likes of which haven't been seen outside the firehouse in months.

"Peanut butter and jelly sandwich!"

"Hi, Tommy," I said.

Big ole bear of a man hugged me before I could get out another peep.

"Fellas, you see how grown-up she is? Look just like your mamma when she beat your daddy at the junior rodeo."

"It was the summer of 1985, hotter than blue blazes," Jesse chimed in.

"Earl could ride a pony like nobody had ever seen," Horse added, "but your mamma could ride a pony like Jesus in a convertible. Now, ain't that right?"

"Sure enough!" the boys agreed.

"Cocky son of a gun thought he had it in the bag, so he bet Dottie five hundred dollars—"

"Oh, I'm familiar," I said. "I could tell this one in my sleep. *Five hundred dollars if he lost and a kiss if he won.* She won and used the five hundred dollars to buy herself a new horse. The kiss she gave him for free."

"Well, alrighty then. I guess we won't embarrass you with the hairy details," Jesse said, crestfallen.

I'd have loved to be a good daughter and humor these fellas. They've stayed cooped up in that old firehouse for so long that I'm sure a trip to the Chickie Shak felt like Disney World. Unfortunately, I didn't have time to waltz down memory lane. Linda was pointing two "I'm watching you" claws at me and gesturing back to the kitchen. Rabid little thing. Couldn't blame her today, what with the crowd. She was sweating so much her hussy upper was about to Niagara fall.

"I'm sorry, y'all, but I've got to get back to it. If you need anything else, Boof here will take good care of you."

"Of course," Tommy said. "We don't mean to keep you."

"We just wanted to say good luck. We're betting on you, sweetie," Horse said.

"Lordy, please don't."

Tommy patted me on the shoulder and said quietly, "I miss your daddy every day."

"Me too, Tommy."

"If there was something we coulda done, we'da done it."

"I know that."

I also know what it feels like to think you could have done more. I could have come home for Daddy's birthday that year. Tommy or Jesse or Horse could have run into that burning barn first. Mamma says, "Ain't no such thing as what mighta coulda." Doesn't stop any one of us from imagining it.

It's funny, when you lose someone you all a sudden remember every time you ever blew them off. Every *Maybe later.* Every missed call. Memories bob to the surface like dead fish on a nuclear lake—don't get me started on the Hog Club's 2014 project, Get That Shit Out of Our Damn Water—and you're forced to look at them up close. As Boof checked in on the boys, I recalled the lecture Daddy gave at the Nickelfiddle bandstand a few years back.

Now Nickelfiddle's just a hair bigger than Pennywhistle, but they do have a sense of history, seeing as one of the most famous Civil War snafus happened right there on Main Street. Rumor has it that as Robert E. Lee was passing through town, Union soldiers captured his horse in the dead of night. When he woke up and scrambled to find his trusty steed, the soldiers rubbed the horse's teeth with pepper. They sent General Lee on his way with the sneeziest, wheeziest bronco this side of the Mississippi. Couldn't hardly lead an army what with all those *Bless yous.* Folks down these parts claim that event was the beginning of the end. Folks elsewhere believe it's a hot dollop of horseshit. Daddy himself had researched the story up and down. For weeks he devoured books and scoured garage sales for anything that might shed some light on what many believed was nothing but a tall tale. The thrill of the chase, he had. See, Daddy wasn't a fan of Lee, but he did take great delight in the idea that something as small as a peppercorn could bring down an army, could change the tide of history, could make a bad fella fall.

"Think you can come down on Saturday to hear my talk? I just know you'd get a lot out of it."

When he called to ask, I was tangled up with my first college girlfriend, a lanky Bostonian who took my breath away and mocked my Southern accent. I didn't feel like dislodging myself from her sultry embrace, especially not for Daddy, who would tell me the whole story later.

Turns out, it was true as can be. Riffling around at one of those yard sales Daddy had located a firsthand account of the incident. Had the document verified and notarized over in Memphis. Kept it under lock and key until the day of the event and then presented the unlikely but true story in a lecture called "The Big Achoo." For his work and dedication Daddy received a standing ovation and a plaque from the Nickelfiddle Historical Society. They even sent him a five-hundred-dollar gift certificate to the local bookstore, which he used to fill up the Pennywhistle library. Meanwhile, for my selfishness, I received a breakup text a few weeks later. The Bostonian wanted to see other people. Frankly, I couldn't blame her.

MAMMA PINS THE next section of the dress onto Bruce, completing the skirt's lengthy train. Looks like if Princess Diana ran away with Toby Keith. Which happened to be Lee Ray's and my favorite bedtime story growing up. And the sleeves! I didn't even know denim could bend like that, but somehow, she's achieved maximum height. Much like the wooden roller coaster at Daddy's Dimples Theme Park, this is redneck engineering at its finest.

"Do we feel like we're taking this all a little too seriously? I mean, what if Boof shows up in jorts and a T-shirt and I'm out here looking like I *tried*."

"You are trying," Lee Ray scolds. "Linda will be trying so hard her mole's going to hop right off her face, jump in the river, and build a dam."

"It's a million dollars, sugar," Mamma says.

"It's stupid."

Lee Ray grabs the scrapbook, as I'm apparently being too ridiculous to hold his precious creation.

"I don't want to look stupid in front of Boof."

"Well, well, well. If you're so worried about it, let's call her," Lee Ray says.

"No!"

"Too late."

In five seconds flat, he's across the room with my phone pressed to his ear.

"Hi! This is Lee Ray, PJ's friend. Yes, from the boat. Yes."

He gives me a thumbs-up.

"Um, thank you! Anyways, I'm calling because we need you for a secret mission. Pageant recon. Excellent! We'll pick you up in twenty."

He hangs up and tosses my phone back.

"You're welcome."

"The speed at which you squash romance is downright frightening."

"Squash?" He tuts. "I think you'll find I'm the fertilizer of your sex life."

"How am I supposed to explain that to the Hog Club? I'mo have to make new pamphlets." Mamma sighs.

"Not what I meant," Lee Ray says. "Pivoting. Brush your hair and get your bike."

"Fine."

"I'm going to need a flashlight and baby's worst condiment. Don't ask me why."

Pennywhistle's low and flat like Mamma's rear, which makes for easy biking. We skitter through gravel roads strewn with pine needles and buckeyes, Skoal cans and Mountain Dews. Biking always renders me a sentimental fool. See, other towns may have things like STD testing and TGI Fridays, but here we got stars. Big swatches of night sky all to ourselves. Makes me feel a little guilty for ever moving away. Lee Ray says those first few weeks after I left were the longest of his life. He built so many boats and kissed so many Memphis-bound FedEx drivers he almost forgot how to feel. Then there was Lionel. Lionel, who was almost everything to Lee Ray. Lionel, who left right before Daddy died. Life's funny that way. Every now and then when something devastating happens, something good and small will happen, too. The toy in the cereal box, if you will. I lost Daddy and Lee Ray lost Lionel, but when the dust settled into the potato we found ourselves awful grateful to be back in the same zip code.

He guides us down the highway, a starlit, star-crossed hero in high-tops, all the way to an exit sign boasting This Way to Sticky Ricky's. I would much rather see Rock City.

"Tell me we are not going to whatever the hell franchise that is."

"I'm afraid we are."

Turns out, Boof lives in an apartment building that used to be a seedy motel but has since rebranded as a seedy motel attached to a mini-golf franchise. The sign declares Sticky Ricky's: Once You Stay, You're Stuck! and truth be told, it seems like most of the guests are here to stay. Lawn chairs and strollers litter the walkway like passed-out drunks. A Doberman sleeps soundly on a Hooters sweatshirt. Boof's door, number 32, even has a handmade beer-cap wreath. I like a girl who makes a wreath. She opens the door in jeans and a tank top, curls flying every which way. I think I'm in love.

"You biked," she says.

"I always bike."

"I just figured when you said you were picking me up there was a car involved."

"Ah, yes. Common misconception," Lee Ray says. "A boat we have. A car we do not."

Well, technically, I do. It's just been sitting like a kid in time-out in Mamma's garage ever since I came home. We don't talk about it, but every few months Lee Ray changes the oil and Mamma drives it to the Mega Beauty Store in Memphis to pick up her latest supply of Reba Red hair dye and That Tramp gold nail polish.

Boof gestures to the bike rack, where a lone, pink bike with training wheels sags against a rusted chain.

"It's just," she says, "I don't have a bike."

"You can ride on the back of PJ's. She's got that little seat where she used to cart around her stuffed animals."

"Did not!"

"Did too."

"Boof, this man is slandering me."

"Hey, I think it's cute," she says. "Besides, I carted my Lonestar Lindsey bear everywhere when I was little."

"More on that, please."

"Lonestar Lindsey? Y'all didn't have something like Jenny B. Tennessee?"

"We got a knock-off Build-A-Bear called Bump-A-Rump," I say.

"No," Lee Ray corrects. "Remember, they went out of business after the copyright lawsuit. Bump-A-Rump Gentleman's Club International shut them down."

"Not that Lee Ray's ever been there."

"I should be so lucky. Closest one is fifty miles."

Boof smiles at us in a way that reminds me she too has a brother. If only a measly twin and not the bona fide universe-throws-you-together sort.

"Sorry, Boof, you were saying?"

"Lonestar Lindsey, Betty Bluebonnet. They were these bears local politicians would give out. 'Collect all fifty bears!' You know, getting kids in on it so their parents would vote for Republicans. My brother got George W. Bear. Threw him off a cliff."

"So, you're from Texas?"

"Try not to spread that around." She winks.

Winks have a way of suspending time, don't you think? Next thing I know we're pedaling away from Sticky Ricky's and off into the wild blue yonder. Lee Ray leads the way while I try to make biking for two look effortless. Thank God I pumped up the tires this morning. Otherwise this smooth sailing would feel a lot more like, well, bump-a-rump. As we whir past mailboxes and plastic deer, Boof holds tight to my waist like I'm something special. Maybe I am, maybe I ain't, but I like to think at the very least all those corn dogs lend me the perfect little tummy for squeezing. The way Boof holds on a little tighter at the turns seems to confirm this.

"Might should have asked this before I let you two whisk me away, but where are we going?" she says.

"If it makes you feel any better, I don't know, either."

"I will answer you via riddle: What's ugly in English, but pretty in Spanish?"

"Linda!" we exclaim.

Lee Ray whips his bike around to reveal a dingy mailbox and hand-painted yellow sign. Keep the Hell Out!

LINDA'S
BOUNTY

The fine print reads: *That means you, Mormons, exes, vacuum salesmen, Dierks Bentley, and the U.S. Census Bureau.* Frankly, a list I can get behind. Cobwebs crowd the graveyard of deserted flowerpots and garden gnomes around the mailbox. A pack of mangy cats darts past. Tabbies, calicos, even a Tennessee rat cat, our answer to the Maine coon.

"Logic stands that because we are not Mormons, vacuum salesmen, et cetera, we are technically welcome," Lee Ray declares, starting down the gravel driveway with the confidence of a man who's never been told off by an inch-long, rhinestoned, press-on nail.

"We're barely welcome at work," I say.

The Tennessee rat cat hisses.

"Funny, Linda's always struck me as a dog person," Boof observes.

"Oh, she is. I scoped the place out yesterday. Here, take a can."

Lee Ray arms each of us with a twenty-four-ounce can of I-Believe-It's-Not-Cheese. Now, hear me out. While it lacks the creamy texture of its highfalutin competitors—your Whippy Cheese, your Can O'Cheese, even your Breezy Cheese—I-Believe-It's-Not-Cheese is buy one, get three free at the Piggly Wiggly. Boof and I shake our cans and await further instruction.

"I'm confused. Which one of us is ringing the doorbell?"

"PJ, this is hardly a simple matter of ding dong ditch. We're here to gauge Linda's strategy for Friday."

"Juicy!" Boof says.

"Funny, Linda always struck *me* as a *gun* person. Lee Ray, you're gonna get us killed."

"Oh, come on, baby," Boof says. "Live a little."

Lee Ray points to her and nods in agreement. He practically invented the word *cahoots*.

"Fine, but we gotta be fast and quiet. And I want ice cream after."

"Deal."

We hide our bikes in the bushes and creep along the tree line until we spot the house. Linda lives in an old-timey cabin, the kind of place that's settled into the land like a TV remote in a couch crack. Ain't never coming out. No glass orbs or plastic deer, but there's a shed out back that's either a woodshop or a gutting room, and your guess is as good as mine. Lee Ray approaches a rickety doghouse, cheese out.

"She's got three: Gator, Brawny, and Easter Bonnet."

"Easter Bonnet?" I whisper.

"I did not name them."

Gator, a chunky yellow Lab, waddles toward us like an uncle at a barbeque fixing to tell the same three stories all night long.

"Hi, darling," Boof coos.

She scratches under his ears just right, the way people who have had dogs all their lives do. It's a little different when you grow up bringing possums, raccoons, and the occasional skunk to your tree house. Wild, but fleeting.

Gator's eyes flutter closed. His mouth relaxes into a tonguey grin.

"I think this threat has officially been neutralized," Boof says.

"Roger that," Lee Ray says. "Give him a little spray anyways."

Gator laps up the make-believe cheese and plops back down in the dirt. Next comes Easter Bonnet, a sprightly mutt with a red bandanna. The brains of the operation. She looks at us like she's church and we're muddy shoes.

"Get down and let her smell you," Lee Ray says. "Trust me."

We kneel down and present ourselves to her curious, wet nose. I guess the Chickie Shak smell never quite leaves our hair, because after a few sniffs she wags her tail, satisfied by the familiar scent of deep-fried humans. Lee Ray sprays a swirl of not-quite-cheese into the grass for her.

"So, that just leaves Brawny," Boof says.

We glance around for the type of dog so covered in muscles and pointy teeth it could own a dental practice. And, shoot. Nothing but an empty clothesline and a breathy barn owl in sight.

"She's probably inside somewhere. I get the impression she's the favorite."

"Do you smell that?" Boof asks.

She walks toward a window that appears to be smoking. Or steaming? I can only just make out a floral shower curtain. I'm not sure if the thought of Linda taking a shower or smoking on the toilet's more barfworthy. We walk a little closer. Lee Ray stops in his tracks.

"The Bernadette Peters perm kit. I'd know it anywhere."

"She's perming?"

"That's bold."

We hear Brawny before we see her, which is how we know we're screwed. Little terror comes running at us with all twelve pounds of her Tina Turner–wig body, plum ready to murder us. I've always said tiny baby dogs are scarier than the big ones. Ever since that Pomeranian stole my bathing suit, I've steered clear of the wee ones. Shoo-ee! Brawny's bark's liable to break my eardrums. That is, if Linda doesn't break our necks first.

"Shut up, Brawny," Linda calls from somewhere inside the house.

We freeze. Brawny does not shut up.

"Do something!" I curse at Lee Ray.

He shakes the can furiously.

"My nozzle's stuck!"

"Use mine!"

Lee Ray beckons Brawny with a fat swirl of orange goop. She takes one lick and resumes her howling.

A screen door screeches open.

"Brawny?" Linda calls.

Boof scoops Brawny up and tucks her under her arm. Praise Jesus in Graceland, the wailing ceases. We breathe a collective sigh of relief.

"She just wants a little attention, don'tcha, honey?" Boof says. "You're all bark and no . . . ouch!"

"I see a cape. Gold lamé pants. Boots," Lee Ray says. "She's doing Elvis!"

Boof drops Brawny and shakes her hand out.

"Devil's spawn!"

"Brawny?"

Linda's voice is closer than a cousin at this point.

"That's it," I say, grabbing them both by the collars. "We're getting out of here right now."

We run as fast as we can, shoelaces and pebbles be damned. Fear's a pretty good workout routine, if I do say so. As soon as we're safely to our bikes, Lee Ray's phone blasts the opening chorus of "Margaritaville," which speaks of sponge cake and oily tourists. Boof and I will have to add this to our parody to-do list.

"Excuse me, ladies. EFP calling."

"EFP?"

"Elderly Fisherpeople of Pennywhistle," I explain. "He's their Moses."

Lee Ray cups his hand over the speaker. "Ernie. He gets very anxious about the water levels.

"Well, what does the Almanac say?" Lee Ray yells.

Boof and I laugh and look up through our little funnel cake of relief.

"Ernie's on the brink of a hissy fit. He told me to, quote, *Get Google on the phone right away*. So, if you'll excuse me, I need to head home and *call Google* about the expected rainfall during the Summer Paddle Adventure."

"When duty calls." Boof nods.

"PJ, I trust you can get Boof home in one piece."

He grins conspicuously. I want to slug him and hug him at the same time.

"Oh, no, *I fall to pieces*," Boof sings.

"Patsy gets it." He winks. "Good night, you two."

Some city slicker might not catch the reference, but "I Fall to Pieces" is the quintessential I-want-to-be-more-than-friends thread in country music's colorful tapestry of love songs. Boof falls to pieces. Boof falls to *pieces*. As we bike back to Sticky Ricky's I swear she holds me tighter than before.

I'm not gonna lie. There's a part of me that wants to take off into the night the minute she hops off the bike. Fight or flight, you know. It's not like I've never kissed anybody. Back in Nashville I had a couple serious girlfriends and more flings than you can shake a stick at. I had a red leather jacket with tassels hanging off the sleeves and spurs on my boots. Hell, I even had a hairdresser. But that all feels like a long time ago. The girl who left Pennywhistle had wheels. The girl who came back had flats. So, she applied for a job at the Chickie Shak, worried about her mamma, and spent Saturday nights watching reruns of *Toddlers & Tiaras*. After a while, change doesn't seem so sexy anymore.

"Never thought we'd make it back alive!" Boof says.

She braces herself on my shoulders as she lifts off the bike. Oh, these moments! Look, I'm not one to spill my guts on precisely why I like women. You get asked in gas station bathrooms and Greyhound buses one too many times and you get tuckered out. You start saying, "I just do!" and leave it at that. But to tell you the truth, the way Boof touches my shoulders is exactly why. Being with a woman's like taking all the best things about having a friend—the anticipation of Friday-night sleepovers, the easy Saturday afternoons, the teasing, the knowing of things like periods and the way your thighs stick to the seat of a car on hot summer days—and adding the desire to get naked and jump in a lake. In her hands, on my shoulders, hell, all the way to the tip of my ponytail, I feel the knowing.

"I've got some ice cream sandwiches in my freezer if you want to stick around." Boof smiles.

"Sure."

We sit side by side with our legs in the motel pool. Kicking the swirl of pool noodles and horseflies back and forth like we got nothing but time.

"*Wasting away again in Sticky Ricky's pool,*" she sings in mock Jimmy Buffett. "*Searching for my lost bathing suit top. Some people claim that there's a janitor to blame. But I know, do, do, do, do, do, it's that damn sleeping dog.*"

She points to the Doberman.

"It was Kenny. I know it."

"Boof, what the hell is somebody as talented as you doing in Pennywhistle?"

She nudges me with her shoulder.

"It's pretty pathetic."

"I don't think you're capable of pathetic."

"How about dramatic?"

"Yeah, that neither."

"Soap opera level dramatic."

"Okay, I'm listening."

She takes a deep breath and looks out at the mini-golf area. A big plaster dinosaur shimmies from side to side, blocking most of hole number twelve.

"I told you I'm from Texas, but that's not really true."

"It's a relief is what it is. Crushing on a Texan. My daddy would be rolling over in his grave."

"Did you know that Pennywhistle was one of the last towns in Tennessee that had a home for unwed mothers? The Blessing House. Sounds like something straight out of the sixties, right?"

I nod.

"The last one here closed in 1999. A few years after my brother and me were born."

"Oh."

We pass a dead horsefly back and forth between our toes until she's ready to talk again. I look deep into Boof's eyes, hoping my face can say the kinds of things my mouth ain't so good at. She takes a deep breath.

"Our birth mom stayed there. By the time she had us, the ladies at the home had it all worked out. My parents picked us up in their white minivan and drove all the way back to Texas without looking back."

"I reckon you get a lot of Lonestar Lindsey bears if you're adopted."

"Dozens. A lot of bears and a lot of hugs. A lot of deep talks. Why do you think I'm such a natural when it comes to calming people down?"

"Yeah, that's starting to make sense."

I reach my hand out and when she takes it there's a firmness, a holding on that makes me feel right chosen.

"I don't even know her name. I came down here and I guess I thought I'd just know her when I saw her."

"And did you?"

"Not yet."

"How long you fixing to wait?"

"That's the question. My brother came to see me because he wants us to do it officially. Get the records. That just sorta feels like chasing a cat with a broom, you know?"

"Sounds like part of you's waiting for her to recognize you," I say.

"You're a lot sweeter than you let on, you know that?"

"Don't go spreading that around. I got a reputation to uphold."

Boof pulls me in for a kiss that is vanilla ice cream and curls and chlorine. Summer wrapped up in one long, delicious moment. Sweeter still is how we linger there after the kiss. Nose to nose, her hand in my hair, mine grasping her waist. When she pulls away to look at me, I know just what to say. Or, rather, sing.

"Possums in a creek. That is what we are."

Her laugh ricochets off the sleeping Doberman, the dinosaur, and the Once You Stay, You're Stuck sign. She kisses me again. And again. Unfortunately, if we want any chance of looking like hot chickens on Friday we gotta get some beauty rest. It's goodbye for now. As I bike home I replay the evening over and over.

By the time I reach home, I have learned it by heart.

NASCAR DISHRAG

Mamma's cooking corn pudding and sausage casserole for the neighborhood pageant pregame potluck. It's early yet. In a few hours, just past cicada o'clock, she'll start setting up card tables and broken wheelbarrows—anything that could call a table cousin—for people to gather round. Christmas lights will kiss the aboveground pool and garden gnomes will mark which trees the fellas ought not piss on if they don't want their junk set ablaze by poison ivy. Daddy's firefighter buddies learned that one the hard way. One barbecue later and they were arborists.

Mamma slops the mayonnaise into the corn mixture. I make sure the fried Oreos don't burn.

"You been practicing your walk?" she asks.

"Course I have."

Lies. Only thing I've been practicing is my nervous shuffle from the kitchen to the couch to the window where my strays eat their dinner, blissfully unaware of the pageant.

"Don't embarrass me now. Lot of people are rooting for you."

More than she even knows. Daddy's ghost has been real active this week. Just like everybody else in town, he seems pretty dang excited about the whole thing. Been leaving confetti in my mailbox and folding my jeans every day. A new horn even showed up on my bike this morning. I've never mentioned Daddy's visits to Mamma, a topic you'd think would have come up between the frozen macaroni dinners and the tampon tossing. Nothing doing. Maybe I'm worried Daddy's only checking in on me, which hardly seems fair. Mamma made sure they served pork rinds at his funeral; Lee Ray and I ate most of them.

"Vandy called me," Mamma says, not casually but fake casually. The faux snakeskin tube top on the rack of honesty.

"Did they now?"

"I'm your emergency contact."

"What's the emergency?"

"You are. Specifically, the fact that you've been TMI."

"You mean MIA."

"Whatever you are, they wanted to know how much longer you plan on stayin' gone."

I flip an Oreo, taking care not to slosh the oil too much. I'm looking to keep my eyeballs, thank you very much.

"Why do they need to know right now?"

"Only so much university dollars to go around, baby doll."

I drop the Oreo. A hot drop of grease scalds my arm.

"Ouch, dammit! They're giving away my spot?"

Mamma hands me a bag of frozen peas.

"They said they don't *wanna* give away your spot. But you gotta start answering their calls before the fall semester starts or they might have to."

The burn stings only slightly less than the comment. I sit down at the kitchen table, where I can look down and pretend to fold napkins.

"So, you want me to leave?"

"All I'm saying is call 'em back."

"Why are you pushing this?"

"That's what mammas are here for," she says as she dumps another can of corn into the bowl. "Pushing you out and pushing you forward."

Suddenly I feel like the corn, all spilled out and aimless.

"I thought you were proud of me. I could win this."

"Shoo-ee!" She cackles. "Look who cares all a sudden."

"Don't mock me. You started it. I know you put those earrings on my soap dish."

"Look," she says, wiping her hands off on a NASCAR dishrag I've never seen before. "Every change that ever did happen started with somebody doing something different than the last time. 'Bout time to move on, I reckon."

"Says the woman who carries Daddy around in a potato."

"I might be a little more moved on than you think."

"Sure, Mamma. You're juggling five different boyfriends and a karaoke gig on the side."

"People ain't always what you think, baby girl. Take Linda."

"I will not."

"She's really made something of herself after all these years."

"Last I checked she's still mean as a snake."

"The sisters'll do that to a girl."

"Sisters?"

"Long story," she says. "Now either get your rear in gear or go bother your girlfriend. I got work to do."

Like a clip-on earring does a saggy lobe, I oughta let the matter drop. But something makes me wonder. Makes me ask.

"Hey, Mamma?"

"Yes?"

"Was it the secretary who called or . . ."

"Said his name was Dean Jackson. Seemed to think right highly of you."

THE FIRST TIME I met the dean was at Percy Warner Park. Just over two thousand acres, it sits at the bottom of a long boulevard of the oldest, prettiest mansions you ever did see. Big, busty columns, sleek slate roofs that glisten like a school of trout. And hedges! No such thing as a hedge in Pennywhistle, unless you count that wall of kudzu covering up the old Blockbuster. I swear, if I blindfolded Mamma and brought her to this street she'd believe we'd made it all the way to Beverly Hills. Mamma's never been to California on account of some Gold Rush superstitions passed down from her meemaw, but she knows glamour when she sees it.

Dean Jackson waved from where he crouched, tying his shoes. Huh. I expected he'd look akin to the KFC mascot, trimmed with a bow tie and a spritely little goatee, but in reality, he was closer to the fellas who work at the firehouse. Like he might ask you for Prilosec after a big meal or use the phrase *set down* instead of *sit down*. The only thing that screamed "professor" was his delicate tortoiseshell glasses.

"Miss Spoon, you made it."

He stood up and shook my hand enthusiastically.

"Robert Jackson, pleased to make your acquaintance."

"You too."

"I hope you like the outdoors," he said, gesturing to a grove of trees. "I try and hold as many of my meetings out here as I can. Tends to strip the air of all that fussy, academic jargon."

"Yes, sir."

"Not to mention, a place like this is brimming with history. Come on, I'll show you the World War One memorial up the hill."

And oh, what a hill it was! What seemed like a single slope just kept looping up and up into a series of never-ending mossy ridgebacks. I was impressed by the band of mothers jogging their babies up the hill and envious of the bikers soaring down it. Mostly I was thrilled I had worn my tennis shoes to this particular rendezvous.

As we made our way up Everest Junior, Dean Jackson gave me a brief history of the park. Back in the twenties, somebody named Lea thought there oughta be some nature in the city, so he bought up the properties and spread the park out like a picnic blanket. Fella also went to law school, served in World War I, and was the first publisher of *The Tennessean*. History's full of these hooligans, people who took *can't nevers* and turned them into *might coulds*. I may not be a history maker myself, but I've always loved their stories.

After considerable huffing and puffing, we eventually reached the lookout point. Damn near all of Nashville sprawled out below and boy, was she huge. Made Pennywhistle look less like a town and more like a pesky pebble wedged into the shoe of Tennessee.

"Do you live in the neighborhood?" I asked Dean Jackson as he wiped his brow with a hankie.

"I do, but I pray you won't cast your judgment based solely on that fact."

A blonde jogged past us, her wedding ring hefty enough to best not one but two Goliaths.

"Seems quite highfalutin."

"Ha! Precisely the term my mother used at our wedding. Bless her heart, my wife happens to come from the hoity-toity set. Although she wasn't hoity-toity when I met her. No, I found the future Mrs. Jackson hanging upside down from the chandelier in her sorority, drunk as a skunk, singing 'Ring of Fire.' I daresay I fell in love with her right then and there."

He smiled warmly at the thought.

"And you?" I asked.

"I was so rough around the edges you could have used me to cut down a tree. Football scholarship. Luckily, I had some professors who appreciated my unique perspective as, how shall we say, a hayseed from Georgia."

"Must have worked. You're running the whole department now."

Something about this saddened him. Was it rude to call a king a king?

"Miss Spoon," he started.

"PJ's fine."

"PJ, do you mind if I speak plainly?"

"Go ahead."

"Growing up, we didn't have a pot to piss in. Six brothers and sisters. No daddy. I like to say the Helpful Hamper at the church was the closest thing we had to a mall. You get the picture. So, when I took that Greyhound up here, I told myself I'd never look back."

He stopped to catch his breath.

"These damn hills. I always forget."

The pack of stroller pushers lapped us again, those braggarts.

"You might feel the same urge to eschew your origins. As for the academic side of things, I have no doubt you'll be successful. You'll learn how to navigate the academic scene, you'll get a feel for the research. In essence, you'll fit right in. However, I would caution you this: Don't forget where you came from. Your roots, your town, that's what makes your work come alive. So, eat with the proper fork and all that, but, PJ, don't you dare lose your accent."

Nashville glimmered below, an invitation. A warning? There I was, the Redneck Odysseus, about to board the ship.

"You're telling me I should do my homework but stay country," I concluded.

"Yes! Precisely. Stay country, hot damn."

Right then and there I knew we'd be friends. And, as a friend, I decided to put him out of his misery.

"In the spirit of staying country, what do you say we ditch the hike and go get something to eat?"

"Praise the Lord," he cheered. Then, steering us swiftly down the hill, "How do you feel about pimento cheese?"

I DON'T TELL Mamma this story or let on how much I miss those hikes-turned-brunches. Somehow, I feel it'd break her heart. Truth is, Dean Jackson always kind of felt like Daddy in an alternate universe. Daddy if he'd gone to college and started wearing polo shirts. Daddy if his hair was all but rubbed away in the middle. I used to picture the two of them meeting at my graduation and, finding each other like long-lost brothers, starting a book club.

"Your father sounds like a smart guy," Dean Jackson would say, tucking a brochure for the extended learning program in my backpack. "He could come up on the weekends for the lectures."

"Just what every girl wants, her daddy camped out on her couch every weekend. No, thank you."

"So, he can camp out on mine. Not everybody gets a chance to buy that Greyhound ticket when they're young, PJ."

There it was again, the similarity. Daddy let anybody and everybody sleep on our couch. Lovesick uncles, weary Avon salesladies. With a good night's sleep, he reckoned, any one of them could amount to something great.

Which is probably exactly what the voicemails say, if I ever mustered the guts to listen to them. Instead, I turn on the *Hee Haw Ha Ha Hour* on KR46 and let old Korny Deets take the mic.

"How y'all doing on this fine June afternoon?" Korny croons.

"Turn it up," Mamma says.

"This week's riddle was submitted by Jenny Q. in Farragut. What do you get when you combine a cow, a car, and a banana peel? A milkshake!"

Mamma chuckles. Apparently Korny Deets is just a stage name. The real fella probably does something boring like sell insurance or count money and lets his alter ego have all the fun. I wonder if he wishes he could be Korny Deets all the time. More than that, I wonder what's stopping him.

After the *Hee Haw Ha Ha Hour* it's the weather update. No disrespect to Cloudy Douglas and his endless supply of weather puns—that fella's shepherded us through more tornadoes than you can shake a stick at—but as soon as he confirms the sun's here to stay, we flip the channel to the country station.

The song that plays is "Any Man of Mine," by Shania Twain. We both pause, remembering how Daddy used to scoop Mamma up for this particular number. First, he'd drum a spoon on the counter to the beat of the music. *Boom, boom, tap. Boom, boom, tap.* Then, when the first chorus drew near, he'd get the biggest grin on his face. Not a lottery grin or a new father grin, but that randy smile he used to wear at the rodeo, the one that could lasso anything. Once the smile set in, Mamma knew she was a goner.

"Earl! You put me down now," she would say, rosy as a perfume sample.

Wasn't so much of a square dance as it was a squiggle dance. They do-si-doed around the couch, Daddy's beanbag, old shoes, and stacks of magazines. When the house got too small for their mirth, he'd kick open the screen door and dance them clear across the backyard.

"PJ, baby, turn it up."

"Don't you dare!"

I always did.

The song's four minutes long, so by the time the key changed she'd be dancing a blue streak right along with him. Stomping molehills to the beat and dipping low in Daddy's arms. And then, as quickly as the magic came, it was gone. We always resented whatever song came after "Any Man of Mine," because it was usually a slow one. "Whiskey Lullaby." "Concrete Angel." Like they knew you'd need a breather after Shania. Maybe we didn't want a breather.

The song doesn't fill the kitchen the same way it used to, but I offer anyway.

"You want to dance, Mamma?" I say.

"No," she says quietly, "let's just leave it there."

I feel like the girl cowering under the disco ball, the one dying to ask, "Can I cut in?" but who's too tongue-tied and bowlegged to approach. Fact is, Mamma and I never had a dance. Never had to. Always took turns being the third wheel.

She hoists the corn pudding into the oven. Is it too late, I wonder, to buy the corsage?

"Anything else I can help with?"

She waves me off with the NASCAR dishrag.

"Go on, get."

"I'll be back before the party."

"Young lady, you better."

LEE RAY ANCHORS us firmly on Best Friends Shrimp Island, a tiny strip of sand and cattails we claimed as our own when we were little. Our mammas would keep watch from the shore while we swam out there using Fritos bags for floaties. Never once lost us to the gators. They had something of a book club out on the shore, a pile of old magazines and battered romance novels, crossword puzzles and takeout menus, they would swap back and forth, back and forth, until we grew sun-sleepy enough to return to their cozy, towel-bearing arms.

As he unpacks our provisions, I catch sight of something shiny. Not a fancy lure or a rogue piercing, but the bright face of a jester.

"You still wear that?"

Lee Ray cradles his treasure, a long, gold necklace garnished with a Mardi Gras doubloon.

"Don't judge," he says. "It's my good luck charm."

"I'm not judging, I'm just wondering what the hell you gave Lionel to wear around his neck, seeing as the only things we throw at Pennywhistle parades are horseshoes and Band-Aids."

"I always went with flowers."

"Smart."

We set up our folding chairs, crack open a pair of beers, and spray on enough OFF! to render the whole of the mosquito kingdom extinct. I watched a *Dateline* episode about New Orleans a few weeks back. Learned a lot. Apparently, they throw out those doubloons by the thousands. Funny how something so common becomes a precious artifact when it comes from someone you love, like how Mamma still has the last pair of dirty underwear Daddy ever threw in the hamper.

"Why didn't you ever go down there and look for him?"

"Maybe I did."

"What? When?"

"Remember last February when I told you I was too sick to watch the extended edition of *The Raccoon King of Raisin Lagoon* with you?"

"I believe your exact words were 'Can't come. I have party butt.'"

"Those do not sound like my exact words."

"Well, that was Mamma's interpretation of your voicemail."

"She's a lousy editor."

"You did eat, like, seven pounds of crawfish at the church barbecue that afternoon."

"Be that as it may—"

"It was a lot of crawfish."

"PJ!"

"Sorry, yes, so you bailed on *Raccoon King* and, what, drove to New Orleans?"

He nods.

"And?"

He spins the doubloon. A tadpole jumps at the sight of the sparkle.

"You know what they say. Small fish, big pond."

"I take it New Orleans is a pretty big pond?"

"I don't think we brought enough beer today for me to explain just how big a pond it was."

Lee Ray gazes out across the cattails, where a pair of dragonflies darts and dances, lover-like. Leave it to mother nature to make a person feel single as hell.

"It was huge and exciting and the moment I caught a glimpse of it I turned around and drove right back home."

"I'm sorry."

"It's okay." He shrugs. "I'm just bummed I missed the anniversary edition."

"There were a lot of good deleted scenes."

"Really?"

Sweet Lee Ray looks utterly crestfallen. Times like these I wish Best Friends Shrimp Island had a little more to offer, like a time machine or an outlet mall. I guess sometimes you just gotta make do with what you got. I can't shrink New Orleans but I can offer up the next best thing.

"Mamma taped the whole program. We could watch it tonight if you want."

"Can you make those frozen wings I like?"

"Does the pope pray? Course I can."

Lee Ray smiles at me.

"Thanks."

"Sure thing, party butt."

"So help me God, I will maroon you, PJ Spoon!"

WE FORGET ALL about the pageant potluck until we're riffling through Mamma's ancient VHS collection—including such gems as *The Passion of the Christ*, "PJ's Second Birthday," and "That One Real Funny Episode of *The Beverly Hillbillies* Where They Think Jethro's a Genius." Her TV is so old and so thick it puts an elephant to shame. Hell, that VCR's older than I am. Back when we could still fit under the coffee table—before my rack and Lee Ray's shoulders kicked in—we'd build forts that spanned all the way from the antenna to the couch. All it took was an old floral sheet and half a dozen bungee cords to festoon the world's littlest theater. Throw in Lee Ray's Princess Diana Beanie Baby and my Bump-A-Rump creation, Elton John, and we had ourselves a regular palace. Shoo-ee! I can smell the butter now, still wedged like a memory into the carpet. Aha! Just when I think Mamma must have taped over *Raccoon King* for something stupid, like the pope's funeral, I discover the tape between "2004 Olympics" and *"Australia's Hottest Hunks* (NOT FOR PJ'S EYES)."

"Boo!" Mamma says.

We jump.

"Jesus, Mamma. Wear a bell or something."

"What in the hell are those outfits? I know I didn't raise you to show up to a party halfneked."

"Shoot," I say, "I totally forgot. Do we have to go?"

"Yes, you have to go. It's our backyard and you's the main event."

Lee Ray looks at me with his big, brown, forlorn eyes.

"Thing is, Mamma, we were really hoping to watch the *Raccoon King* special edition tape tonight. We don't hardly get to see each other with work and the pageant and the EFPs. It's a damn shame is what it is."

Lee Ray nods.

"Nice try. You saw each other yesterday."

"Can't you just tell everyone I'm sick?"

"Young lady, you better get your ass to the dresser and find something decent to put on before I pop you. Lee Ray, honey, you can wear something of Earl's."

"How sweet," he mumbles.

Nothing says party-wear like a dead man's Hawaiian shirt. And as for me, well, the best I can do is wiggle into my high school graduation dress and pray it doesn't bust at the seams. I swear I grew an extra set of ribs since the last time I wore it. But also somehow lost half my arm circumference?

It's always the old guests who arrive on time, scuttling up the driveway with a casserole that weighs more than they do, blue hair lit by the setting sun. Mrs. Heller gives us a wave.

"Hi, cuties," she says.

"Hi, Mrs. Heller."

She grasps my hand in hers and shakes it gently.

"We are just so excited to see your performance tomorrow."

"Don't get your hopes up."

"Do get your hopes up," Lee Ray corrects. "Dottie and I have outdone ourselves."

"I bet you have. Do you know I still have the programs from all your musicals? *Fiddler on the Piggly Wiggly* was my favorite."

"You're too kind."

She releases my hand to take his.

"Now whatever happened to that sweet little boyfriend of yours? The actor? He used to come sing with me at the library sometimes."

"He went back to New Orleans, ma'am."

She clucks like a peeved chicken.

"He'll never do better than you, son. Never. But, if you're searching for somebody new, my grandson lives just a few hours away in Arkansas. He's got a wife and children, but his pants are a little too tight, if you know what I mean."

"Thank you, Mrs. Heller, but I think I'll be just fine."

"Offer stands. You just let me know."

"Will do. Now, if you'll pardon me for a moment, I could use a drink."

Lee Ray dips toward the moonshine while Mamma unburdens Mrs. Heller of her casserole. I'm catching a strong pork smell. Mayonnaise base. And is it just me, or is that a cigarette butt?

"Nice to see the two of you together," Mrs. Heller observes, "seeing as PJ was such a daddy's girl."

People always used to call me that. Preachers, teachers, even the cashier at the gas station who watched me chew my Hubba Bubba and spit it out just like Daddy did his tobacco. I gummed up just about every inch of Daddy's car in pursuit of his particular flourish. Eventually he encouraged me to switch to Tic Tacs. We'd chew the bit and spit the spit every night in the backyard while Mamma stirred her way through the Cracker Barrel cookbook and drew up plans for the next Hog Club protest. She was busy; we were in cahoots.

But as Mrs. Heller chatters on, I notice the way *daddy's girl* hits Mamma. She closes her mouth tight like you do underwater, holding your breath. Makes me wonder if she wasn't stirring after all, but gazing out the window at the two of us, just waiting for her invitation.

Lee Ray returns with two Dixie cups.

"When did I become the go-to for everyone's closeted gay grandson?"

"He sounds like a real catch. You like kids, right?"

"Speaking of catches, I must say, I'm quite a fan of Boof."

"Really?"

"PJ, you're allowed to gush. Just because I'm . . .' "

"Thinking of getting busy with Mrs. Heller's grandson?"

"Single," he corrects, "doesn't mean I'm not delighted for you."

"You sure?"

"Yes. Now get out there and mingle before Dottie wrings our necks."

Lee Ray gives me a tender shove toward the fray of overalled Penny-whistlers. Cheerful grandmas, bearded Tupperware salesmen. I think of the doubloon just under his shirt, glimmering quietly in the hopes of reunion, and wonder how long he plans on wearing it.

"You should call him."

He rolls his eyes.

"Come on. What do you have to lose?"

"PJ."

"I mean it. I'm sure he thinks about you."

"Who says I think about him?"

"Ahem, the spring musical."

Don't get me started on *The Last 5 Beers*, Lee Ray's take on the already depressing musical *The Last 5 Years*. Peep and Nina at the adult store sent him a few free samples after that one, if only in the hopes of catching something upbeat next season.

"So it got a little dark," he admits. "I'm working on *Annie Get Your Gum* for the dental school commercial, which promises to be delightful, and I just got my summer cut, so I'm actually feeling pretty good about things. Next topic."

A Don't Tax My Hoo-Ha T-shirt catches my eye.

"Fine," I concede. "Do you think this tampon thing is actually going to work?"

"It might help if you believed it could."

"Hold up. Last I checked I am not a member of the Hog Club."

"You're a member of the Spoon family."

"We still calling it that?" I mumble.

"PJ!" He tuts.

"I'll write to my senator, okay?"

I wave to Mamma across the crowd, where throngs of speckled heads nod and bob to the timbre of her voice. She mouths something. *I'm so proud of you.* Or maybe, *We're out of booze.* Someone spills the Kool-Aid punch and the whole thing gets lost in translation.

By the time I'm napkin-mopping, the moment's up and gone.

GOD'S BRILLIANT GRACE

To quote the Raccoon King, "It was morning. The kind that comes after night. But not just any morning. Friday. The first bite on the pizza of the weekend. The morning everything would begin." If Emmens Clementine doesn't win a Pulitzer for this one, then I'm a monkey's uncle. He's got a real talent for capturing things exactly as they are.

Sure enough, as I bike to work I see the signs of pageant preparations everywhere. There's a billboard above the gas station with pictures of us from the worst possible sources. My junior year yearbook photo. Boof's Chickie Shak ID card picture. And what one can only assume is the beauty shot Linda intends to use in her obituary. Better than the usual billboard for Hansel Hickory's Hair Transplants, but still rough.

That's not all. As far as the eye can see, people have strung up yellow and red bows—the official Chickie Shak colors—papier-mâché chickens, tiaras, balloons, the whole nine yards. Peep and Nina even dressed up their "lady companion dolls" to look like me, Boof, and Linda. I'm oddly flattered to see my body rendered in silicone under a sign that says Good Luck, Hot Chickens! They captured my rack, Linda's mole, and Boof's can perfectly. Love is in the details, as they say.

Nobody's as excited as Mamma, who's settled into her role as a pageant mom quite nicely. She loved being a softball mom—she got to yell at umpires and tell a whole team of youngins how proud she was of them every week. Mamma wanted buckets more kids than just me. Nothin' doin'. So, Lee Ray scratched the second kid itch and the rest of the team scratched itches three through eighteen. She can't show off her team anymore, but she can show off her denim creation and the ten-step pageant strategy that she and Lee Ray drew up this week. She's invited damn near all her friends over to see the thing. Man alive! If I have to hear "Team PJ" one more time I'm going to spit.

Much to the chagrin of my double chin, this is only the beginning. This week it's beauty, next week talent. Whoever gets the highest combined score wins and advances to the finals in Nashville. Like I said, I don't give a lick. Soon as the required bit's over, it's back to the fryer for me. Not that I would mind a trip up the body of the raccoon. Nashville's the heart, after all. I guess I could eat a few biscuits at the Loveless Cafe and catch up with my old classmates if I win. I bet Boof would sure like to step back on a honky-tonk stage and strut her stuff. Strange to think we were both in the heart of the raccoon at the same time. I wonder if we ever passed each other on the street or shared the same port-a-john at Pride. It's possible. Then again, Nashville's big enough that we likely never overlapped, just buzzed around like two mosquitoes biting the same leg.

Come to think of it, I've never mentioned my life there to Boof. She's probably heard about it from Deedoo or seen one of the PJ's Going to Nashville! T-shirts Mamma sent round when I got in, but she's never brought it up. When the time is right, I'll make like the arthritic cashier at the Piggly Wiggly and spill the beans. For now, the allure lives on.

I DON'T KNOW if it's summer or something else, but this morning my hair looks a little less brown sugar and a little more butter. It used to blond right up every summer, brighter and brighter until my eyebrows disappeared, but by the time I went to college I figured the heather'd set in for good. Maybe I was wrong. My cheeks have welled up with freckles lately, too. Nothing like Boof's, but enough to think of constellations.

I get a little blonder when she smiles at me from the back door.

"What's in the basket?" she asks.

"A present. Saw this at the library and I thought it might be helpful."

Boof laughs at the familiar teal cover.

"*Are You My Mother?*"

"Essential literature. No, I also picked this one up," I say, heaving a ten-pound tome from my backpack. "Might be a little more informative. It's got all the Pennywhistle population records from the nineties. And it nearly popped my tires this morning. Worth it, though."

"Do you wanna get married?" She smiles.

"Can't. Lee Ray and I have already used the fake newlywed trick on all the Olive Gardens to get free desserts."

"That would still make me your first wife."

"Good point. I'll think about it."

Boof lays a hand under my jaw, lets her fingers rest at the foothills of my hair, and kisses me softly.

"Thanks for the books."

"Anytime." I shiver.

A few kisses later, she pulls back.

"And if you ever want to show me what's in that notebook . . ."

"Don't push your luck."

We share one last clandestine smooch behind the trash cans before walking in together. Never thought I'd be so keen to make out three inches from day-old ground beef and caked-on mustard. Crushes'll do that to you. Linda waits at the register, freshly permed and surly as ever. She's got a new, slightly more practical manicure, featuring red and yellow glitter but no key chains this time around. The tips, however, are filed so sharp she could slice a Christmas ham.

"Morning, Linda."

"What do you want?"

"Nothing. I just thought I'd say good luck tonight."

"Me, too. Best wishes." Boof nods as she ties on her apron.

Linda parts her kudzu-esque curls with a claw. I'm sure "to perm the bangs or not to perm the bangs" was a tricky decision, but Linda seems to have doubled down on "to perm the bangs" because the hairs in the front are especially mobile, as if they've been permed and re-permed a few thousand times.

"You must think I'm pretty stupid," she says.

"No," I say hesitantly, sensing a trap.

Linda sidles up to me and gives my sternum a hard poke. Jesus, that claw is sharp! Suddenly my chances of walking out of here alive are slimmer than Lee Ray's mamma on the Lose Weight for Jesus diet.

"Do you have a dog?" she asks.

"Excuse me?"

"Are you the owner of a canine?"

"What is this, *CSI: Pennywhistle*?" Boof tries.

"I'd watch the hell out of that."

"Clearly, you don't." She pokes me again. "Or you would know what kind of pure hell I-Believe-It's-Not-Cheese wreaks on a dog's colon. Lava. Piping hot lava on my couch. In my Reeboks."

"That's awful."

"I take it your dogs aren't feeling well," Boof says.

I have to stifle a snort at her tone of mock concern. Even as Boof keeps Linda's gaze, her quizzical expression shakes with 'bout-to-burst laughter. I've got about three more sentences in me before I break. In short, we're terribly unconvincing for two people whose lives depend on denying the existence of a three-for-the-price-of-one cheese replacement.

"I could have both of you fired in five seconds flat."

Boof drops a roll of silverware. My stomach goes right with it.

"All I'd need to do is call up Lawson at HR. Y'all probably never heard of ole Lawson, but we go way back. He used to clean my gutters, if you know what I mean."

Her false eyelashes lock as she attempts to wink. Looks like a couple of spiders in a lovers' embrace. She clears her throat and flicks them apart with a pinky claw.

"Linda, we're awful sorry about your Reeboks—" I mumble.

She cuts me off.

"Then again, turning your asses in would ruin all the fun of shoving my one million dollars down your throats."

The bell on the door rings, signaling the day's first customer. I silently praise old Mrs. Heller for saving me from the whooping of a lifetime. She can have all the honey biscuits she wants, on me. Linda takes a step back, flashes a fake smile at Mrs. Heller.

"If the two of you ever set foot on my property again," Linda whispers, "I will personally decorate your paychecks with a fat splash of orange dog shit. So, don't talk to me no more and don't you dare go wishing me good luck. I don't need it."

"Why's that?" Boof counters.

"Because you two wouldn't know God's Brilliant Grace if it Frenched you at the drive-in."

Boof and I don't have time to correct her. Frankly, we ain't got time all day because come to find out, pageant day is the busiest day we have ever had at the Chickie Shak. Hell, we served so many people today we had to call the fire marshal to kick some of them out. Unfortunately, he got stuck talking to table two and that was the end of that. Now I have a mere forty-five minutes to degrease my womanly figure and make it to the pageant.

PEERING THROUGH THE side door I can see close to three hundred people. Jesus Christ, Superstar, I might just pass out.

"Easy does it," Mamma says as Lee Ray hoists an armful of garment bags onto the rack in my makeshift dressing room.

Linda got the girls' bathroom, Boof got the fellas', and I'm in the janitor's closet. The pageant committee apologized for putting me in there, but Mamma told them it's the reverse.

"Shows you're the one to watch. Like Jesus in the manger."

Ole Jessie Christ had the company of donkeys and wise men, and I, too, feel strangely comforted by the mops and buckets keeping watch over me. I might even borrow that snappy little jumpsuit for my first official date with Boof. Enough pockets for all my yo-yos and besides, it's spill-proof. Doodle Barnum, who's been mopping halls and busting would-be blow jobs for forty years, keeps quite the little museum in here. Banners from basketball championships. Buttons from unsuccessful prom queen campaigns. I like that she holds a place for both. Life's one part tiara, one part swirlie, and a whole lot of in between.

"Not too shabby," Lee Ray says.

"The room's peachy keen," I say. "It's the bags that worry me. Lot of bags for one dress, y'all."

Mamma and Lee Ray stare at the ground like a pair of poodles who have just destroyed a couch.

"Mamma?"

"Don't shoot the mailman, darlin'."

"Lee Ray?"

"We didn't tell you because we figured if we did you'd skip town under the cover of nightfall."

"Not a bad idea. If I leave now I might could make it on the next bus to Nickelfiddle."

"Oh, hush," Mamma says with a wave of her hand. "Nickelfiddle's nothin' but a one-horse town with a fancy Arby's."

Lee Ray sits me on an upside-down bucket and delivers the news as if by presidential podium. I'm reminded of his famous dugout speeches.

"Ladies and gentlemen, tonight's competition consists of three rounds. 'Walking in Memphis'—that's casual wear. 'Blue Velvet'—formal wear. And, well, 'Six-Pack Summer.' The bathing suit section. But it's in the middle, so I promise it will go by in a snap."

"Bathing suit? Onstage? Oh hell, no."

"Now, don't you worry your pretty little head, sugar," Mamma says. "Lee Ray talked me out of the bikini."

"And into what? You and I both know I have only two bathing suits and one of them is my swim team Speedo from junior year."

"And there's a longer conversation to be had about the shelf life of bathing suits, feminine hygiene, et cetera," Lee Ray says.

"Grrr."

"Good, let it out. Now shut up and trust me for a minute. Dottie wanted a bikini, but I know you'd rather be skinned alive with a butter knife, so we've got you in a tasteful, grown woman's black one-piece from Old Navy. Can you work with that?"

Like an overdue colonoscopy, I'm afraid this shit's mandatory.

"I reckon."

"Good girl. As for casual wear, I'll have you know I went all the way out to Quarterflute, where they actually have a Dillard's."

"And a Disney Store!" Mamma gushes.

"She came with."

"Picked up some new pajamas and a couple of stuffed animals to hang out with your daddy on the mantel. Oh, and you'll love this! I got you one of them sparkly princess wands so you can reach the button when the smoke detector goes off."

"Thanks, Mamma."

Lee Ray unzips the bag to show me the full array of tonight's ensembles. Even I have to admit that he and Mamma have made this as painless as possible. My shoulders relax a few inches.

"Obviously, the gown is our magnum opus."

"That's Latin for biggest octopus," Mamma adds.

"Right."

"Everybody knows formal wear is the most important. The rest is just gravy. So, it doesn't matter if you bomb the first two. Just be confident in the gown, capisce?"

"Okay."

Mamma and Lee Ray stare down at me expectantly. They clearly can't smell my neck sweat. Or my rack sweat. Or, for that matter, my back sweat, which has trickled all down my T-shirt like a liquid rattail.

"Dottie, could you give us a second?" Lee Ray asks.

"Don't you get her pregnant, now."

"A joke that never gets old."

She pats me on the shoulder and shimmies her scrawny rear out the door. Meanwhile, Lee Ray takes a silky sachet from his backpack. The kind of bag you use for marbles or handcuffs, depending on the day of the week.

"Here." He hands it over. "Dillard's was having a lingerie sale."

"Lee Ray!"

"Do not fight me on this. I have already burned your other undies."

I look at the sensible but pretty pair he's picked out. Lee Ray knows I usually dress my can from packs of ten from the Fashion Barn. Which, I suppose, might create some ugly lines for the biggest octopus dress. He really does think of everything. I reckon everybody needs at least one person in their life who thinks of everything and I got two. Comprehending the sheer dumb luck of it all, I spring forward and hug Lee Ray tight. Last-day-of-school tight. Funeral tight. I have done nothing to deserve this sweet boy, and yet here he is, throwing out my baggy drawers and keeping me afloat.

"Why're you working so hard on this?" I ask.

He unpacks my casual wear.

"I'm a perfectionist."

A perfectionist who suddenly won't meet my eyes. Mamma says busy is the first exit on the highway of grief. A better choice than the liquor exit or the mattress outlet, but it sure don't get you where you need to go.

"Liar, liar, pants on fire. Nose as long as a telephone wire."

"My nose is just fine, thank you."

"Come on, Lee Ray."

"Fine. This is the first interesting thing to happen here since Lionel, and despite the absurd nature of it all, I might be a little bit excited."

"Thank you."

"Now put on your casual wear and hand me the flat iron before I change my mind."

"Aye, aye, Captain."

Twenty minutes later, I'm all spiffed up. Eyebrows sharp, hair did, undies invisible. So good-lookin' that if I washed your car for a school fundraiser, you might even whistle at me. We know it's time to go when the junior brass band starts playing the sports warm-up medley. You know those songs? Get you all fired up and hungry for a corn dog. Apparently, they can get you all fired up for a pageant, too. Lee Ray fusses with my hair one last time and leads me down the hall toward the backstage door. Now he's the one sweating.

"Here's your one chance. Fancy, don't let me down," he whispers.

"How long have you been waiting to use that Reba quote?"

"Ages. Absolutely ages."

The horn section toots out the first few notes of "Rocky Top." A better ode to Tennessee there never was, but bless their hearts, it's gonna be a long night if that's the best they can do.

"Wait. Can you do me one favor before I go out there?" I plead.

"As discussed, I will not drive you to the bus station."

"I need your phone."

"Hmm, no."

"Hey, let's not forget how you stole my phone to invite Boof over. You owe me."

"Fine. Don't scroll. I mean it."

Lionel's number isn't hard to find. It's the one with a heart next to it.

I HATE TO disappoint, but in case you were wondering, Mr. Puddin is not tonight's emcee. He's got bigger chicks to fry. Instead, the privilege goes to Mayor Delilah Fisher-Trapper, whose church hats put the state of Kentucky and its wimpy little derby to shame. At six-foot-three, she is not only a head above the town, but a hat, too. She trots onstage to start the show.

"Good evening, Pennywhistle! I am proud to welcome you to what I hope will be the first annual Chickie Shak Hot Chicken Beauty Tour."

The crowd hoots and hollers.

"Meet tonight's judges: Tammy Applebaum of Tammy's Tam Tams: Hats for Every Occasion; Sean Donne, general manager of Pennywhistle's Used Car Emporium; and the lovely Boudreaux Beanie, Miss Tennessee Junior Baby, 1985."

Tammy is just exactly how you'd picture her. Short little dumpling of a lady. Hair cut in that blender-swept mullet style that is neither matronly nor sexy, just confusing as hell. She's wearing a pink blazer with shoulder pads so wide you'd swear she was a general. She could be anywhere from forty-two to seventy-five and your guess is as good as mine.

To Tammy's left is Sean Donne, widely known as Pennywhistle's Fabio. His teeth are real, his tan is fake, and his dimples are said to be the result of a hockey injury way back when he played for the Pennywhistle Partners. His hand is so close to Tammy's leg he might as well be her rosacea.

Finally, there's Boudreaux Beanie. She put Pennywhistle on the map at just six months old. Came back from Junior Baby nationals with pneumonia and a peanut allergy, but it was well worth it. She's been coasting on her title ever since. Which, if I had to say, does make her the most qualified judge of the bunch.

Purveyors of beauty, masters of industry. The three of them strike an impressive panel.

"Let's get things started," Delilah says. "Our first round this evening is casual wear. Sponsored by Piggly Wiggly: I'm Big on the Pig. Leading us off tonight is Boof Kidston."

"Cotton Eye Joe" blasts as Boof walks onstage. "Where did she come from?" is exactly what we're all thinking. She looks one pony away from perfect in her red patchwork dress and her dainty little lace-up boots. Shoo-ee! And is it just me or are her curls extra bouncy today? I wonder if she did it all herself or if there's somebody back there—her very own Lee Ray—clutching a can of hairspray for dear life. I still got so much to ask her.

"Miss Kidston hails from Dovetail, Texas. She enjoys writing and performing music, line dancing, and meeting new people. Tonight, she's wearing a vintage dress from Lenny's Once Worn. Let's give it up for Boof."

She blows kisses at our regulars. The junior hockey team, the mortuary college. If it were up to the audience, Boof would get more votes than a cat in a flea election. Quick as she come, she's gone. For all this hoopla, our stage time really isn't much. In between the rounds, local kids compete in relays and challenges. Catch the greased chicken, pin the tail on the teenager. You know, the usual.

When Boof's applause fades, Linda's song starts up. We didn't get the full scope of her perm today on account of the baseball cap. I figure she wanted to keep her secret weapon under wraps until tonight's performance. Hate to say it, but her noggin don't look half bad. Somebody ought to call Miss Bernadette Peters and personally thank her for rehabilitating the once limp locks of the Volunteer State. Funny, with curls, she and Boof almost look alike.

"Born in Knee, Tennessee, Linda Carter Creel has been a bona fide Pennywhistle resident since 1997. She enjoys hunting, fishing, and watching QVC. She's wearing separates from the Fashion Barn."

Linda's contingency is fatter and wider than you'd expect. Hunters and dog enthusiasts, Gretchen Wilson groupies, stranded long-haul truckers. And a man in the front row, holding up a handmade sign that says I Love My Hot Wife! Linda's married? Who'da thunk it? Despite the twisted ankles and ill-fated fingernails, it's clear that Linda has mastered the art of pageantry. She flirts her way across the stage, flexing her cheetah-print leggings and shaking her can in an airbrushed T-shirt that says Baby's Girl. Does that make the man with the sign Baby? Or is it more like Baby is Girl? Whatever it means, a shirt like that really talks to people. Says I've been places. Places being Gatlinburg or behind the dumpster at homecoming.

Next thing I know it's me. My grandmother used to say, "Well, ain't you just been to Memphis" when somebody dressed up nice. Apparently, I've been to Memphis, because the moment I walk onstage

Tommy Robertson, Jesse Dupree, and Horse Wilson lead the fire department in one big hog whistle. Man alive! That just about shoots my hearing for the rest of the night.

"PJ Spoon was born right here in Pennywhistle. Her hobbies include reading, canoeing, and trying new recipes. She's wearing Reba for Dillard's."

In case you're wondering, Reba for Dillard's amounts to jeans that actually touch my legs all the way around and a yellow blouse with little daisies embroidered on it. We're going for "girl next door." Which, technically, I am if you ask the residents of 23 and 27 Dogbark Lane. Lot of people expect queer folks to look a certain way. They think we're like paper dolls. Come with a few outfits, a few hairstyles, and that's it. Really, we're more like the whole dang toy store. Some days I dress like Twister, other days, Ken. Every now and then I throw in a fairy princess look, just to keep you guessing. Point is, it's kind of cool that each of us is doing our own thing with the casual wear look, even Linda, who's as straight as nobody's teeth.

As I strut my stuff, I spot Mamma in the fourth row. She's got Daddy's ashes propped up in the seat beside her, the little potato hands lifted up like he's cheering. The potato is happy, but I wonder, would Daddy be proud of me, too? He was less inclined to watch *Miss America* than to spend hours in front of the History Channel, elbow deep in a bag of pork rinds.

He and I, we had big ideas for the kind of person I'd grow up to be. He'd recognize the girl who was getting her PhD in American history, but probably not the girl I am right now, a Hot Chicken contestant shimmying into a bathing suit and rubbing Vaseline on my thighs to make them look extra juicy.

"Can I have my phone?" I ask as Lee Ray pins my hair back into a tasteful Twinkie shape.

"No, ma'am. Eyes on the prize."

"What would I even do with free Chickie Shak for life?"

"I can think of a few things we could all do with a million dollars.

Listen, you looked good out there, but you need to work the crowd a little more. The good lord gave you eyelashes for a reason."

"You gave me eyelashes," I point out, batting the false ones he just glued on me.

"And?"

"And I feel like a Shetland pony."

"Then start prancing!"

Unfortunately, by the time I get backstage, Boof has finished her lap of the communal swim meet. How she manages to make a half-zipped wetsuit look sexy, I'll never know.

"Hey, stranger," she says.

"What do you think?" I ask, gesturing to my suit.

Boof does a loop around me. Hums like a cat with a question.

"I think you look like the hottest mom at the tanning salon."

"Damn, I didn't realize that whale at SeaWorld coughed you back up."

"Do you like it? I thought it was a fun nod to deep-sea fashion."

"Does that zipper go all the way down?" I say in my best version of a bedroom voice, which lands closer to a kitchen voice.

"For you it does."

A pimply stage manager gives us the stink eye.

"As per Mr. Puddin's latest email," I remind her, "we're not supposed to fraternize during the competition."

"How 'bout after?"

"Definitely after."

The stage manager maintains his surly stare. We turn our backs. By the sound of the crowd, Linda's doing famously out there. Nothing compliments her Redneck Woman song medley better than her bathing suit, a strappy two piece with enough strings to staff a high ropes course.

"Look at her back." Boof points.

"I'd rather not."

"No, look."

Four tiny tattooed footprints dance just above her can.

"She doesn't even have kids," I whisper.

"Have you forgotten about Brawny, Easter Bonnet, and Gator?"

"So, they should be paw prints."

"We may need to saddle up for another recon mission."

"Baby, that dog don't hunt."

Before she can tempt me into another trespassing rendezvous, the music fades, signaling my turn.

"Shit in a basket," I curse.

"You'll be fine. Go on, get!"

Boof rushes back to her dressing room before Linda can see us together. I'm not really worried about her finding us out from a romantic standpoint. Linda once told me she liked queer folks better than straight folks, "on account of queer folks always treat dogs good and they don't never burp when they finish eating." Not sure where she got this info, but I always think about it when I see a dog or finish a meal. Frankly, she's more likely to get angry about the practical side of things. The whole working together and spooning on the side mess. And, I guess, the whole competing for a chicken-tender-studded crown thing.

Lucky for Linda, I trip within seconds of walking onstage, before Jimmy Buffett can even get to the chorus. It's not the nerves, but the footwear. Mamma and Lee Ray know I'd wax my lip with a flytrap before I'd wear heels with a bathing suit, so they paired the suit with a cheerful pair of yellow flip-flops. Now I have a sneaking suspicion that my knee's bleeding from the fall. Blood or no blood, I'll be damned if I'm gonna sit on my can for all of "Margaritaville." Work the crowd, Lee Ray said. I stand up, snatch the shoe like this was my plan all along, and swing it around sexy-like. The crowd hoots. Exclamations of "yeah, baby" and "woo, doggy" embolden me even further. I zing that busted flip-flop into the audience as far as it can go. Despite aiming for one of the firefighters, I snag Mamma instead.

"Here you go, baby!" she yells as she Frisbees it back to me.

Embarrassed, but undaunted, I fling it again. This time it lands among the EFPs, who couldn't be more delighted to be singled out.

The EFPs, like everybody, just want to be noticed. That, and to make it down the Mississippi before the good lord grabs them by their mullets and takes them up to heaven. An enthusiastic little bunch, they whistle for me with the twelve collective front teeth they have left. I'm happy to have the support.

I parade back and forth for a few more minutes until Jimmy lets up and I can retreat back to my dressing room. Sure enough, blood is streaming down my knee.

Lee Ray hands me some gauze.

"For the amount of blood you lost, you did pretty well out there."

"Thank you. Do you think I tanked the whole thing?"

"No, you're at least second. Boof's going to be penalized for the wet-suit. The guidelines specifically stated that seventy percent of the body must be visible for that round."

"Jesus."

"I have to say I admire her spunk."

"I'm pretty into it myself."

"It's fun seeing you like this," he says, lacing me into the denim mas-terpiece.

"Like what?"

"Open."

"Was I closed before?"

"Like a Blockbuster in a blizzard."

"Touchy," I say, Mamma's rendition of *touché.* "Now hurry up so I can go see Boof twirl around."

We were instructed to pick a love song for our formal-wear debut. Romance the crowd, something like that. Boof has chosen "Bless the Broken Road" by Rascal Flatts. Could she be talking about me? My lov-ing arms? It's way too early to be talking—or singing—about love. But I get the gist of the song, that feeling of finally making it to the right place at the right time after one too many sad detours. It reminds me of my last day in Nashville. I went on a first date, one of those coffee shop do-si-dos that can either last thirty minutes or four hours, depending on the quality of the coffee and the conversation. This girl seemed perfectly nice. Funny, vivacious. Even had her own store selling roadside souvenirs. That day I felt as good as my red leather jacket, as free as the tassels that flowed from the arms. Fifteen minutes in, I got the call from Mamma. Nay, five calls.

"She's usually not this persistent," I told my date. "I hate to do this, but do you mind if I step out for a minute?"

"No problem."

"I promise this isn't one of them fake phone calls to get you out of a date."

"I believe you." She smiled.

When I came back inside, Nashville was my roadside souvenir.

"It's my daddy, he's a . . . was a . . . well, right now it's somewhere between *is* and *was*. There's been some kind of accident."

She understood. She sat there and ordered me some food I couldn't even begin to eat. Rubbed my shoulder and gave me a ride back to my apartment. When she finally left, we hugged like old friends, knowing fate had made its decision. Like a cell phone kiosk at a Renaissance fair, it was the right place, wrong time.

And then there's Boof.

Breathtaking Boof in a purple gauzy gown. Waiting to recognize her long-lost mamma. Like someday she'll come round the cornbread aisle with a spray of red curls and a map of freckles that lead to treasure. *Is that you?* they'll say in unison. And by golly, it will be. Maybe that's what kept me and Boof just coworkers for so long, the fact that we were in our own time warps, the both of us stuck in that in-between space before you pick someplace to go next.

When she comes offstage I want to make like overalls and pull her into my denim embrace. Instead she heads for the side door.

"Boof?"

"Gotta pee," she whispers. "Keep an eye on Linda for me, will you?"

Hard to miss her in what can be described only as a negligee Elvis suit. The ensemble features not only a hussy upper but also, it seems, a can trampoline. Indeed, her buns are more buoyant than beach balls in a bayou, bobbing up and down as she walks out to "Burning Love." Sean Donne fans his face as she shimmies his way. Someone rips a "Yee-haw!" from the front row. Even our preacher, forever single Skippee Robinson, blows a kiss to the lady in gold.

I'm starting to wonder how she stayed behind the counter so long. Why shake what the good lord gave her now and not, say, ten years ago? Maybe it's the promise of a million dollars. Maybe it's the perm. She's still bouncing by the time our paths cross backstage.

"That, PJ, is how it's done."

I wait for her to poke me again, but instead she gives my gown the old up and down.

"Your mamma didn't do half bad."

This is just about the nicest thing she's ever said to me, and frankly it'll do. A stagehand nudges me forward. Daddy used to say, "When you don't know where to go, go on." Seems the only direction I'm allowed.

Nervous as I may be, I feel downright regal as I walk onstage to Dolly Parton's "I Will Always Love You." Now, a lot of folks think Whitney Houston's version is the top trout. With respect to Miss Houston, legend has it that Dolly wrote "I Will Always Love You" and "Jolene" on the same damn day, which is kinda like McDonald's coming up with the McRib and the Filet-O-Fish on the same day. Dolly's got one of them deep Tennessee accents, too. The kind of Smoky Mountain tinny tune that sticks with you late at night. You can hear the crickets and the Cracker Barrels, the heartaches and the chipmunks. Somebody yelling "shut your trap" at a dog on a porch.

Needless to say, "I Will Always Love You" is doing the beaver's share of the work for my formal-wear routine. But, sit tight! I'm about to up the ante. We practiced this dozens of times. Once the second chorus hits I pull a hidden string—okay, fine, bungee cord—and release the train of the dress. And bam! The junk in my trunk spills out for all to see. Hundreds of rhinestones sparkle as I stroll to the far side of the stage and fan out the full ten feet of the train. Pennywhistle goes wild. Yaps and yelps and whistles and kazoos. A bona fide redneck orchestra confirms that Mamma's engineering and Lee Ray's bejeweling has more than paid off. This here's a denim miracle.

"Thank you, everybody. Thank you," Delilah Fisher-Trapper says. "Our judges will tally everything up and give us their scores momentarily. In the meantime, the Little Volunteers."

After an age-inappropriate rendition of "Whose Bed Have Your Boots Been Under?" from Mrs. Juniper's third grade choir, the three of us return to the stage to hear the verdict. Delilah Fisher-Trapper starts another round of applause.

"Let's give it up one more time for our hot chickens! Beautiful, just beautiful. Each and every one. Now, for the juicy bits. Boof, Linda, and PJ will each receive a score out of thirty. Tonight's scores and next week's results will determine who will advance to the national competition in Nashville. Judges, it's all up to you."

She tips her hat and passes the mic to Tammy. Sean whispers something in her ear that causes her to snicker "You devil!" loud enough for all of us to hear. She clears her throat.

"In third place, with a score of twenty-one, Boof Kidston. Casual wear, eight out of ten. Bathing suit, four out of ten. Formal wear, nine out of ten."

Huh. I guess the wetsuit really did piss them off.

"In second place, with a score of twenty-four, PJ Spoon. Casual wear, seven out of ten. Bathing suit, seven out of ten. Formal wear, ten out of ten.

"And in first place, with a score of twenty-six, Linda Carter Creel. Casual wear, seven out of ten. Bathing suit, ten out of ten. Formal wear, nine out of ten."

The audience claps nonstop for a good four minutes, but I've got only a thirty-second head start to make a break for my phone, jog to the second-floor ladies' room, and lock myself in before anybody can come congratulate me. Sure enough, Lionel has answered my shot in the dark text. I'd better respond before Lee Ray comes to unlace me or, like a nose job in a tornado, the whole operation will be blown.

Hey, Lionel! PJ here. Lee Ray's friend.

The famous PJ! Nice to virtually meet you. To what do I owe the pleasure?

"Phenomenal performance, just phenomenal!" Lee Ray shouts from outside the bathroom door.

"Jesus, Mary, and Joseph." I wince. "Can't a lady have a moment alone to urinate?"

"Quickly. If I don't unlace that thing soon you might just turn blue."

I'm typing. I'm sweating. I'm holding ten feet of denim aloft as I squat.

"Uh, might be a while. I had stanky fries for lunch."

"So it's a number two?" he yells loud enough for the entire tristate area to hear.

"One and a half."

What are you doing two weeks from now? I ask.

Fighting cockroaches and lizards for the last beignet. Nothing much. Why?

How'd you like to watch me play a banjo and humiliate myself in front of the entire town?

The pageant, right. I saw a bit about it in the news.

Lee Ray sure would love to see you.

A long pause. Perhaps I've gone too far.

I'll be there.

SECRETS

Keeping a secret from Lee Ray is tougher than fighting diarrhea on a white-water rafting excursion. Maybe I should tell him so he has the chance to get a haircut and do a few crunches before Lionel arrives on Friday. Then again, he might just steal my idea and skip town before he has the chance to fail. I've never met Lionel, but I spent enough hours on the phone with Lee Ray to picture the rise and fall of their relationship. They met—where else?—on the river.

Lee Ray had just docked the EFPs for the day. They spread out their blankets and unpacked their coolers. Fished tuna salad sandwiches from greasy paper bags. The whole scene looked like that French painting except with more jorts and fewer parasols. Then, a few quilts over, somebody moaned, the kind of moan Peep and Nina sell at the adult store for $14.99. It just kept getting longer and louder. Lee Ray turned to see what pair of fools was daring to make whoopee in broad daylight on the banks of the Loosahatchie. Instead, he saw a handsome young man eating a PB&J.

"That must be one hell of a sandwich," he called.

Lionel grinned, gave Lee Ray the old up-and-down gaze.

"Why don't you come see for yourself."

"No, no. I believe you."

"I insist. Come over here and have a bite."

Usually guys flirted with Lee Ray only in the nooks and crannies of Pennywhistle. The port-a-john line. The gas pump. The VHS section of the public library. The whole broad daylight thing—not to mention Lionel's thick eyelashes—was throwing him off.

"Just one bite," Lionel said, "and maybe your phone number."

Lee Ray looked to the nearest EFP, Asberry Judd, for guidance. Setting his hot dog down for emphasis, Asberry gave the idea three teeth and two thumbs up. Lee Ray went for it.

"So how was the sandwich?" I asked.

"Utterly ordinary." He grinned.

It was four months of sandwiches, Scrabble, and Sunday-afternoon naps. After that, Lee Ray never snuck around again.

Sometimes you know what a phone call means before you answer it. For example, a call one week after the gynecologist means something funky's in your Crock-Pot. A call from Lee Ray at three thirty in the morning on a Tuesday means heartbreak. Lionel, apparently, had finished his stint in the Quarterflute Playhouse's rendition of *Cat on a Hot Tin Roof*, and intended to go back to New Orleans.

"You know where to find me," he told Lee Ray.

"How on earth would I—"

"Boy, you got a boat."

A boat he had. The guts to use it, not so much. In his despair, Lee Ray turned to the great Twains: Mark and Shania. When he wasn't on the Mississippi with Huckleberry Finn he was sobbing the lyrics to "Any Man of Mine" in his bathtub. Funny, when he called me, I couldn't offer much in the way of sympathy. My heart hadn't ever been broken. Hell, it had barely been bruised. A few weeks later, when Daddy passed, I understood a little more about loss. We switched the radio to Sarah McLachlan and sat in the aboveground pool until our fingers were as warped and pruny as we were.

You can understand, then, how keeping Lionel's visit under my toupee feels a little itchy. I'm hoping it's worth it. Hoping that by inviting

Lionel to Pennywhistle I'm bringing back all of the giggles and none of the shits. Maybe my second-place victory's got me feeling risky.

It's certainly got me feeling frisky. Shoo-ee! Boof and I have been flirting within earshot. Kissing with our eyes closed. With Linda all fluffed up from her win, we figure she's not paying us much mind. She may have won by only two points, but that old coot's as cheerful as a leech on a leg. Customers she once scorned with *sweethearts* are now lining up to flirt with her. Teenagers are buying her sweet teas. Her husband even stopped by with a new T-shirt—I'm Horny for Linda—to which she batted a bejeweled eyelash and said, "Hush!" Bless the poor airbrush artist who had to take that request. Nobody has ever been horny for a Linda.

Boof peeks her head into the kitchen around two thirty. I love the way her curls poke out the corners of her Chickie Shak baseball cap like happy little SpaghettiOs. More and more she's letting them show. More and more I'm wearing my crappy brass hoops. Guess this is what Lee Ray means when he talks about opening.

"Can I get a mayo cup for table five?" she asks, loud enough for Linda to hear.

"Sure thing, but don't they need hot sauce, too? They're like salt and pepper. Rude to pass one without the other," I say in my best stage voice.

"Wanna come over tonight?" Boof whispers. "*Ernest Goes to Camp* is on TV. We could watch it or . . . not watch it."

"Sounds like a win either way."

Linda slaps the counter, announces her smoke break, and heads outside. The only folks still eating their lunches are a pair of retired teachers who would sooner burn their chunky, wooden necklace collections than rob a register. Been quiet all day. Seems everybody's too tired from a weekend of pageant barbecues and fireworks tennis to make it in today. Boof watches Linda until she makes it out the door, then joins me in the steamy poultry sauna that some call a kitchen.

With nothing much else to do, I start shaping burgers for the dinner crowd. Delilah Fisher-Trapper likes hers in the shape of Mickey Mouse. Teeny Wilson likes hers in the shape of a grown man's ding-a-ling. To each her own, I say.

"You know what I hate?" Boof asks.

Funny question from a woman with her arms wrapped around my waist. I try not to jab her with my elbows as I mold the beef.

"What?"

"When they say, 'Pick you up at eight?' in movies. It's always eight. But that feels too late to me. Pick you up at seven is more like it."

"Makes sense. How 'bout I shower and shoot for seven thirty?"

"Deal. Hey, I ran into your mamma at the Piggly Wiggly yesterday." I stiffen.

"What did she have to say?"

Boof glances out at the dining room. Still no thieves or peepers.

"Just introduced herself. Told me to get you while the getting's good."

"Dammit, Mamma." I sigh. "She acts like she wants you to knock me up when I've explained to her time and time again that two hoo-has don't make a baby."

Boof laughs, but I can hear the slightest catch in her voice.

"Kinda got the impression you were going somewhere."

"Daytona," I lie. "Mamma's taking us to Daytona for Labor Day."

"Well, if that's all."

"That's all? It's the redneck Disneyland."

We debate the merits of NASCAR until Linda returns. I don't know why I didn't tell Boof I'm not going anywhere. Shoulda been easy. Just like that little alien in a basket says "I'll be right here."

Will you? Daddy's voice echoes in my ears.

I wish he'd stick to picking out my outfits and sleeping in potatoes.

BOOF'S APARTMENT IS the kind of messy that looks totally intentional. Like a screenwriter said, "She's messy, but in an adorable way."

As opposed to my place, which is messy in a "where'd them Skittles come from?" kind of way. I notice her bookshelf is organized by color.

"I've got all the great Southern writers."

I arch my brows.

"What?" she asks.

"Sure, you've got all the usual ones. I like Tennessee Williams as much as the next girl, but where's your Rita Mae Brown? Your Lee Smith? And where in the hell is your Emmens Clementine?"

"Who?"

"Who? He's only the most famous author ever to come out of Penny-whistle."

"Never heard of him."

"*The Raccoon King of Fiery Gizzard? The Raccoon King of Destiny Hole?*"

"You're making these up."

"I could never."

"He sounds like a real visionary."

"He is!"

"Okay, okay, I believe you."

"I'll lend you my copy of *The Raccoon King of Lake Tomorrow* when I finish it. Though I'm running slow on my reading. Been a little distracted of late."

Boof leads me to the couch.

"Is that so?"

She plops me down on the orange-and-yellow-tweed cushions. Cushions like these are practically historical landmarks. I can only imagine the cans upon cans that have come before me.

"You were saying?"

"I was saying some gorgeous Texan's been taking up most of my brain cells so I don't have many left for finishing my book."

Boof sets her hands on my shoulders and looks at me. Her look is like a bird landing on a tree branch: soft, testing to make sure nothing breaks.

"May I?" she asks.

"Please."

One knee at a time, she lifts herself onto my lap. I wrap my arms around her waist and pull her closer. God bless poultry and timing. I finally have Boof all to myself.

"Well, now that we're comfortable," I say, "what do you wanna do tonight?"

I can feel her blushing as we kiss, which makes me so happy I could spit. A blush like that doesn't mean she's embarrassed. It means she's getting exactly what she wants after a long time wanting it. I love how her skin betrays her like that.

As she leans into me, I feel the weight of her, how her can is bigger and better than I could have even imagined. Every redneck loves a hearty woman. Don't let nobody tell you different.

"Do you mind if I?" I ask, gesturing to her ample backside.

"I'd be offended if you didn't."

I let my hands explore down her back to her can. Damn if it's not the best thing I've ever touched.

"You're so . . ."

"What?" she asks.

"Unprecedented."

"Is that a compliment?"

"Yes," I assure her from the tender spot below her ear. "You're also very hot."

"So are you."

Our clothes come off faster than a loose wig on a Tilt-A-Whirl. Look, I've been forced to explain sex between ladies to one too many cousins, and it always goes something like this: "No, Jerry Jack, it ain't just naked pillow fights and the pillows burst open and the feathers get everywhere. Who even has feather pillows?" Or "Joey, those movies ain't accurate."

The questions get more and more personal until all I can do is pull up Google, wring my hands, and head for the hills. It's exhausting, all this sex education, so you'll forgive me if I care to leave out the nitty-gritty. All I'll say is this: I've never made whoopee with somebody who smiles as much as Boof. Every time I open my eyes I see an effortless grin sprawled across her face like litter on a highway. Sex with her is fun and intuitive. And, frankly, exhausting. I'm gonna need a Gatorade and some orange slices before I can get back out on the field again.

AS WE LIE there, she plays with my hair. This is the part where somebody usually says something sweet like "nice tits" or "you got a cig?" Boof's gaze is talking big.

"New game," she says. "Words romance novelists use to describe getting busy."

"Oh, let's see," I say, shifting onto my elbow. "Nape of the neck."

"Where the hell is the nape?"

"I think somewhere below the chin but above the crack."

"So, the torso?"

"I think you mean the womanly hourglass."

"Where the bosoms are?"

"And the flaming passion."

"Right, right. And I think there's some kind of rule where if the author doesn't say *pleasure* at least fifteen times they're disbarred from the whole genre."

"If nothing trembles they're out."

"If nothing trembles *with desire* they're out."

"If nothing *swollen* trembles with desire they're out."

"If no velvet bosoms tremble with swollen, forbidden desire while also kissing the nape of the neck with pleasure . . ."

"Then, that's it," I conclude. "Go back to selling insurance because, buddy, you're fired."

We laugh and laugh until I don't just need a Gatorade, but also a bathroom break.

"First door to the left."

"Roger that."

Just as I suspected. Bar of soap, jar of shells. Why do people keep a jar of shells in their latrines? What're you gonna do? Run out of toilet paper and scrape yourself clean with nature's bounty? Daddy preferred a jar of dominos or tangled necklaces, so you have something to do while you're in there.

I snag the robe from the bathroom door and wrap myself tight. A very girlfriendy thing to do. Oh, well. Dress for the job you want.

"So, listen," Boof says. "I've been working on something new, and I think it might be worth doing for Friday."

"You mean you don't want to go with 'Possums in the Creek'?"

"While it is our magnum opus—"

"Biggest octopus."

"Our biggest octopus, this might be a chance to perform something, I don't know, real."

She hesitates. Real is scary. It's waking up four counties over with nothing on your person but a poker chip and a Snickers bar.

"Alrighty, let's hear it."

"I wrote out the music, so you can play along if you want."

She hands me a yellow notepad and a banjo. You gotta love a girl who keeps a banjo lying around. The song's called "Mamma's Two Left Feet" and shoot, Boof's handwriting is so nice you'd want to bring it home and introduce it to your parents. I scan the notes. One, two, three and we're ready to go.

They say Moses was floated down the river
In a basket toward a better destiny
Past the letdowns and the hard luck
Past the pity and the potlucks
Past the sign that always says "No Vacancy."

I don't know how to part the sea,
But my mamma did the same with me.

She sent me off to someplace warm and dry.
Now there's no return to sender
Not a voice I can remember.
There's just one thing that I have to prove I'm yours.
When you gave me up you thought you gave me nothing.
But you left me with my mamma's two left feet.

My mamma's two left feet don't make for dancing.
My mamma's two left feet, they trip me up.
Can't waltz to save my life.
Can't keep a partner by my side.
Because I'm dancing with my mamma's two left feet.

These two left feet they always walk away
from the people and the places
that I really ought to stay.
They seem to know that home ain't worth the trouble
for every time I love someone
I only lose them double.
Moses had commandments.
Bet his buddies couldn't stand him.
Was he walking with his mamma's two left feet?

My mamma's two left feet don't make for dancing.
My mamma's two left feet they trip me up.
Can't waltz to save my life.
Can't keep a partner by my side.
Because I'm dancing with my mamma's two left feet.

Now I'm trying to keep my two left feet a'planted.
Trust the ground I'm walking on won't be quicksand.
So I'm sending back the basket.

Life is good now.
You can have it.

Call me up someday.
I'd really love to meet.

She grabs a cup of water and takes a long drag, the classic hide-my-face-until-I-know-what-you're-thinking maneuver. Funny, she's usually so sure. Are my introverted ways rubbing off on her? Is she fool enough to think her voice is bad? Maybe we've just accidentally stumbled onto one of those things that matter.

"Boof, this is beautiful."

"It's not too mushy?"

"All apple, no sauce."

She breathes out.

"That's a huge relief."

I kiss her forehead, pull her into my robey embrace.

"If you're not a famous singer-songwriter in ten years, then I'm a monkey's uncle."

Fragile as she seems, Boof holds me tight.

"Do you think maybe she'll be there?"

"Who, your mamma?"

"Yeah."

"It's very possible. And if she's not, she's probably watching on TV. This whole thing's on channel ten, you know."

"I was thinking if I made it all the way to the big one she'd have to see me."

"Shoulda thought of that before you walked onstage in a wetsuit."

Boof sighs.

"Look," I say, "when Mr. Puddin first barged in, I thought this whole thing was one pound of stupid, two pounds of misogyny."

"Don't forget two tablespoons of country and a heap of weird."

"Right. I guess when I got up there and saw all those people I realized this pageant might actually serve a higher purpose than just getting Linda to shave her mole."

"Though it was an excellent bonus." Boof laughs.

"It's like, seeing everybody get so excited about it makes me weirdly proud, you know? Like we're giving them something to get out of bed for. Peep and Nina told me they got some customers in from Memphis the other day. Somebody drove *here* from Memphis. Can you believe that?"

"So, what's in it for you if you win?" Boof asks.

"That's not going to happen."

"You were neck and saggy neck with Linda on Friday."

"If I win, Mamma can go to the Disney Store a lot more often. And Lee Ray can buy a bigger boat."

Technically, I could pay off my student loans and fund a heck of a lot of research, but I still haven't told Boof about any of that. Not Nashville, not school, not even Daddy. Fry me up and call me an oyster. I may be opening up, but I'm a long way from showing my pearl.

"Come on, you don't have something you want?" She nudges.

"Checked that box half an hour ago."

"They do say the best things in life are free."

We practice the new song until it's time for me to go home and get some beauty sleep. More like ugly slumber. I keep waking up from bad dreams, convinced the Raccoon King's kidnapped me. We're on a motorboat speeding away from everybody I know. By the time I realize I can swim, it's too late. I wake up.

"ALMOST DONE. JUST a few more pins."

Mamma tailors my suede pants for Friday, tighter and tighter despite my pleas to leave something up to the imagination. At this rate she might as well glue them on.

"Mamma, do you know anything about the Blessing House?"

"Your meemaw used to threaten to send me there whenever I got a little too frisky in the tree house."

"It's for my research."

She stops pinning.

"For school?"

"Sure."

"So you called them back?"

"Yes," I lie.

"That's wonderful! When do you start?"

"They can take me in the fall."

She pulls me in for a hug. The pins in my pants poke my dirty, rotten, lying legs.

"My prayer's been answered. I told Jesus if you went back to school I'd stop stealing Helen Robinson's marijuana plants for my rheumatoid arthritis and I really mean it."

There's just too much to unpack there, so I continue my questioning.

"Do you know anybody who went there?"

"Where?"

"The Blessing House."

She glances away.

"Sugar, that place closed a while back."

"I'm sure you remember somebody."

"I don't care to gossip."

"You gossip all the time. Come on, Mamma!"

She rubs her forehead with the heel of her hand.

"All right, I'll tell you. But I don't want you to think any less of her."

I roll my eyes.

"No, I mean it. Your generation's different about these things. Before that it was rough out there for a girl."

"You did all right."

"I's one of the lucky ones." She sighs. "When I hopped off that four-wheeler and found out I was pregnant, I thought, Whew! Thank Jesus I shacked up with the kind of fella who'll make an honest living and love our family right. The girls who went to the sisters were not bad girls. Matter fact, I don't believe in such a thing as bad girls. That there's some bullshit. Those girls simply went there to escape the horse piss things that had happened to them. Trust me, it wasn't one of them rich homes for girls who just needed to pop that baby out before they could go back to Charleston or Atlanta and marry some senator. It was more like a sanctuary. Kept out the abusers. People who shoulda never touched those girls in the first place."

"So who was it?"

She tugs on my ponytail in that sweet way that only a mamma can. *Ding dong, I love you.* I smile back at her.

"Situation like that can make a person hard. Closed up. Little mean even."

I wait. She goes back to pinning my pants.

"I think you can do the arithmetic on this one, baby girl."

FUNNY HOW TROUBLE means different things to different people. I remember the first time I ever got into it. I'd stolen into Mamma and Daddy's room to look for change in Mamma's purse—how do you think kids afford those great big gumballs at the bowling alley?—but had, instead, ended up cross-legged on the floor of the closet reading from the oldest book I'd ever seen. The pages flaked and tore under my fingers. The binding sagged and shifted like Meemaw's jowls during a Thanksgiving tirade. Somebody had written their name in inky cursive on the front page, which struck me as blasphemous, seeing as Daddy was always telling me not to write in books. Well, I thought, seven and stupid, if he can write his name, so can I.

Mark Twain said the ink. *PJ Spoon* said the crayon.

"Oh, sugar." Daddy wept when he discovered his ruined first edition. "I was saving this for you."

In my young life I'd seen Daddy cry over many a Super Bowl commercial and Christmas card. But never, ever, and I mean never, had I been the cause of the waterworks. The very thought rendered me a mess. Daddy cried over the book, I cried over Daddy, and the two of us watered the carpet like expert gardeners. Only thing to do, I thought, was to start reading this thing I'd spoiled. Wiping my nose, I turned to the first paragraph and began.

From then on out, Daddy and I haunted the public library with Halloween-like fervor. Took long drives to garage sales that promised piles of books. I don't know how precious the book was before I ruined it with my chicken scratch, but I do know it shot up in value the moment the man who owned it died. Mamma thought we oughta donate it to the Tennessee Historical Society. I argued they had enough books. She was all set to mail it, but before it could be lost to the haunted postal service and the cobwebbed historians, I tucked it into my purse. Under my name I wrote *Earl Spoon* and thought about how funny—and not funny at all—it was to be the only person still alive to read it.

"Hey, Mamma? These pants got me thinking."

"What about?"

"Just, you know, it's been a while since we rode together. Weather's nice. Maybe we could borrow Trusty and Showboat?"

"You want to do a trail ride?" she asks, setting her sewing down. "With me?"

"Yeah, why not?"

"Does Lee Ray have a date?"

"No."

"And Boof?"

"I'm not sure what she's up to."

"Huh."

"It's fine," I mumble. "You don't have to if you don't want to."

"No, I do. Lemme see if I can get Peep and Nina on the phone. They's usually bumpin' rumps around this hour but maybe not so much after the hip replacement. Sit tight."

Half an hour later we're two Appaloosas up a mountain. Well, not mountain exactly, but the hilly part of Pennywhistle, where wild strawberries grow and brooks spring up after powerful rain showers. We used to come here when I was little to let the dog run. Gloria was her name. We'd turn her loose on the fauna and keep a hot sack of Krystal cheeseburgers in the saddlebag to ensure her eventual return. Gloria's been dirt napping for at least ten years. Has it really been that long since we've been up here? Mamma wipes her brow with a pink bandanna. Trusty and Showboat pull up clovers by the pound.

"Sorry if I've been a little pushy lately," she says.

"Lately?"

"I'm just tickled about your research. I know that was more your daddy's cup of noodles, but I'm interested, too."

"Thanks."

"So, what's it about?"

"What's what about?"

"Your whole darn thing. Catch me up."

The horses amble forward toward a purple patch of hill in the distance. Side by side, tail swatting tail. Too close to gallop onto another topic.

"Well." I sigh. "I started out thinking I was gonna focus on Southern lit. I did my senior thesis on that."

"I remember."

"You read it?"

"Took me a while, but yes."

"Okay, so then I read this book last summer about Southern rituals. A lot of it had to do with the way food's been served throughout history."

"Mostly with forks, I reckon."

"It's more like the idea of hospitality and communion."

"Really?"

"Nothing too churchy, but that figures in a little. I'm looking at how food's a way to include people."

"Might be the only way," she observes.

I'm reminded of the cooler our preacher hauled over after the funeral, the pies Mamma doled out in return. Jesus did a lot with loaves and fishes, but imagine what he could have done with Crisco.

"Maybe you should start throwing casseroles with those tampons," I suggest. "Might bring in a few more constituents."

"Hey, that ain't a bad idea. I'mo write that down when we get home. I got a rump roast recipe from the Martha Stewart magazine I been itching to try."

"Since when do you spring for the good magazines?"

"Got myself a subscription, don'tcha know."

"Fancy."

"Well, if you ain't growing you're dying."

We fall silent, the both of us, at the mention of death. Sure, we lost the same person, but sometimes it feels like we've got no more in common than two campers in the same cabin. I'm the one who got homesick. She's the one who learned how to swim.

"So, tell me more about this rump roast."

Mamma breathes in like she's got something to say. I wince and grip my reins a little tighter, but instead of a lecture I feel a soft hand on my arm.

"We don't have to talk about it now," she says.

"Okay."

The horses make for the strawberries the way the dog used to make for the cheeseburgers. Trusty, the hungrier one, canters ahead, leaving me and Showboat at the rear.

Mamma looks back.

"I'll be here when you're ready."

SATURDAY

Saturday morning Boof and I wake up when the sun's almost done with its paper route. The dew has left the buttercups. The continental breakfasts wind down waffle by waffle. Nevertheless, my stomach protests with a fierce growl that it is still most certainly morning. Maybe not at Denny's, but here under the orange blankets and messy pillows, we have not yet fathomed lunch.

Boof chuckles into my hair.

"How do you like your eggs? Over easy? Fried?"

"Talk more about eggs. It feels good on my neck."

"Scrambled eggs," she coos, "poached eggs."

"Go on."

"Sunny"—kiss—"side"—kiss—"up."

"That one."

"Can do."

The light hits her freckled shoulders as she paws around for her robe. I sit up on one elbow.

"You don't have to cook for me."

"I don't have to. I want to."

At first, I thought grief was like sandpaper. That it would whittle me down to the tiniest person alive, toothpick size. I was wrong. Grief's an expander. It stretches you out bit by bit until you think the balloon will pop and then, handing you a plate of eggs, it stretches you again.

"What is it?" Boof asks. "Too much salt?"

"No, they're perfect."

She relaxes.

"It's just that I forgot what this feels like."

"What what feels like? Eating eggs in bed?"

"Sure, let's go with that."

The thing about Boof is, she knows I'm not talking about eggs. Setting her fork down, she starts to say something. My name, maybe, or one of those deep questions I love to skirt.

"I'm working on it," I promise.

"Okay," she says, a little sad, a little wondering.

I don't want to lose the orange sheets and the orange hair and the warm something in my shoulders that made me feel safe enough to sleep in, but the better things are, the easier they seem to squander. I eat my eggs and kick myself. Try, I think, just try.

"How about a little miniature golf?" Boof asks, pivoting. "I'm entitled to four free rounds a month. More if I find any cockroaches in my bathroom. So, technically, seven free rounds this month."

"Delightful as that sounds . . ."

"Ten free rounds. I forgot about the baby ones."

"I'm supposed to meet up with Lee Ray at noon. Rain check?"

"Anytime."

Kissing her from cheek to forehead to nose to cheek, I hope to convey the kind of softness I never manage with words. She squeezes my side. Maybe it works.

THE LOOSAHATCHIE, MURKY chocolate milk of a river, will take you straight to Cleat County if you let it. If you fall asleep, say, or if your paddles grow lazy. Maybe we're giving up, but today Lee Ray and I let the Loosahatchie waft us as far downstream as it'll go.

"Do you think we've passed the Fayette store already?" he asks drowsily.

I blink the orange out of my eyelids.

"Depends which Cracker Barrel that is."

He squints, zeroing in on a set of rocking chairs that look like they haven't seen a heinie in years. Cobwebbed and wishing. Everybody wants something.

"Gotta be Battle Creek."

"Home run," I murmur.

"You didn't have to quit softball when I did. You were good. You could have kept playing, maybe even played in college."

I start paddling toward the shore.

"Maybe."

"No, really. Why'd you stop?"

"Because sometimes it's scarier to be good at something than it is to be bad at it."

Lee Ray knots the boat to the dock, as Boy Scout as you can be when the Boy Scouts wouldn't take you.

"Like the accordion," I joke. "Scary to be good at the accordion."

Shaking his head, he lets me slip into silly. Lee Ray's always been good at that. It's like he's the knees and I'm the toddler. When the world gets a little too grocery store big, he lets me hide out for a while.

"Shall we?" he says, offering a hand.

"We shall."

Just Thighs settles into the mud as we sally forth in search of lemonade. It bobs back and forth, goodbye for now.

THE WOMAN AT the ice cream counter recommends the double fudge. No can do. With my bubblegum cone and his cookies and cream, we trust our childhood taste buds and take to the town. Battle Creek's familiar the way an old toy is. It's like we left this place in the attic and only just remembered it. So many softball games over the years, victories and popcorn littered over the dusty fields, and yet we haven't been back.

"Look"—Lee Ray points—"it's us."

A little girl with a long blond ponytail sails across home plate. The dugout clamors to congratulate her before the next inning starts. Life is short, but this much matters.

"Do you mind if we watch for a little while?"

"Of course not," Lee Ray says. "Now I'm invested."

The bleachers scorch our britches the way bleachers are born to do, and a woman with a pink umbrella offers us paper fans. She waves at the homerunner.

"That's my granddaughter. The little one who just scored."

"She's good."

"'Bout the only one, I tell you what."

The Dancing Unicorns, visiting team, purple shirts, lead ten to two. They wear glossy ribbons on the ends of their braids and boast an endorsement from the Chevy dealership, while the Butter Biscuits look like somebody ran them through a blender.

"Who's coaching?" I ask.

"Nobody. They're feral."

"What?"

"They had a coach at the start of the season but he took a promotion at the plant. Same with the next one. Busy. Not enough daddies around to coach."

"Where we come from the mammas coach."

"Well, Mamma," she gestures to the dugout, "have at it."

The dugout smells exactly as it did when I left it, all dust and Gatorade, all waiting, all wishing it was over, all praying it would last. I stand on the bench and clear my throat before the dust has a chance to settle in.

"Hello, Butter Biscuits."

"Hi." A girl with a blankie waves. Another chews what I hope isn't tobacco.

"My name's Miss PJ and today I'm gonna be your coach. We've got two minutes. Tell me everything you know about softball."

What they know is very little. Never heard of stealing bases or throwing with their hips. The woman with the pink umbrella tosses me a thumbs-up I'm hesitant to return.

"We're good at being crazy," says the one with the blankie.

"Come again?"

"We don't brush our hair," says tobacco.

"They're afraid of us."

"You know what"—I decide—"we can work with that."

I send the girls out into the field as monsters, bogeymen, ghosts, ghouls, every terrible thing that wakes you from your sleep and shakes the sure out of you. They rub dirt into their cheeks and storm the field. My banshees. My babies. My Bee Stings.

And, so help me God, it works.

As the Dancing Unicorns quiver, my girls learn to catch. The pitcher grows wings, the outfielders snarl their way into the clovers, and by the time it's their turn to bat again, they hit like there's no tomorrow. These are girls who've never settled on a victory dance because they've never had to.

"Like this, ladies," Lee Ray shouts.

Two, four, six, eight, kick, turn, clap, jig, jog, roll. I remember what it feels like to win.

Just when we've given all the high fives we can muster, the sun tugs on our T-shirts and reminds us it's time to go home.

"Don't go," the girls beg.

"We have to."

They shower us with whatever they've got—sticks of gum and beaded bracelets, mostly—and wave feverishly as we paddle upstream.

Something warm settles in me.

I suspect it's the opposite of scared.

THREE PEAS IN A POD

When the softball mitt appears next to Daddy's potato Sunday morning, I instinctively head to the hall closet. Can't help it. There the dusty white balls and skinny metal bats hobnob with umbrellas and flashlights, just waiting for a day like this, when the lilies pop up so orange you can't bear to stay indoors. Mamma's church dress sways around her knees like a bell.

"Catch."

I toss her the other mitt, the one that says *Dottie* in cursive.

It's muscle memory. Leaving our Sunday clothes in white linen heaps. Pulling on old T-shirts and digging around in the dresser for a pair of socks. Even the sandwiches we make—bologna and mustard for me, turkey and pepper jelly for her—practically slice themselves. I forget to keep my distance as we walk down the street to the baseball diamond.

"Race you."

"No fair, missy! I've got the bat."

Nevertheless, she barrels forward, keeping up and then some. Fighter in a size six shoe, her feet find the field a moment before I do.

"Woo-doggy!" she cheers.

"Show off."

We head for that old familiar place, Mamma pitching, me batting. The first ball I hit putters out toward third base like a woozy balloon.

"Move your left foot back," she says. "And choke up on the bat a little. That's right. Go 'head."

My rustiness threatens to embarrass me right off the field. I blush with every foul ball, every clumsy strike. It's hard to be new at something you used to be old at. But there's Mamma, calm as ever, ready to pitch until the rust wears off. She wipes her brow and motions for me to go again.

"Swing with your hips."

"Okay."

Forget honey. There's nothing sweeter than the crack the ball makes with the bat.

"Shoo-ee!" Mamma cheers. "That's my girl."

For a moment I'm so happy I almost forget to run the bases.

MONDAY IS *BUSTLING*. As Gabriel's Shiny Whatever draws nearer, up goes the volume at the Chickie Shak, both decibel-wise and people-wise. I tell you what, these past few weeks have been nothing short of a statewide family reunion. Old Connor McGee, who was said to have fallen down the Tennessee River Gorge back in the sixties, came trotting in, healthy as a horse. Lee Ray's uncle Dandy peeled himself away from the nearest slot machine to order a Jumbo Trucker's Plate and wish me luck. The firefighters sat among their constituents, no longer the bashful head-poker-inners they were last week. I've fried so many chickens and dreamed up so many Dippy Whips my fingers might just fall off. When closing time draws near, I ponder heading home for some reading and heat-up macaroni. Then again, Boof looks awful cute as she collects bouquets of soiled forks and greasy paper napkins.

Sure enough, the sun's still got a bit of glimmer to it by the time we lock up, so I ask her to wait up a minute while I give Lee Ray a call. Last thing I want to be is one of those fools who throws her best friend under a train for a little bit of romance. Lee Ray probably just got off work at the old folks home—where you think he sources all his potential EFPs?—and is sure to be up for a little adventure after a long day of spoon-feeding and checkers.

"Question: Does the Best Friends Shrimp Island charter extend to lovers?"

"Only if you never, ever, and I mean never, use that word again."

"Meet you there in twenty?"

He hesitates.

"Y'all don't want the lagoon to yourselves?"

It's one part jest, one part worry. See, when I first got to college and discovered the delights of the queer student union and decent cell-phone service, I forgot to call Lee Ray on his birthday.

His mamma popped him out at the end of summer, so his party usu-ally fell over Labor Day weekend. And, oh, what a party it was! His aunties would drive in from all corners of the state, even as far as Pi-geon Forge, just to spend hours peeling potatoes with their long, witchy fingers. Mesmerizing, they were. Each could take the whole peel off in one long swirl while simultaneously supplying a year's worth of gossip to her sisters. Ruthie, Ruby, June, and Lee Ray's mamma, Julie. Daddy used to say they could cover the whole of Tennessee history between them. We sure thought so. We'd hide under the kitchen table and catch the curlicues and the chitchat, which is how we learned what "gettin' busy" meant, as well as who in town was the busiest and who was busy with whose wife and who hadn't been busy since 1964.

Along with the potatoes, the aunties would fry a coop of chickens and stir up the spiciest gravy this side of hell. Shoo-ee that stuff burned! Al-ways seemed to take forever and a day for everything to come together. Sometimes Ruthie would whip up some hush puppies if us kids tugged on her apron and looked famished enough, but for the most part we just had to wait it out. Kick the can. Hop the scotch. Finally, when the food was ready for feasting, the ladies would gather wily cousins, sleepy un-cles, and everybody else around a great big table made out of at least six mismatched kitchen tables borrowed from around the neighborhood. Long ago, Lee Ray's grandmother had sewn the world's biggest tablecloth for this exact purpose. A hush would make its way over the crowd, including the dogs and the crickets, and the aunties would say grace. That is, they'd pray at the top of their lungs. And then, when we were so doggone hungry we could cry, the meal would begin. You never heard such a ruckus. Clinks and slops. Cackles of laughter. The kind of unrestrained burps that would put a hippo to shame. After supper we'd play capture the greased watermelon and later, jar-handy and nearly asleep, we'd catch the fireflies. By the time the moon took center stage, every last guest was so full of food and life that the lawn would be littered with bodies. Grown men with their legs draped over magnolia branches. Children curled up on the vacant laps of grannies. Long story short, it was the highlight of our whole summer.

All it took was two weeks of orientation and a little romance for me to forget.

Lee Ray's too sweet to hold a grudge, but deep down I'm sure the fear of losing more birthday calls still creeps up whenever I meet a new little lady. I want him to know he ain't got nothing to worry about this time around. Boof's the first person I've been with who can actually keep up with Lee Ray. She gets his jokes. She likes his sneakers. And she survived the trial-by-fire excursion to Linda's house. What could go wrong?

"Listen," I tell him, "getting busy's fun and all, but what I really want to do tonight is hang out with two of my favorite people and talk shit about Linda."

I can feel his shoulders relax across the telephone line.

"Deal. I've been meaning to ask Boof what her intentions with my best friend are."

"Unsavory, I assure you."

"I would expect nothing less."

WE DON'T HAVE our suits, so Lee Ray brings us to the island via *Just Thighs*. He's got a little lantern rigged up at the front, making me wonder how long he can resist breaking out into a *Phantom of the Opera* number. Maybe he's still saving some of himself up, sussing out whether Boof deserves it. Then again, both Boof and Lee Ray are fundamentally brave people, unafraid to seek the diamond in the rhinestones.

"So, Boof, what brings you to our thriving metropolis?" he asks, gesturing to the just visible Hansel Hickory's Hair Transplants billboard in the distance. "The culture? The canker sores? If you're looking for the haunted post office I'm afraid Geoffrey's been gone for ages."

That he has. I miss that old coot trying to read my letters and pinch my rear.

"She's searching for her birth mamma," I say, then catch myself. "Sorry, was that supposed to be a secret?"

"No, I figured out a while back you two share just about everything." He shrugs.

"Pretty much."

"Getting pretty tough ferrying the one toothbrush back and forth, though," I say.

"You're an animal. Do you know that?"

The cattails sway with the evening breeze as we lay our blankets out. Lee Ray and I have managed to wear the grass down over the years, so there's always a stretch of land ready to be tanned or cried on, depending on the day.

"Why do you want to find her?" Lee Ray asks. "Besides the obvious reasons."

She peers up at old Henry Hansel's toupee. A north star in its own right.

"I think I need to understand where I came from if I'm going to be a successful songwriter."

"What are you talking about?" I tease. "'Mamma's Two Left Feet' is amazing. You could sell that kind of song for your whole dang career."

"No, I couldn't."

"Why not?"

She sits up on her elbow. The humidity's gone and done freed her curls from the tidy barrette she tries so hard to trap them in.

"Can I give you a bit of a schooling?"

"Please."

"Ladies, at least wait until I make it back to the shore," Lee Ray jokes.

"Hush, you. Go ahead, Boof."

"So, you remember a few years back when all the songs on the radio were about country boys partying?"

"Lord, yes," I lament. "Every other song was about so-and-so in his truck drinking with the boys and the girls didn't hardly have any clothes on."

"Precisely," Boof says. "It's called Bro Country."

"Okay."

"The songs were fun, so they did well on the charts. But they also happened at the same time this real particular brand of toxic masculinity was running wild in real life."

She takes a breath, looks around to see if we're still with her. We mime-eat popcorn, urging her to continue.

"In all those songs you basically had your hot girls and your bar buddies. Everything was from the male perspective. And not the sweet, Randy Travis, Hank Wilson perspective. The rapey asshole perspective."

"Boooooo!"

"Female singers and songwriters were getting totally edged out. But then, little by little, you started to see these songs like 'Buy My Own Drinks' by Runaway June and 'Girl in a Country Song' by Maddie & Tae. Kacey Musgraves and Maren Morris were on the rise—"

"I love me some Kacey Musgraves."

"The *hair*! I mean!"

"'Rainbow' always makes me tear up, I swear."

"Ahem."

"Right, go on."

"Women like Kacey started bringing back storytelling. Their songs had history and emotion and eventually they got so popular that the Bro Country guys simply couldn't keep up with them."

"Where'd those fellas go, I wonder?"

"Oh, they're still here," Boof says. "They just caught on that they couldn't play the party-boy angle forever, so they pivoted. Now their songs are all unity and respecting women, things like that. Bottom line is, female singers can't be one-trick ponies. They have to constantly reinvent and reinvigorate the genre. And if I'm going to be right there with them, I need all the source material and all the parts of me I can find. So, yes, I'm gonna need my mamma."

We can't help but applaud. Damn, to have that kind of candor *and* that kind of can? Sometimes the good lord works in scoops.

"Did I ever tell you you're brilliant?"

"I'm just practical is all. Besides"—she pulls her curls away from her face—"I'd love to know where I got these tiny little ears."

I have a feeling I know exactly where she got them. In fact, I could solve all Boof's songwriting worries right here, right now, if I wasn't so chicken.

Lee Ray shakes his head in awe.

"PJ, how long have you known?"

"Known what?" I scramble.

"That Boof is a phenomenal speaker. You should give a lecture to the EFPs. I'm sure they could all benefit from a schooling in feminist country music history. We could put a fishing spin on it. Something like 'What's the Catch: Country Music's Biggest Fish.' Maybe we could even write something together?"

"I'd like that."

As they chatter back and forth about potential titles, I promise myself I'll tell Boof eventually. The water laps at *Just Thighs*. The crickets trade snickers and Powerball tickets. And just when I think I might fall asleep to the sound of their banter, Lee Ray elbows me.

"You haven't shown her 'Clemens and Clementine'?"

"What's that?" Boof grins.

"Only her brilliant senior thesis comparing Mark Twain and Emmens Clementine."

"It was fine," I demur.

"It was sublime," Lee Ray corrects.

Boof cocks her head at me, like she can't for the world understand
where all my confidence scurries off to when presented with a compliment. Didn't used to run off so fast. I didn't always make for the other
side of the highway at the first sign of an emotional 18-wheeler. Hell, I
used to apply for grants and ask girls out via karaoke song. Back then I
fell asleep knowing there'd always be Daddy's voice on the other end of
the line. He'd say just keep on being yourself. And maybe try wearing
your Easter dress to the gay bar. Who can resist a girl in tulips?

Lee Ray and Boof await my answer. I suppose I'd better get used to
jumping without the net.

"I can make you a copy at the library," I concede. "But if she gets to
read my piss-poor thesis, she definitely gets to watch the DVD of *Fiddler
on the Piggly Wiggly*."

"That was my early work and you know it."

"If you ever need a good place to stage a musical," Boof observes,
"the mini-golf course outside my room has great acoustics. You can
hear a toddler scream on the eighteenth hole and swear it was happening right in your bathroom."

Lee Ray wags his Coors Light at her.

"I like the way you think."

"So," she says, sitting up on her elbows, "who wants to swim?"

"We're much better at drowning," I murmur.

"Huh?"

"Sorry, long story. Also we don't have suits."

She whips off her T-shirt with finesse. I was always the kid who
snuck out of my gym clothes in the bathroom stall, so this sort of casual
magic baffles me.

"Watch out for the leeches," I call after her.

"Pretending I didn't hear that," she hollers back.

Boof swims out past the island toward the blurry tattoo of moon. Even in the dark, I can see the spray of freckles across her shoulders, the pull of the water on her curls. Uncanny, her ability to move forward. Eyes closed, breath steady, she dares me to follow. To forget the squish of weeds, the threat of leeches, and every unknowable danger that lurks in the cool, dark marsh below. The farther she swims, the longer it will take to catch up.

Lee Ray gives me the nod. Daddy, too.

Flinging my shirt to the wind, I swim like an Olympian.

THE SHIT & THE FAN

alling you in 5 to discuss tonight's hair, Lee Ray texts. *Don't you dare screen me, PJ.*

PJ who? I respond, but when the phone rings a few minutes later, I pick up.

"If I've told you once, I've told you a thousand times. I will not be seen on national TV looking like Marie Goddamn Antoinette. Put the hairspray down and go back to the drawing board."

"Pardon?" a familiar voice asks.

"Lee Ray?"

"It's Dean Jackson."

"Oh, hi."

My heart plummets, down, down, down to the fuzzy blue carpet. Lookee here, I think vaguely, there's that orange Tic Tac I lost last week. And one of Boof's earrings. Maybe if I stare at this carpet long enough I'll find the will to live.

"It's good to hear your voice," Dean Jackson says. "I was starting to worry you'd fallen down a well."

"I know I haven't exactly been easy to reach."

Hell, you'd have a better chance of catching Jesus on his landline on a Sunday morning than getting me to pick up. Even as I rush to explain this, I can feel the miles in my voice doing it for me. The girl I was in

Nashville lives half a state and a world away. No lesson can lasso her back to me now.

Dean Jackson sighs.

"PJ, please understand this is a very difficult call for me to make."

"Slow down, there. You're starting to sound like my ex-girlfriend. Or my dermatologist. Or, frankly, my plumber."

I wait for a chuckle we both know won't come.

"The department understands you've been through a lot this past year, and I've done my best to hold them off, but there's only so much I can do to influence their decision."

"Decision?"

"On whether or not you can stay in the program."

"Oh."

"They need to see concrete evidence that you plan to come back. That you want to come back. You have to want to come back."

"I see."

"Well, do you?"

Lee Ray's call beeps through.

"I'm sorry, but I'm going to have to call you back."

"PJ, please don't hang up."

"I'm sorry."

"The hearing is July thirteenth at noon. Meet me in my office. We'll go in as a united front. Maybe we could even grab a bite to eat afterward. PJ? PJ?"

Mamma saunters through the kitchen door with her sewing machine tucked under one arm and a bolt of cow-print fabric under the other.

"Thought we'd make some last-minute alterations to your pants," she says. Then, noticing my expression, "Who you talkin' to? And why do you look whiter than a ghost's teat?"

"Nothing. Nobody. I'm talking to Lee Ray."

"Well, hang up. We got work to do."

"Yes, ma'am."

I keep quiet all through Mamma's sewing and on the walk to the auditorium, up until I see Boof in her outfit and can't help but feel chatty again. Mamma probably suspects I've just got pageant jitters. Truth is, I've been playing possum so long I'm riddled with fleas.

LINDA'S TALENT ISN'T your run-of-the-mill dance with batons number. Nor is it some sort of *Annie Get Your Gun* skeet-shooting variation. It's not even ventriloquism. When she walks onstage in a red leather jumpsuit, the only thing waiting for her is a bowl full of cherries and a bucket.

Tammy and Sean Donne make eyes at each other while Boudreaux Beanie leans over to see just how many cherries Linda plans to, well, who knows? Juggle? Spit? Maybe if we'd done another spy mission, I could say for sure what she's up to. Whatever she's planning, it's got Boudreaux Beanie stumped. She pats Tammy on the shoulder and attempts to whisper a wager, but Tammy waves her off. Beauty that she is, Boudreaux Beanie looks like a woman who's about to be thoroughly bested. Wouldn't take much, really. When she won Miss Tennessee Junior Baby, her talent was breastfeeding.

If I had to guess, Linda's probably about to hit us with some close-up, redneck magic. Couple of rabbits and a hat. Maybe some dry ice. That bowl of cherries'll end up on the mayor's head or down the coroner's pants. Boudreaux Beanie and I both run out of time to wonder because quick as a tick, the lights go down. The crowd hushes to a halt.

"Welcome back to the Hot Chicken Beauty Tour," she says. "First up we have Linda Carter Creel."

Linda's husband belches out a long squelch of support. True love really does exist.

"Tonight Linda will be performing the Waitress's Secret."

The audience murmurs with theories.

"I know that one," Tammy declares. "Never could make it past two without getting tired."

"Linda, how many of those cherry stems you think you can tie in a bow tonight?" Sean Donne asks.

"How much time I got?"

"Four minutes."

She clucks her tongue like she's really considering, but if I know Linda, she already knows her number by heart.

"Four minutes. Well then, let's make it a hundred."

Murmurs molt into yeehaws. Knee slaps of disbelief ricochet off the hot dog stand and the 1997 *Most Likely to Almost* Tennessee Semifinalist basketball banner. Even the EMTs in the back sit up a little straighter.

"Ladies and gentlemen, you heard her. One hundred sweet little cherry-stem bows. On your mark, get set, go!"

I used to work at a lizard sanctuary. I sold Popsicles at my childhood lemonade stands. Hell, I've even watched a few unsavory films with titles like *Down on the BaYOU* and I have never, ever, and I mean never, seen a tongue work so fast. At first the crowd tries to count with Delilah Fisher-Trapper, but after twenty it's a lost cause. Linda's popping those bows out like a paintball gun on the Fourth of July.

When the clock finally stops, a pimply stagehand rushes out to give Linda a glass of water. She throws it back with the reckless abandon of a plumber in a waterpark. The audience watches intently. We're all thinking the same thing. That thing being, "Dear Lord, I hope there's not a dozen of those little stems clogging up her throat and blocking her windpipe."

Linda takes a big gulp—you could hear it from a mile away—and says, "Ahhh."

The crowd bursts into theatrics, like Christmas come to town. Delilah-Fisher Trapper taps her microphone and displays her clicker.

"Ladies and gentlemen, one hundred and fifty bows!"

They hoot and holler all over again. Maybe 150 cherry stems doesn't count for much in places with Costcos and clean water, but here in Pennywhistle, we respect anybody who can go upward of six bows per minute on the Waitress's Secret.

I wonder what kind of talents the ladies of Knoxville and Nickelfiddle are showing off tonight. Skinning things, weaving traps, brewing moonshine in their toilet bowls. Whole lot of culture to be had out here. All of it stuck between the red-and-yellow walls of the Chickie Shak.

AFTER A BRIEF demonstration from the Pennywhistle Snake Safety Commission—"When in doubt, get the hell out"—we're up.

I squeeze Boof's hand one last time before we go onstage. She squeezes back. To think, just a few weeks ago if we'd touched hands accidentally in the kitchen I'd have apologized. Now it feels like we're two paws on the same coyote.

"Next, we have a special combined performance," Delilah Fisher-Trapper says. "Boof Kidston and PJ Spoon will be displaying their talents together."

Sounds like a euphemism for gay sex. *We caught them displaying their talents in a parked car.*

"Is that allowed?" Sean Donne asks.

"Technically, yes. Judges, you're encouraged to consider each performer's contribution as well as the performance as a whole. PJ, Boof, the floor is yours."

Between my suede pants and cowboy hat combo and Boof's short jean shirt, we look pretty darn believable as an up-and-coming country duo.

I start things off with the delicate intro medley. A pluck here, a pluck there. At this point, a few people are still whispering to their husbands. They're not rude, they're just not all that interested in us, either. That is, until Boof starts to sing.

"They say Moses was floated down the river . . ."

Now our crowd is stunned silent. Not armadillo on the side of the highway silent, but the kind you get when you're gently rocked to sleep. Back and forth. Floating. When things seem too plum good to be true, which, of course, they are. The song is perfect. From the riffs to the key change to the turn in the last lines. And Boof ain't just singing. She's calling out her siren song. Whole lot of mammas in the audience are already bawling their eyes out, whether they left their kids years ago or they're sitting right damn next to them. This one's for them.

Country music always did love mammas best. Loved the way they tell it to you straight and feed you up right. Protect you from trains and whiskey. Shoo away boys who only want one thing but don't have no diamond ring. And sure, it's a great honor to be written about this way, like you're sweeter than God's bathwater and clever to boot. But not all mammas are flawless. What I like about Boof's song is that it scoots over and leaves a little room on the couch for error. It says, *You're human! Me, too. Now, where's the remote?*

"Call me up sometime. I'd really like to meet."

It's just like Mamma doesn't believe in bad girls. Boof doesn't believe in bad mammas. No matter who she came out of is A-OK with her.

I strum us out and look to the audience hesitantly.

They sob. They roar.

And for a moment it seems like life couldn't get any better.

"THAT WAS AMAZING," I say. "You were amazing."

I'm so topsy-turvy from the spotlight and the applause that I don't catch my breath until we make it backstage. My words sound rough, cigarette spun. Boof kisses me with everything she's got, stagehands be damned.

"Bathroom," she says, and for a moment I think she means meet her there.

"What?"

"I'll be right back."

"Right, okay!"

Wiping sweat from my brow, I hang back and watch the EFPs do their CPR demonstration. As I search for the perfect vantage point I catch sight of a yeti-esque phenomenon. As in ain't nobody ever witnessed it, ain't nobody ever will. It's Linda, sobbing. And not about her performance, neither. Linda killed it tonight. It's all to do with those four footprints on her back. Turns out, we both know who they belong to.

How could Linda not know? Somebody comes out of your hoo-ha, you ought to recognize them in the Piggly Wiggly. Worse than that, if she *did* know, how could she not say anything? Mamma likes to say shame is the tapeworm of the soul. Eats you up. Makes you sick. Gets so big you either die or have the thing wrenched out your ass with a pair of tweezers. Whether she's known all along or only just now, Linda's bound to be riddled with it. I don't have the time to wring my hands or offer my compassion. Before I know it, the EFPs are mid-drowning and Boof is back.

"Do you think my birth mom was in the audience? I kept trying to spot redheads but the stage lights were too bright."

I can't do this any longer.

"I don't think she was in the audience."

Like a cheap flamingo floatie on a shell-strewn tide, Boof deflates. I can't stand the sight of her like this, eyes watering, mouth taut. Breaks my heart.

"You said she was bound to be here. I mean, everybody's here. The whole town's here."

"Boof, she wasn't in the audience because she was . . . on the stage."

I gesture to Linda. With her head in her hands and her hair pulled back, we can see her ears. The shape, small and neat with a little puppy-dog flop on the end, looks mighty familiar. Boof reaches for hers. She looks back at Linda again, scrutinizing her every feature.

"You knew?"

"No. Well, yes. But not forever. At first, I only suspected. Once she got the perm and when we saw the tattoo things started to add up."

"And then what?"

"I asked my mamma. She didn't know everything but she confirmed my suspicions."

Boof looks back and forth between me and Linda, her face shaking like a building on the brink of collapse. First her eyebrows, then her mouth. She swallows hard. Even her little hands are shaking. I want to steady her—hell, I want to marry her—but she steps away. Not toward Linda, not toward the door, just away.

"I swear I was going to tell you after tonight. We worked so hard on the song and I thought if you knew it might stress you out."

"No, PJ," she says, taking another devastating step back. "You don't know shit if you think keeping this from me was the right thing to do."

I wince at the way she says *shit*. When sweet people yell at you it really smarts.

"Boof, I'm sorry."

Another step back.

"Sorry is not enough."

I don't want to cry my way out of this argument. Still, I can't help but give way to the trembling in my voice, the snot in my nose. A tear falls on my banjo. Dear God, I might actually understand that old Taylor Swift song now.

"What can I do?"

She shakes her head. Over yonder, Linda wipes her eyes off on her jumpsuit sleeves. That red vinyl ain't too absorbent, so the tears fly right off.

"Boof, what can I do to make it right?"

Delilah Fisher-Trapper is calling us back to the stage. I want to tell her to shut the hell up, get some choir or home hair-waxing safety demonstration back up there. Who cares who won? It doesn't matter who managed to wow a bored town full of have-nevers and won't-nevers. I got bigger things on the line. But time is up. Delilah gives a stern shake of her head for us to get going.

"Look," Boof says in a measured tone, "I am not someone who flies off the handle. I hate that about as much as I hate 'pick you up at eight.' But I'm angry. I'm really angry. And if you're interested in knowing me at all, you will respect that I need to be angry by myself for as long as it takes to work this out."

This moment, of all moments, is when I feel the words *I love you* float to the surface of my brain like a lone noodle in a pot of chili. Right words, wrong time. I love her for keeping up her kindness even in her anger. I love her for the way she can come right out and say things. I love her and I cannot let her know.

"Okay," I manage.

I can't muster the rest of it. My words are always stuck at the bottom of my stomach. She waits anyway. Just like everybody else been doing. As she walks onstage, I think, Why on earth has every person I love been wasting their precious time on me?

LINDA WINS BY the hair on her chinny chin chin. She's going to Nashville.

I LOOK FOR Mamma in the crowd, but I don't see neither hide nor hair of her. Instead I find Lionel presenting Lee Ray with a big bouquet of magnolias. He's even better than the half dark, still asleep, sneak photos Lee Ray used to send me. Awake and well lit, Lionel wears big, funky eyeglasses and a floral shirt that even Jimmy Buffett would find too flashy. A catch if there ever was one. I can just see him in those Mardi Gras parades, strewn with beads and feathers. On summer nights I bet he plays the trumpet to the palm trees and the strays. Oh, he's marvelous. Simply marvelous. It's no wonder he couldn't stay here.

I watch Lee Ray's face as I approach. Am I about to be smacked or kissed? Or maybe I barely register, just float closer like a hanky on the breeze. From the way Lee Ray's looking at Lionel I gather he's not too pissed at me. It's like Mamma always says, "Buy my favorite flowers and I might just forget the smell of shit."

I clear my throat. Lee Ray turns.

"Oh, hi! PJ, this is Lionel."

"We're long-lost friends." He smiles.

Even while talking to me, they keep their gazes across the short lake between them.

"What did you think of the song?"

"I think you were robbed," Lionel says.

"Robbed," Lee Ray agrees, though I suspect he'd agree even if Lionel had called our performance the worst thing since the pickled Snickers.

Across the auditorium, Boof whispers something to her brother. I haven't even learned his name and I've already ruined his life.

"Not that I don't respect a good rendition of the Waitress's Secret," Lionel clarifies. "But your girlfriend can really sing."

"How does Lionel know you're official before I do?" Lee Ray teases.

Now Boof and her brother are leaving. I feel like a dog at the edge of an invisible fence. Not knowing what's worse, the shock of leaving or the smallness of staying put.

"He doesn't. We're not."

There are too many people here. I need to go home.

"What's wrong?" Lee Ray asks.

Don't cry. Don't you dare cry.

"I think I just majorly fucked everything up."

I wish I could tell Lee Ray the whole story right now. Call an emergency sleepover with heaps of booze and candy corn, but it's his turn. Been his turn for a while now. He holds on to my elbow, that subtle motion of catching someone in case of a sudden fall, but I shake my head.

"Y'all go have some fun. See if you can get a table at Le Fried Pantouffle. My treat. I'll be fine. Really."

"Really?"

"Yes," I lie. "You seen Mamma?"

"She ran out after they called it," Lee Ray says.

"Hope she's not too heartbroken."

"Looked it."

"Shit," I curse. "I'm glad you could make it, Lionel. Get into some trouble for me, will you?"

He doesn't have to promise. Trouble's on tap today.

THE SUEDE PANTS don't make running easy. How cowboys ever managed to escape the law in these things I'll never know. Rounding Craw Street, I pass my silicone likeness at Peep and Nina's adult store. I feel sorry for anybody who picked up this model, because they ain't fooling around with a winner. Eventually, I spot Mamma ambling up the road.

"Hey, wait up."

She keeps going.

"Wait up! Mamma, it's me."

She swivels on her purple flip-flop.

"Dean Jackson called me."

"Mamma, I need to talk to you. It's important."

"No, this is important." She gestures with her run-down cigarette. "He begged me to talk some sense into you. Said he hadn't heard from you all summer and if you don't make it to the meeting on the thirteenth, your time is up. Imagine my surprise, seein' as just this week you said you were working on your research. Don't sell me a donkey when I paid for a horse."

"I'm not. I'm going to figure something out."

She throws up her hands, cigarette and all. The smoke twirls out.

"You're going to lose your spot. Your daddy and I did not work tooth and tit so you could just throw in the towel. He practically sold his kidneys so you could go to college and if he were still here he'd tell you to march your sorry ass up to Nashville and beg those nice people at the university—"

"Well, he's not here and it's my life, so I guess I can do whatever the hell I want with it."

She scoffs.

"Shoo-ee! I swear my sixteen-year-old is standing in front of me again. What's next, you gonna sneak out and pick up girls by the river?"

"Shut up, Mamma."

It comes out more sixteen than I want, dammit.

"I expect more from you than this."

"Well, I'm sorry I couldn't win the pageant and pay you back for all the years of strife. Consider this an IOU."

She grabs my arm in that particular way that's not rough but ain't gentle neither. Southern Mamma Claw, Lee Ray and I call it.

"It was never about the money and you know that. It was about you getting excited about something again. You used to be joyful. Where's that girl?"

I shake her hand off and start walking toward my house. My bike isn't where I left it, leaning like a lover against the church marquee. Figured nobody would steal a bike right outside of church. And yet. I walk ragged circles around the sign, hoping my beloved has just wandered a few yards. I scan the parking lot, the wishing well. There's nothing left of my chariot but a few measly indentations in the grass. Dammit. Just when I stopped locking it to things. The urge to cry wells up, threatening to break through my stony expression. I love that bike.

"Where is my joyful girl?" Mamma asks again.

We both hear the crack in her voice. Same one she had when Peewee Dupree asked her to stop buying up all the flour and deal with herself. Something about loss. I'm too damn sad about my bike to fix things right now. Where's my trusty ten-speed? Where's Mamma's joyful girl?

"The hell if I know," I say.

And tonight I mean it.

I'M SO LONESOME I
COULD SPIT

To live near the train is to constantly be reminded of coming and going. It prowls along like a house cat, the blaring horn like the little silver bell on the cat's collar. Both say, "Listen, I'm coming." When I first moved back, the train passed by only every now and then. Now it seems to be after something. Like the kitty who discovers the mice in the attic and vacates the sunny spot in the window to investigate.

As it meows past, it asks, "Are you really still on the couch? Didn't you say you were going for a walk?" Shamer, blamer. "If I can make it to Memphis today, surely you can make it to the grocery store." It's raining, I'd like to point out.

Four blankets deep, I peer out the sliding door to see if any of my strays have stopped by. Seems even they're pissed at me, camped out on my neighbor's porch in protest. My menagerie has grown rather skinny during the pageant, I'm afraid. Wasting away to nothing, the poor critters, while I dared to dream outside of my three-mile radius. Next door at Mrs. Hubbard's, the goose taps a half-empty bird feeder while the cats wait for somebody to empty out the kitchen garbage. They know the schedule. Right about now, on the other side of the door, Mrs. Hubbard will be feeding her spoiled tabby, Okra, a tin of Fancy Feast, the remnants of which might just end up in a loosely tied trash bag if they're lucky. The dog, I notice, is long gone, hopefully having Lady-and-the-Tramped his way indoors.

As for me, I waste the day watching Westerns.

Nothing says sorrow like a covered wagon on fire and a burned Hot Pocket in the microwave. As I wallow in my blankets, I start half a dozen texts to Boof:

I'm sorry.

I never meant to hurt you.

I miss your can.

I'm an idiot.

You're the best thing that's happened to me since Daddy died. By the way, Daddy died and I deferred my PhD and I'm scared of just about everything.

Like an adult DVD with a scratch down the middle, I start, but I don't finish. Boof said to give her space. That includes texts, calls, and those little paper airplanes you loft at people you love.

My Hot Pocket beeps, ready to scorch me.

I check my phone in case she's changed her mind. No new messages.

My phone dings. *Big Pig Savings from Piggly Wiggly! Your coupon of the week is: Buy One Get One Free Bush's Baked Beans. Exclusions apply.*

"Jesus Christ," I scowl, tossing the phone into the cushions. Thunder growls at my little house like the big empty stomach of a giant. Mamma would say that giant's God and that he just needs his supper, but I don't want to think of Mamma-isms right now. She looked so tiny when I left her. Half her size and twice her age.

I try to focus on the cowboys instead, and soon I fall asleep to the sound of Jessico Jax, outlaw, galloping away from his troubles. By the time I wake up, the next movie is on, the next cowboy riding his way out of town. An endless loop of wild blue yonder boys. I promise myself I'll stay awake long enough to watch him get the girl, just as soon as I make some dinner.

Well, shit.

The pantry's got more tumbleweeds than the Westerns. When did I last go shopping? Wash my sheets? Falling for Boof has taken up so much of my heart—and my stomach—that nothing else has really mattered. Seems foolish now that I look at my shelves. Usually I'm so careful.

I consider my options. Woman cannot live on beer and raisins alone, neither can she show her face in the Piggly Wiggly with last night's stage makeup still streaking her cheeks. I rack my brains for an alternative food source. The freezer's empty, the canned beans sparse. Even last year's Christmas jams are long gone. It occurs to me that humans could stand to learn a lot from squirrels. If I were a little more rodent-like I'd have a year's supply of Nutter Butters buried under the house right now. Come to think of it, I do know one person with enough buried Zebra Cakes to survive zombies, chicken pox, or nuclear war, whichever comes first. Someone who likes to share.

I walk to Mamma's house in my rain boots, hoping for some sympathy and maybe a sleeve of Oreos, but there in the driveway sits a car I've never seen, and on the dashboard, a dancing, grass-skirted woman with no shirt but a coconut, the surest sign that I've been ousted from Mamma's heart.

The girl does not bob from side to side.

She doesn't even hum to a stop.

No, this car's been here awhile. Been here enough times to park just shy of the gnomes but not so far down the driveway that it's stuck between the dogwoods. This may be Mamma's house, but that there's a man's car.

I stand in the family of gnomes, feeling like an orphan. The rain runs into my boots. My ears turn red. Here I thought Mamma would stay put, as waterlogged by grief as me, but the spray of laughter coming from the kitchen begs to differ.

REMINDS ME OF the time I lost her in the Quarterflute Dillard's. I was about five or six, knee high to a cricket, and we were looking for dresses to wear to my uncle Rusty's fourth wedding. Same bride, just three divorces later.

"He treats that woman like a Cheeto done fell under the couch," Mamma had said on the car ride there. "Just dusts her off and eats her again."

"Waste not, want not."

"I guess so, baby girl." She sighed. "Truth be told, I don't think he's worth a Cheeto, even a dusty one."

We held hands through the parking lot. Scrawny Mamma and freckled me. I remember thinking I had the funniest mamma in the world, something neither money nor horses could buy. I was totally unaware that she could up and disappear. My small voice trotted through the dressing rooms like a foal.

"Can you button me?"

I waited. No response but the Randy Travis song on the loudspeakers.

"Mamma?"

Dress wide open, I plodded out of the little carpeted hallway and into the store. Mamma was gone. Left, right, up, down, gone. I zigzagged through the floral dresses, the white slips, even the naughty lingerie until I finally caught sight of her. Worse than being gone, she was fussing and cooing over some other little girl. The nerve!

"Mamma!"

"What do you think about this one?" she said.

It was then that I realized the other little girl was a mannequin. Her cheap wig seemed so obvious now. Her plastic mouth, a dead giveaway. She was wearing a yellow dress dotted with irises, my favorite flower and Tennessee's, too.

"That's nice," I mustered, embarrassed.

She glanced at my bare back and laughed.

"What you running around halfneked for?"

"Nothing."

"Let's try this on and then if you're real good we can go to the Bump-A-Rump and make a teddy bear."

I breathed a deep sigh of relief and reached for her hand.

"You're not gonna have any more kids, are you?"

She looked at me funny. Like I'd found her diary or stepped on her toe.

"Couldn't if I wanted to, sugar."

"Good."

"I'm all yours," she said, and until today I believed it.

NOW HERE I stand, crying all the way down to my socks. No Mamma, no Boof. Even squandered the chance at free chicken for life, ridiculous as that predicament would have been. The little voice inside me—the mean one, not the horny one or the occasional Elvis—says, You're pretty darn good at screwing things up. This is precisely why I stuck to the deep fryer. Shaded by steam, steeped in grease, I could have spent the rest of my days filling people's bellies instead of letting them down.

Where's my joyful girl? keeps playing in my head. What could I tell her? Feels like I left dozens of girls behind when I drove home from Nashville. The girl who could write a thesis, the girl who could make a speech. They're so missing, Lassie's stopped checking the wells.

So has Dean Jackson, apparently. No new messages. He usually gives me a ring on Saturday afternoons after brunch to report which eggs have his benediction, but I must have scared him off for good. Of course, there are other students to mentor, other eggs to fry. I just thought his faith in me would last a little longer. At least a year. Maybe two.

PJ Spoon, what in the hell are you doing out here?

Not Mamma's voice but Daddy's.

I'm not sure.

Well, pop an umbrella, angel, 'fore you catch a cold.

But I don't have an umbrella. Truth is, I don't want one. The longer I stand in Mamma's driveway, the browner my hair gets, no hint of gold, just water. How it should be. And while I've managed to lose the last handful of people who believed in me—not to mention my bike—a few feet away in the warm light of the kitchen, Mamma turns the radio up. Shania Twain. "Any Man of Mine."

They must be dancing.

BACK IN THE SHAK

Sunday night I dream of dancing Zebra Cakes. Of a teenage Emmens Clementine working the fryer with one hand and writing his debut novel, *Steamy Reno Dreamboat*, with the other. Just before I wake, the notebook falls headlong into the fryer.

Not exactly a good omen. And yet, the hoop earrings return to my sink. A little shiny, a little tarnished. They've got to be the work of Daddy, not Mamma, who probably wouldn't offer me a *howdy*, much less an earring after what I said to her on Friday night. I cradle the hoops in my palms. I guess when Daddy left them on the soap dish a few weeks ago that was his way of saying *I'm still here*. Strangely enough, we all are. Me, Linda, Boof. Despite the rumble of the pageant, the whole town's stayed put.

As I click the hoops into place I wonder what I'll be walking into at the Chickie Shak today. One thing's for sure: it can't be good. Like that pile of paternity tests in the Pennywhistle landfill, there's just too many unknowns. Have Boof and Linda had their come-to-Jesus talk yet? Are Boof and I vamoose? For all I know, she spent the weekend revenge-smooching a slew of our flirtiest regulars. Giggle Shivvers. Lexi Bow-right. Hell, Bootsie Trample's been trying to get into my khakis for years, so I'm sure she'd be thrilled to make it with Boof.

In a perfect world, she'd have passed the time painting her nails and mining the country music channel for parody ideas. Making amends with Kenny the Doberman. Taking long walks with her brother along the river, long walks that ended with forgiving me.

My hands instinctively reach for the handlebars. Instead they split the humid air.

Grief is the step that isn't there.

A POGO STICK leans against the cellar door, courtesy of Deedoo's last visit, but having already embarrassed myself enough for the month, I decide to lace up my running shoes instead. I notice that most people have kept their decorations up, except for Peep and Nina, who removed Boof and me from the window display. Where'd they stash us? I wonder. Are we gonna end up in the town Nativity scene in a few months like the rest of the lady companion dolls that don't sell or are we too tarnished to reenact the birth of Christ? This nettles me more than it ought. Maybe I'm not pageant material, but I'm good enough for the first Noel.

A buckeye nearly kills me as I round the final curve. By the time I reach the hose rack I'm soaked with more sweat than a Coors Light in church. I wring out my ponytail and step inside.

I don't know what I expected. War? Graffiti? Instead it's a forty-ounce cup of awkward with a jumbo side of quiet. Linda's unlocking the register while Boof refills the salt shakers, a polite murmur passing between them every time Boof picks up the next set of shakers from the back. They're acting like a couple of twelve-year-olds who just held hands in the movie theater and now have to face each other in the lobby. Tongue-tied and twitchy. Neither wanting to make the next move lest the next move be the last move. How the hell did I become the most confident person in the building?

Each time I try to catch Boof's eyes, she looks away.

"One Reuben and a Chicken Frisky ready to go."

She takes the paper bag with a look I can't quite decipher, something south of angry but north of come hither. A curl considers the ledge of her ear.

"PJ?"

"Yes?" I brighten.

"I need a double fry for this one," she says softly. "It's Mr. Tucker. He always gets the double fry."

"Oh. Okay. Just a second."

"Thanks."

And that there's the most intimate conversation we have all day. I watch as Boof fairy-godmothers table four with extra silverware, picks a card, any card, from the plumber-magician at table two. Even the way she winks at the firefighters stings. As she orbits the checkered tablecloths with an uncomplicated love, the distance between me and a good thing gets wider and wider.

Fine, I think. I'll focus on something else. Lo and behold, my something else has gone missing, too. I scour the mustard, topple the ketchup, and tear through the kitchen with an anger that surprises even me. It's probably got something to do with the inscription at the front of the notebook. *We took our dreams and made you. Here's a little paper to make some PJs of your own. Love, Mamma and Daddy.*

Daddy loved whipping things up on his typewriter, so it's one of the only pieces of his handwriting we have left.

Not even the bills or the to-do's.

Not the grocery list.

Mamma threw all those loose bits of handwriting out along with the expired cans of Ro-Tel and the broken Christmas ornaments. I'm sorry, but I just can't stand to lose another thing today.

"Did you take my notebook again?" I ask Linda in a too-loud voice.

"No."

Liar. I follow her through the kitchen door and across the restaurant.

"Just give it back."

"Excuse me, I'm trying to go to the ladies' room. By myself, preferably."

"Linda!"

"I told you, PJ, shoo."

"Can you just give me back my fucking notebook?" I shout.

Suddenly lunch comes to a screeching halt. The diners fall silent, save for the kids at table three, who try out the new expletive like you do a fresh soccer ball. Kick, kick, kick. Fuck, fuck, fuck.

Linda turns on her heel.

"I don't give a rat's you-know-what about your notebook. It doesn't matter. You're not using it. You gave up, PJ. Remember?"

"Says the woman who abandoned her children," I spit. "Any more you want to drop at the fire station while we're at it?"

Deedoo looks up from the claw machine. The firefighters frown through their sweet tea. Even Mrs. Heller, whose hearing aid is no more than a repurposed Barbie shoe, heard that one. Boof storms over before I can utter another word.

"You, come with me."

She hauls me into the kitchen by the elbow and pulls the notebook from her apron pocket.

"Here."

"Why, why do you have this?" I stutter.

"Jesus, PJ." She sighs. "Maybe because I want to know you and you won't let me."

"That doesn't mean you read someone's journal. That's private."

"Can Lee Ray read it? Can your mom?"

"No."

Boof steps back and shakes her head. I reach for her hand.

"Boof, please."

She swats it away.

"I don't know who you're saving yourself up for, PJ, but I can't keep waiting around and hoping it's me."

"Boof."

"No, let's just go back to the way things were before. I won't ask you to share anything and you don't have to feign any emotional lasagnas, okay?"

The cash register dings. Linda turns back to look at us, eyes narrow and wet, and we all know the only thing to do is keep cooking, keep taking orders, keep pouring sweet tea. Our only mistake was looking up.

"What can I get you, baby?" Linda asks Deedoo through a forced smile.

"Deedoo?" Trumpet prods her.

She crosses her arms.

"I'm not hungry anymore."

"It's lunchtime," Linda says. "You need something in your belly. You sick? Boof, why don't you bring her out some ginger ale."

"I'm not sick."

"Well, then, let's get you an Ankle Biter Meal."

Deedoo unravels the braids Linda must have woven this morning. I think she just realized her mamma ain't taking too long at the gas station.

"You're not supposed to leave your babies behind," she says.

"I didn't," Linda pleads, "I didn't."

The whole restaurant goes quiet again, EFPs and senators and Peep and Nina's regulars. Boof hands Deedoo a ginger ale.

"If that's true," she says quietly, "then how'd I end up in Texas?"

Linda looks at the pair of them, Deedoo with her unspooled braid, Boof with her puppy-dog ears. Maybe if she could just braid Boof's hair. Maybe if she could just wrestle Deedoo's mamma back from that Bible man. Maybe if she could just utter a simple apology, things could turn around. We're all, the regulars and the biggie shakes and the claw machine, hoping for it.

Instead, she punches a key on the cash register.

"Next."

A BOOT SCOOTIN'
OPPORTUNITY

Lee Ray stops by my house on Monday night with a Velveeta quiche and a smile so bright it could power a tanning bed. Scares the bejesus out of me. Not the smile—he looks positively radiant—but the sudden appearance in my kitchen. I swear I started locking that door after the suck-the-gay-away vacuum saleslady slipped through last month. Nevertheless, Lee Ray paws through the drawers for a pair of clean forks.

I put down my book. With no word from Boof I've had plenty of time to read it. Feels like school getting canceled but only on account of a tornado. At this point in the plot, the Raccoon King has successfully reached the future in his trash can time machine, but now he can't get back to the past. Damn it if I don't relate to the poor little scamp.

"How was your weekend?" I ask.

Lee Ray hands me a fork.

"It was heavenly, thank you."

Swaying around the room, he tidies a knickknack here, kicks a dust bunny there, and hums Amy Grant's "Baby, Baby" like he wrote it.

"Ahem?"

"Sorry. Quiche?"

I scoot over and let him under the blanket. We take down the quiche like emperors.

"I reckon things went well with Lionel?"

"Indeed they did."

He flashes a neck dalmatianed with hickeys.

"Go on."

"You know I want to gush," Lee Ray sighs, "but I can only stay for a few. We're going to the drive-in."

"What's playing?"

"*Scooby-Doo on Zombie Island*. Lionel's never seen it."

"And with that look on your little lovesick face he never will. Just don't give all us homos a bad name when you fog up the car."

"No promises." He smiles. "I just wanted to say thanks and make sure you're eating."

"Oh, I've been eating all right. Been working my way through the family-size frozen aisle. My toilet is none too pleased."

"Boof still mad at you?"

"Hasn't called so I can only assume. Mamma sure is. And Linda, probably. Feels like you're the only person who isn't mad at me right now."

Lee Ray straightens my coffee table with his foot. We haven't covered the fact that I lied to him, too. Lying to Lee Ray is probably the worst of the bunch. Everybody lies to their mamma. *Yes, I brushed my teeth. No, that's not my thong on the roof.* Most people probably lie to their girlfriends. *You're way cuter than Jessica Simpson in the* Dukes of Hazzard *remake.* But lying to your best friend shouldn't come as naturally. It should feel wrong, like a burger made out of eggplants or a boat in Kentucky. It should chafe.

The last time I lied to Lee Ray was way back when I told him I kissed Abraham Maloney at the seventh grade Little Debbie Dance Off. We bickered on the jungle gym while passing a bologna sandwich back and forth.

"Did not," he said.

"Did too. With tongue and mouth and stuff."

"When?"

"After they played 'Cotton Eye Joe' but before 'The Devil Went Down to Georgia.'"

"Liar," he said. "That's precisely when I was kissing him."

The bell rang, signaling fourth period, but later that night we talked the whole thing out over a plate of Ritz crackers and I-Believe-It's-Not-Cheese. Consulted the Magic 8 Ball and the stars. By the time we fell asleep he had forgiven me for lying and I had confessed it was Abraham Maloney's sister, Toni, that I really wanted to be smooching, and that I was sorry to have risked our friendship over the wrong Maloney. We traded Beanie Babies and called it a day.

"It occurs to me that lately I've risked too much," I offer.

It's no Beanie Baby, but I hope it will do. Lee Ray taps my foot with his.

"You should have told me Lionel was coming, but frankly I'm too delighted to be mad."

"Promise?"

"Yes. I would have never plucked up the courage to call him. This was the kick in the pants I needed."

"Spare me the sexy details."

"Oh, hush."

Lee Ray ferries the quiche to the kitchen.

"Let me know when you're ready for your kick in the pants."

"Can I get a little time first?"

"It's coming fast, PJ. All this opening, it's not just going to close back up."

"Thanks for the quiche."

"My pleasure."

I wish I could have him all to myself, but I can tell he's ready to make like a moped and scoot.

"Go on, get."

He gives the door a little *tap-tap* on his way out.

"Start with Dottie. Work your way up to Boof. It'll all turn out."

"Can I ask you one last thing before you hit the town?"

"Shoot."

"Did you know Mamma had a boyfriend?"

Lee Ray takes a moment to compose himself, the way he used to in the final inning of a Bee Stings game, when everything depended on him. It doesn't seem so long ago that we'd chew our Hubba Bubba with anxious maws, praying for victory, and watch him step up to the bat, nod to the girls on the bases, and swing us all the way home.

He tells me that despite his joking on the matter, he never got around to setting up Mamma's dating profile.

"Nor do I think she set one up herself," he says. "Your mother's technology skills are abysmal."

"She still doesn't understand why I wouldn't let her use 'save a horse ride a cowgirl' as her email address." I sigh.

"I shudder at the thought. No, a few weeks back I was getting my eyebrows done out in Horse Creek and I just happened to run into the two of them at a coffee shop. She looked so joyful. It seemed too new to interrupt."

"Anybody we know?"

Lee Ray shakes his head.

"Must be from Horse Creek."

"Since when does everybody go to Horse Creek?"

"They've got cappuccinos."

"I see."

"Do you?"

"Not yet."

"Want me to sit with you while you wait?"

For this I rise from the couch and give him a proper hug. For this I let him go.

AS I WORK my way through the rest of the quiche, I think of things lost. Of things found. Of Mrs. Heller, who noticed my silver bike necklace last week.

"Nice bike," she said.

"Thanks."

"Where'd you get it?"

"Daddy's ghost."

She chuckled.

"I reckoned he'd still be here."

A flock of tots ran past us, shoelaces woefully untied, overalls three siblings old, toward the forever-there pillows in the children's section. They must have traveled by red wagon. They were clearly loved. Eventually, their mother arrived, pregnant.

"My daddy stuck around for a long time, too, you know," Mrs. Heller said. "Good thing he did. I was so lost. Had three little ones. Didn't know what on earth I was doing most of the time. Honey, I swear his ghost got those kids to sleep every single night for the first few years. But, you know how it is. You learn on the job. One day I looked around the house, all those teddy bears and wooden blocks everywhere, those tiny shoes, those tiny jackets, and I realized he hadn't been home for a while."

"Did he ever come back?" I asked.

"No."

"Why not?"

"He didn't have any more unfinished business."

"Huh."

As I wondered how long I could keep my business unfinished, Mrs. Heller leaned across the counter and took my hand.

"One of these days, a little while from now, when you're doing real well, you're gonna look up and realize he's skedaddled. And it won't be a bad thing."

"How do you know?"

"Because I'm still here."

I guess she's right. You can't just puddle up and melt into the dirt. If you did, I wouldn't even be here. Before I came along, Mamma and Daddy had already lost two youngins. No wriggling arms and legs or names, just big dreams they woke up to find staining the happy, yellow sheets. In a town where most folks had enough kids to staff a Denny's, coming up empty was unusual. They tried getting busy in all sorts of forbidden locales. They tried praying on it. Even dumped a jar's worth of wishes into the fountain at the Quarterflute Mall. After a while they told Jesus and the adult store they'd received the message and would go back to their normal lives. But, after dreaming so hard, their regular lives didn't fit anymore. They'd grown smaller, like leather shoes left out in the rain.

So, Mamma ran for mayor and Daddy started taking classes at the community college. They'd stay up late at night, Mamma's pork rind casserole warm in their tummies, and chart the course of the rest of their lives with Magic Markers and almanacs, newspapers and kisses. They'd go to Nashville, Washington, Paris. Places you'd never want to bring a car seat anyways. And yet, somewhere between the maps and the moonlight, they made me. One morning when Mamma was filling up at the gas station old Jed Murdock looked her up and down and said, "Growing yourself a beer gut, ain'tcha Dottie." Mamma didn't drink beer. A pregnancy test revealed the gut was me.

Seeing as the others had startled easily, the doctor put Mamma on bed rest for most of the pregnancy. This meant no more campaign speeches, no more campaign at all. She couldn't even watch Westerns while she waited, in case the gunshots spooked me into coming early. Seems awful boring, but Mamma talks like it was the happiest time of her life.

"We couldn't wait to see who you'd turn out to be. And whose nose you'd get," she likes to say.

One morning when Daddy had gone to work, she woke up with a wild hair. No, she really oughtn't be walking, but how about a little trail ride for old times' sake?

"I wanted to do one last thing, just the two of us, before you came into the world and started making it yours."

She saddled up Queenie, the pony she'd bought with the $500 she'd won off Daddy all those years ago, and made her way through the hills.

Pennywhistle's pretty flat chested compared to, say, Knoxville or Mont Eagle, but Mamma knew the hidden spots where the dandelions were wild, the dogwoods thick with flowers. She rode to the crest and gazed out over the town. She swears she saw a bald eagle and a swan flying over the courthouse, but knowing Tennessee, it was probably just a hawk and the Frisbee chasing it. She's got a way of seeing beauty where there ain't any.

As the birds passed, her water broke. I'm sure she'd have liked to gallop down that hill and get me out quick, rodeo style, but she ambled down slowly, taking the long way to the firehouse.

"Dorothy Summers Spoon, what in tarnation are you doing on that pony?" Daddy asked. "And why's she all wet?"

Mamma and Daddy left Queenie with Horse. Then they rode to the hospital with a full firehouse escort.

"God works in Aquarius ways," Mamma likes to say.

Watching the world from her pony that morning, I don't think she ever imagined it would be just the two of us again. That life would take with the same bizarre rationale that it gave. I guess that's just how it works. When the doctor placed me in Mamma's arms, she was amazed something so small could have a heartbeat. Later, when they handed us Daddy's ashes, we were surprised to learn someone so vast could fit beneath the zipper fold. I suppose all a person can do is try to make the time between the umbilical cord and the plastic baggie count.

The light fades. The quiche runs out. As I think of Mamma on her pony, of the mother in the library, and of Mrs. Heller raising her brood with no help but a phantom, it occurs to me that it would be awfully foolish to spend any of my precious time being angry.

Instead, I grab a pen.

Dear Mamma,

Writing you reminds me of that summer Lee Ray and I went to that YMCA camp out in Horse Creek. We sure were little terrors. I remember we begged you to come get us after they took away our slingshots and you wrote back that real campers would make their own slingshots. You were right. (As usual.)

I want you to know I'm awful sorry for the things I said on Friday. Sometimes I forget that you lost Daddy, too. That things didn't turn out as either of us had planned. It's just, he was sort of a life force, wasn't he? If he believed you could do something, all a sudden you believed it, too. I think I've been afraid of going back to school because if he's not here believing in me, maybe I won't have what it takes anymore.

But while I was busy being afraid I forgot something important. I still have someone magical rooting for me: you. And if you can turn this roughneck into a pageant contestant, maybe I can learn to be brave. All I ask is a little patience.

Love,

PJ

P.S.

Not to be snoopy, but I gather you've met somebody new. Good for you. Just don't come home covered in hickeys, ya hear? Kidding. If he's up for it, I think I'd like to meet him sometime.

When the phone rings, I think, maybe this is it. The answer to everything. I peel myself out of my blankets and Cheeto bags, leap off the couch, and grab the phone from the kitchen counter.

"Hello?"

"PJ, darling. It's me."

Not the *me* I was hoping for. Neither the one who birthed me nor the one whose curls I want to wake up to in my mouth.

"Evening, Mr. Puddin," I grumble. "Didn't think I'd be hearing from you again."

"And why, pray tell, is that?"

"Last I checked I lost your little competition."

"Little?" He tuts. "PJ, do you realize your performance with Beuf was one of our highest-rated clips to date? It's gone viral. Any more viral and we'd have to notify its sexual partners."

"I get the picture."

"My dear, you're a real audience favorite."

"Great," I say flatly.

Outside my strays fight for the last bite of slop. Mr. Puddin breaks the silence.

"I'm dawdling. I can hear it in your voice that I'm dawdling. So, let me get right down to it. Much to my dismay, we've had to disqualify two of our regional winners. Hannah Bluth from Quarterflute and Becky Grimes from Chattanooga."

"What did they get disqualified for?"

"Oh, I hate to be a slander-monger."

"Do you?"

He cackles like we're the best of friends. Hard to imagine Mr. Puddin being friends with anyone other than dolled-up Malteses and tennis pros, but here we are.

"Fine. Twist my arm," he says. "Hannah was apparently doing *favors* for a certain judge."

"Lord."

"Oh, nothing like that. Just a bit of yard work. Power-washed the driveway, trimmed the hedges."

"Phew."

"And Becky was licking biscuits with all three judges. Fellatio, I mean."

"Oh, my God."

I wonder if Mr. Puddin has any children and, if so, what their birds-and-bees conversation must have been like. Was it all food themed? Did they leave the conversation thinking babies were made from onion rings and corn dogs? When I was a youngin, things were simpler. Mamma and Daddy tossed me the American Girl doll guide to my body and hoped I'd pick the rest up off the streets. Somehow the streets missed the phrase *licking biscuits*.

"Much as we all adore a good biscuit lick," Mr. Puddin continues, "we simply cannot let bribery get in the way of a fair competition."

"Of course not."

"What am I saying? You get it. Happy Proud month. Or was that last month? What are we on now? Lust Month?"

"Jesus Christ, Mr. Puddin, I beseech you to get to the point."

"Right. The point is we need you and Beuf up in Nashville on Saturday. Check-in starts at eight a.m."

"We're back in the competition?"

"I thought that much was clear."

"But, why us? I'm sure there are dozens of runners-up."

I can just picture them, the second-rate chickens of the South. Plucked and hopeful, only to be right back where they started.

"Let's just say I have a soft spot for old Pennywhistle."

"Don't we all," I say, half sarcastically, half for real.

He pauses the way Daddy used to when I'd say something ignorant. Something like *Northerners are stupid* or *Hooters is overrated*.

"Listen, I'm not supposed to dole out any wisdom," Mr. Puddin says. "I've sworn to keep things equal, you understand. So, I'm telling you this as a neighbor, not a boss."

"Alrighty."

"Do you know what happens to a dream deferred? Does it smart like a bruise? Does it smell like old ground beef or is it sugary like honey left out to dry? Does it stay a tomato or does it become a sun-dried tomato?"

"Careful, Mr. Puddin. Sounds like Langston Hughes's wisdom, not yours."

"I knew I'd heard that somewhere," he admits. "The point is, you and Beuf clearly have something special inside of you. Don't let that slip away."

I consider this. Friday's train wreck still has me on crutches.

"If we make something of ourselves, who will be left to staff your flagship Chickie Shak, huh?"

"Oh, that doesn't trouble me one bit. There will always be someone ready to work at the Chickie Shak."

I scoff.

"You sound so certain."

"The Chickie Shak, I believe, is like a pit stop. A place to gas up before you head somewhere else bigger and better. And let me tell you, history speaks for itself. Just about every person who has worked at the Pennywhistle branch has gone on to do fabulous things."

"Name one."

"Mayor Delilah Fisher-Trapper. Senator Brill First. And our very own Emmens Clementine."

"Emmens Clementine?" I gasp.

"A talented fry cook much like yourself."

"I thought he went to Harvard."

"With what money, angel? Mr. Clementine attended the school of stanky fries long before he matriculated in Massachusetts."

"Wow." I sigh. "I'm having a record week for being wrong about people."

"Well, take it from me, who is always right about people. Go to Nashville and bring Beuf with you."

Ouch. Heartache and heartburn are close as cousins, so I can't tell which is radiating through me right now. Be it the quiche or the choices, deep down I know Mr. Puddin's offer is my best shot at solving things.

"I suppose I'd better talk to her."

"You should, indeed."

"Thanks for, uh, the opportunity," I mumble.

The line goes quiet for a second, nothing but the sounds of my strays joyfully lapping up the last of their feast, while Okra, next door, barely appreciates her steady meals and air-conditioned life. The strays do better, I think. Mr. Puddin finally speaks, a parting gift of sorts.

"Well, you didn't hear it from me," he says, "but I happen to believe in you."

MAYBE THIS TIME

The next morning, I place *The Raccoon King of Lake Tomorrow* on Mrs. Heller's desk.

"Well, well, well," she clucks, "I was starting to think you'd read it twice."

"Actually, I need to put it down for a while."

Booklover, grandmother. She reads the sadness in my eyes and tells me to stay put while she does the one-two shuffle to the children's section.

"Now," she says, handing me the Elmo puppet, "tell me all about it."

"I think I might have let everybody down."

"How come?" she asks as Peter Rabbit.

"Because I didn't win."

"Oh, I don't think that's it." She adjusts Peter's jacket. "Try again."

"Because I lied to Boof."

"Getting warmer."

"Because I lied to Mamma."

"Toasty, but not quite."

A bespectacled second-grader taps on the desk.

"Where's the Harry Potters at?"

"Behind the *at*," she replies.

"Huh?"

"Children's section, row ten."

"Thank you."

"Grammar matters," she explains. "Go on."

"I'm running out of ideas here, Mrs. Heller. And my hand's getting sweaty. Sorry."

The Elmo puppet leaps onto her hand like a cockatiel. She considers his ponderous eye.

"Maybe what we need is some summer reading. You're never too old for that. Follow me."

Wafting from shelf to shelf, she hands me an assortment of period-related titles.

This Bloody Tax!

Menstruation Legislation

Body Ain't No Wonderland

"Don't question. Just read. When you've got your book report finished you just bring it on back and tell me what you've learned. Look, now, there's a seat right there next to the little fella reading *Chamber of Secrets*. He won't fuss at you."

"It's been a while since I've written anything."

"And that there," she says with both puppets, "might just be your problem."

Mrs. Heller blesses me with pencils, Post-its, and paper the way a mother would bless a brown bag with apples, bologna, and Ding Dongs. It feels good to hold a pencil again. To sketch an outline. While the little boy beside me wades deeper into *Harry Potter and the Chamber of Secrets*, I wade into the ass-backward politics of tampon taxes. Voldemort, misogyny. Kinda feels like we're in this together.

"Are you kidding me?" I ponder aloud at the Florida law that taxes tampons the same as makeup.

"Pretty scary, right?" says the boy.

"Terrifying."

Hate to admit it, but there's a part of me that always considered the Hog Club a little silly, a little ragtag. At Christmastime they decorate mailboxes in exchange for donations for the homeless shelter. Nobody stringing holly to your mailbox can be all that important, now can they? The more I read, the wronger I get. These taxes add up. Every month, every uterus. Mamma's an expert at keeping Pennywhistle safe and warm, but if she can pull this off, she'll save a whole county. Quarter-flute, Dimehorn, Nickelfiddle, and a dozen Piggly Wigglys from here to the Loosahatchie, tax-free.

My outline grows like a beanstalk until it's time to leave for work. I check two more books out. Three to be safe. Fine, five. I'm hooked.

"I'm gonna need a bag."

"Honey, you're gonna need a truck."

WALKING TO WORK, I feel slightly lighter. The firehouse looks peaceful, too, baked in waves of heat and stretches of shade from the maples. They're probably in there playing cards right about now. Or making toffee. They make a lot of toffee in the off hours. Daddy used to say there was a big gulf between danger and waiting and toffee made that gulf sweeter.

I could go in. They might even have some fresh.

Not yet, I tell myself. Not yet because I have to get to work. Not yet, because I'm still a little raw. But I know there's wiggle room in that *yet*. It's like when Lee Ray got trapped in his mamma's wedding dress. We were reenacting Princess Diana's life story and didn't account for his wide shoulders when we stuffed him into that godforsaken cupcake. Zipper got stuck and so did he. We had to confess the conundrum to his mamma, who simply said, "Suck in, boy!" and with that little extra space, he was able to get out. I reckon when I'm ready to suck in, I'll be able to get out, too.

For now, I keep walking, the wheels on my bicycle necklace going *whir, whir, whir.*

As I pass a front yard littered with chickens, I think of Mr. Puddin's call. *You didn't hear it from me, but I happen to believe in you.* It sounds like something Dean Jackson would say. Maybe believing in things isn't as hard as I thought. Maybe it's like these chickens, puttering about, pluck-ing grass, ferrying it back to the coop. They might be building some-thing. They might be playing. It might not matter at all in the scheme of things what happens to the blades of grass, but perhaps it matters because they've decided it matters.

"Good luck," I tell them. "Whatever you're after, good luck."

"YOU HEAR FROM Mr. Puddin?" I ask Boof as she ties her apron strings. It's an offering, an olive branch. A Powerball ticket tucked into an Easter card.

"Yeah," she says, not coldly but not toasty, either. "No clue where he got my number."

"Me neither."

"Your number's on your W-2, you dummies," Linda snips.

"Right," Boof agrees quietly.

She stuffs the napkin holders like a nurse would tuck in a rowdy child with chicken pox: firm, efficient, and just a little bit sweet. We take refuge in the sound of it. *Tuck, tuck.* There aren't enough napkin holders to get us through the day. I clear my throat.

"So, are you in?"

Her eyes light up like a trash-can barbeque, but she douses them.

"I still need to think about it."

"Of course. Sure. Take your time."

By *take your time* I mean get the hell over here and love me already. I cross my fingers and toes she'll sneak into the kitchen when Linda heads out to smoke. At least poke her head through the walk-up win-dow after the lunch rush.

No dice.

Truth is, none of us knows what to do with one another. We knock knees and bungle the orders all day. The customers pick up on the fu-nereal atmosphere. This, however, doesn't stop them from ordering the toughest dishes on the menu. The 50th Birthday Hot Dog Tower, the

Flaming Ranch Chicken. I nearly lose a finger chopping up the two pounds of jalapeños required for the Devil's Whiskers. Plain and simple, I don't know if these folks have got too much confidence in us or not enough. Does the Waitress's Secret beget five-star service or does it remind people we're nothing but a trio of grease slingers who happen to boast decent voices and flexible tongues?

We finally get a moment's rest around four thirty. Linda makes for the door with not one but two cigarettes.

"I'll be back," she tells us.

"Mind if I join you?"

It's the softest we've ever heard Boof talk, and it turns both our heads. She's got a dishrag hanging from her little clutched hands, an image that strikes me as blanketlike. As if she's just come down the hall after a bad dream, a little shaken, a little embarrassed. Come on, Linda, I think. Least you can do is warm her up a glass of milk.

"You don't smoke," Linda mumbles.

"I know, I just thought maybe we could—"

"I'll be real quick. You can take your break right after. Real quick. Just a few minutes."

Linda flees with the speed of food poisoning. Boof stays put.

BY THE TIME we switch off the neon Open sign, we've officially had the longest day in Chickie Shak history. My dogs are barking louder than Brawny. Linda's lost all but two nails. Even Boof looks like somebody shat in her hash browns. I wonder if the two of them will ride home together, but before you can say *Elvis in heels*, Linda shimmies past us and out to the solace of her truck. Boof locks up, watching her go. As for me, I lean against the hose rack, painfully aware of the lack of bike there.

"Can we talk?"

"PJ," she protests.

"I just want to tell you something."

She sighs. Her eyes, usually wide and lively, look tear sunk and sleep forsaken. Maybe her weekend was as lonely as mine.

"Go ahead."

"I heard this old country song called 'You're the Reason Our Kids Are Ugly' and I thought maybe we could play around with it. Like 'Possums in a Creek.' Lot of potential there."

"That's what you wanted to say to me?" She balks.

"Uh, yes."

She shakes her head and starts walking away. Just like her song, I think.

"Wait! You said you needed space, so I thought you meant you didn't want to talk about the Linda stuff. Can we just go back to the part where we were writing songs and having fun—"

"How about sorry? How about you're not the only one going through something? I finally found my birth mother, and she doesn't even want to talk to me."

She wipes her eyes with the backs of her wrists. That's the kind of thing I should be doing, would be doing, if I hadn't screwed the pooch, the poodle, and the whole damn pound.

"Boof, of course I'm sorry. I don't know how to do this."

She turns.

"Do what?"

"I've never been in love before. I'm still getting my sea legs."

The words tumble out of my mouth like marbles from a coffee can. *Clink, clink, clink, clink.* Once released, they're everywhere. It takes about five seconds to realize Boof won't be spilling her marbles.

"PJ, wait."

"Forget it."

Three words, that's all I wanted. Instead I get four that hurt.

"I love that song."

Not me, but the song. Not me, but the mother who gave her away and never once came looking for her. I walk and walk until the Chickie Shak is nothing but a clapboard house with a grease problem.

MY THOUGHTS TAKE me to the riverbank. The rain's swelled the water to arc-bearing heights, but without the blue of *Just Thighs* and the orange of Boof's laughter, it strikes me as nothing but a big puddle. Just the reeds, blowing this way and that, and the dragonflies who know nothing of disaster.

"Hello?" I call across the river. "Anybody out there?"

If the snapping turtles can hear me, they pretend otherwise. Same goes for the drowsy scarecrow. Shoot, it's been a long time since I was truly alone. Years, maybe. Possibly never. Heaving a sigh of defeat, I lose my sandals and sit a spell.

Silt finds the wells between my toes. You're never too old to love something like that. There will always be silt. Will always be a river. God might take your daddy, but on a day like today he seems to be saying, *Look how much I left behind. I didn't take the trout or the dandelions or even the blue of the sky. The whole town remains, every person who loved me before I left.*

Something in my stomach says to leave again would be to make them disappear.

Something else says if they stayed put once they'll stay put again.

A third thing asks what Mamma would do.

Of course, I know exactly what she'd do. She'd get her ass to the Piggly Wiggly and gather up as much flour as money could buy, as many apples as orchards could spare, and as much Crisco as the devil could churn. Rising slowly from the sand, I decide it's time I follow suit.

If grief won't get out of my kitchen, I might as well feed it.

Peewee Dupree lends me her wheelbarrow, for which she will receive the first pie. Then there's Deedoo, for breaking her little heart. Lee Ray for never letting me down. Peep and Nina for being their strange selves. Mrs. Heller for playing puppeteer through years of arthritis. The list goes on and on. I bake through the night and into the morning. As I stir, I turn on Daddy's favorite Randy Travis record and simply let it hurt. All this time I thought maybe if I cupped my sadness in my hands like a firefly it wouldn't be able to escape. Instead, the firefly became a wasp, stinging me over and over in its quest to be let out.

When the pies have cooled and the tissues have run out, I feel not stung but relieved. I reach for my bike. Phantom limb, best loved thing on two wheels, it's still nowhere to be found. But maybe I'm supposed to walk, supposed to feel the miles of apology in my shoes as I place my warm efforts on Pennywhistle's doorsteps.

First Linda's, then Boof's, then Mamma's.

Linda's dogs still lie snoring in their beds. Boof's dinosaur continues to sway from side to side over hole number twelve. Mamma won't be up until the rooster crows. The still-deciding sun is my only company now, peeking out as *maybe* as can be, as scared as me, but still doing the damn thing.

A screen door opens. Deedoo's. Somewhere between the Granny Smiths and the cinnamon I hope she'll taste my apology.

"Miss PJ," she calls, "wait."

Her long hair, scraggly to the point of rodent-hood, skitters behind her back.

"Do you know how to braid?"

"Not particularly. Where's Miss Linda?"

"I told her not to come."

"Oh, Deedoo."

"She's not my friend anymore. She's a traitor."

"Is this because of what I said?"

"Maybe."

"Listen, all that yelling, the things I accused her of, it really wasn't fair."

She crosses her arms.

"But was it true?"

"True, well, what's true is . . ." My answer snags like a sweater caught on a chain-link fence.

"What's true is that Miss Linda can be a real pain in the rear. We all can. Starting with me. Especially me. Point is, she loves you."

"How do you know?"

"Because I'm a grown-up."

"No, you're not."

I have to smile at this. There are about a hundred reasons I don't qualify, starting with my fear of just about everything, but I ask anyway.

"Why not?"

"Because," she says like it's obvious, "grown-ups know how to braid."

LINDA AND BOOF don't shower me with hugs and kisses when I show up to work. Nor does Mamma stop by the walk-up window at lunch to take me back. Still, like a hot-air balloon does at a state fair, I feel something lift.

"Saw a bike for sale on Craigslist," Boof says casually as she grabs a lunch order.

"What did it look like?"

"Not like yours."

"Oh."

"It was pretty cute, though."

"Yeah?"

As she reaches for the mayonnaise, Boof flashes the smallest of smiles.

"Fifty bucks. Some fella out in Nickelfiddle. Might be just the thing for a second chance."

"Nice to know those things come in pairs."

"Exhibit A," she says, pointing to Deedoo, whose braids play double Dutch forgiveness down her back.

AS I START my bikeless trek home, Linda saddles up to me. I'm sure we strike an odd pair. Linda's at least two Twinkies taller than me on account of the heels and the hair. Looks like she's about to give me a makeover or marry my granddaddy.

"Uh, hi?" I say.

She spits her tobacco into the grass.

"I need a favor."

"I'm so sorry, but my kidneys are spoken for."

"Hardy, har, har. My truck's busted."

"I swear to baby Jesus, Linda, I did not mess up your truck."

"I know that. Mr. Creel tried to ford the river like in that Oregon Trail game and now it's flooded. Men are idiots, and you can put that down in writing."

"Agreed."

A squirrel runs across our path.

"Point is, I need a ride to Nashville tomorrow."

"And?"

"And I know you got a car."

I narrow my eyes like a Tennessee rat cat.

"Who told you that?"

"Nobody. I saw your little buddy take it in for an oil change. I know your mamma drives it to Memphis to get her hair dye. And I know it's sitting pretty in your garage right this very minute."

A town this small, she probably knows my blood type, too.

"Linda, I don't—how you say?—drive anymore."

"You don't drive?"

"No."

Nobody has ever made me explain why. It's a bit of a roadkill situation. Lee Ray and Mamma pass it often but they never intervene. Nobody else really notices. Therefore, the idea of talking about it, with Linda no less, turns my stomach to grits.

"Well, how were you planning on getting there, princess?"

"Lee Ray's gonna drive me."

She cackles.

"Let me get this straight. He's skipping the Summer Paddle Adventure to drive your sorry ass to Nashville? Gonna leave those EFPs and his little lover boy high and dry? I don't think so."

"That's this weekend?" I ask.

She gestures to the marquee at the senior center: Summer Paddle Adventure This Weekend. Come Dry. Get Wet!

"Dammit."

"Dammit is right."

I knew there would come a day when Lee Ray wouldn't be around to sponsor my pep talks and braid my hair, but I figured it would be a little later, once he'd gotten hitched or I'd found a new hairdresser. Going it alone feels gaping. Impossible. And just like that, I'm having trouble breathing out. As I totter from side to side, Linda puts a steadying hand on my shoulder. Snaps her fingers in front of my face with the other one. From this angle, she looks almost motherly.

"Hey, now. Let's just calm down."

"I'm trying," I croak.

"What's the matter? You got asthma? I got a Benadryl in my purse."

"No, it's just . . . I can't do this without Lee Ray."

She considers this.

"Y'all are pretty tied at the hip, ain'tcha?"

"Yes."

"Wasn't that boy on the girls' softball team?"

"The MVP."

"The times, they up and change, now don't they?"

"I guess."

She rubs my back. A little rough, like she's got no practice, but nice nonetheless. I can't help but wonder what kind of mamma she would have been to Boof if it weren't for the sisters.

"Lee Ray makes a mean denim dress. I'll give him that. But much like Madea, you can do bad all by yourself."

"I can?"

"Sure." She slaps my back. "Still gonna lose to me, but you'll give 'em a good show first."

"I still don't know if I can get behind the wheel."

"Fine, you big ole wuss. If it makes you feel better, I'll drive."

"Okay." I exhale. "Okay, you drive."

"I like driving. Specially big cars. You got a Jeep, right?"

"Yes."

"That's just dandy, ain't it?"

"Sure."

Linda eyes me with a small glimmer of—I kid you not—genuine concern. Like me fainting might actually stir something in her chilly abdomen.

"You gonna be okay?" she asks.

"Probably."

"Good."

"Hey, wait a minute," I observe. "You didn't call me sweetheart."

"Come again?"

"You usually call me sweetheart when you think I'm being stupid about something. Like, 'Sweetheart, this order looks like shit' or 'Sweetheart, the toilet paper roll's on upside down.' No sweetheart for my childish fears?"

She considers this.

"I used to babysit you when you were little. Did you know that?"

"No." I blush.

"I reckon you wouldn't. You were only three or four. Your mamma found me in the frozen aisle of the Piggly Wiggly one afternoon and decided I was a responsible adult, which, of course, I wasn't."

"She tends to promise the moon when all she's got handy is a tennis ball."

"Exactly." Linda chuckles. "She scooped me up from the corn dogs and from then on I'd spend every afternoon braiding your hair and taking you to the creek. You were always a little shier than the other kids. But you had this bravery, too. You'd catch crawdaddies between your fingers like you didn't know they had claws. And you'd jump into just about any body of water. Half the time I was scared to death you'd knock your teeth out on a rock and I'd have to carry your canines back to Dottie in my hands. Then you met Lee Ray. I thought, Thank goodness that gutsy little thing finally has somebody to play with."

Linda looks out across the dirt road to where the sun touches the trees.

"When you started working here you didn't remember me," she says, "but I remembered you. And the you who walked in was nothing like the you who caught crawdaddies."

She's right. She's oh, so painfully right.

"I know how it feels to not feel like yourself. Trust me, I been there. When I lost the kids . . ."

She pauses, puts a hand up to her eyes.

"It's like you can't remember who you used to be much less how the hell to get back there. It's like you lost the map."

"I feel like that a lot," I admit.

"I know you do. Point is, I was there. And I remember. It wasn't so long ago that you, missy, were just crazy enough to try just about anything."

Once, when it snowed enough to cut the power, Mamma and Daddy took me up a hill to learn how to ski. Latched into my wooden feet, I soared with the kind of confidence only a four-year-old can muster. Again and again I whirred down the mountain. All the children did. It was the adults who faltered at the top. It occurs to me now that I want to love the way children ski, with red cheeks and no fear. I want to be bundled and giddy again, back before I learned of trees, of broken arms and twisted ankles. I want to go down the mountain as fast as I can despite having heard about falling.

"I'm still not ready to drive," I tell Linda.

"Baby steps," she says, heading for the creek we once played in.

FRIDAY AFTERNOON, WHEN the sun's not yet gone lickety-split, Lee Ray and Lionel drop the car off at the Chickie Shak. There's a moment when they're coming up the drive, before they've reached me, when I can see the way they talk to each other. I can't make out the words— some snarky joke, some silly bet—but when Lionel tickles Lee Ray's ribs I know the feeling. I almost want to tell them to take another lap and savor it. Because sometimes joy hides out for months. You get to thinking it's gone. Then, all a sudden, it comes around the corner like the ice cream truck, so full, so hot, you have to lick the riches from your hands just to keep up.

"Your chariot, madam." Lee Ray honks at the top of the hill.

He and Lionel look mighty strapping in their Summer Paddle Adventure shirts and bandannas, the cutest couple of hunks you ever saw. I like how Lionel has cut his shirt in a sort of shipwrecked-underwear-model style. Adds a certain *je ne sais gay*.

"I take it the EFPs have accepted Lionel as one of their own?"

Lee Ray scoffs.

"I've been absolutely and utterly usurped. He caught that big catfish— Hank Williams—that we've been after for months and cooked him up in some sort of Cajun concoction and now the whole club won't let him have a moment's rest without asking for the recipe."

"Family secret," Lionel explains.

"Mean old Helen Duroche claims she was the queen of a Mardi Gras ball back in the forties, when we all know she's never been west of Horse Creek outside of a boat, but I digress. They adore him. I adore him. And we are all of us, every one, rooting for you."

"Thanks, guys."

"We'll be camped out on Hellfish Island tomorrow night, and I'll try to catch a signal, but just in case, here."

He hands me a note.

"Lee Ray, these are just the lyrics to 'I Hope You Dance.'"

"I was strapped for time."

I pull him in for a hug.

"Thanks for everything."

"You too."

"Knock 'em dead, sailors."

"Our average age is seventy-eight. Please don't jinx it."

As they stride off, hand in hand, I survey my loot. I've got a duffel, a pair of Saturday boots, and my banjo. Meanwhile, Linda hoists so much luggage into the car I might as well be taking her to college.

"Keys?" she asks.

I hand over the big ball of souvenirs and key chains. Everything we collected on the road to Dollywood and back.

"Anything in here that could start a car?" Linda groans.

"Think of it as a treasure hunt."

As she flicks through my sweetest years with a freshly sharpened nail, I hear footsteps. I wonder if it's Linda's husband come to give her one more passionate kiss before the road. Or maybe Mrs. Heller, who regularly forgets her glasses at table two.

"Wait up," Boof says.

Linda winks at me. I want to shake her for answers, Magic 8 Ball the woman into saying something I can understand, but for now I accept the miracle for what it is.

"So, ladies," Linda says. "Who's feeling hot?"

THE OPEN ROAD

I have my reservations about Linda steering the ship, seeing as she could just as easily knock us off and fill us with sawdust as she could safely transport us to the big city, suspicions that spike the moment she turns right.

"Highway's the other way."

She spits out the window. The tires kick up gravel like the tap dancers at Randy Rumpus oyster night.

"We gotta get the dogs first."

"And why, pray tell, is that?"

"They're part of my act."

Before I can protest, we're swerving around the pack of cats that guard the mailbox and into the sprawling forest of Linda Manor.

Linda lets out a hog whistle so loud it could put out a candle.

"Jesus!" I clutch my ears.

Sure enough, Easter Bonnet, Brawny, and Gator emerge from the trees at warp speed. In the light, Brawny is even more terrifying than she was under the cover of nightfall. Gator's older than I expected, fringed with patches of white fur, and Easter Bonnet's about as lithe and keen as I would have guessed. The trio pants noisily outside my door. I frown at them. Even though I've all but walked out on this car, I still take pride in the clean seats, the lack of candy wrappers. It's never been hit, scratched, or dented. Nobody's given birth in the back seat yet. Linda reaches across me and opens the door.

"Get on back, now." She points.

"It's my car!"

"Dogs always ride up front."

"No!"

"Tell you what. When you drive, you can make the rules. Until then, scoot."

My annoyance is far outweighed by my delight at getting to share the back seat with Boof. It's the closest we've been since Gabriel's Shining Star, a fact we are both very much aware of as Linda hauls ass out of the driveway. A family of turtles crosses the road, the kind we used to paint our names on with nail polish and let loose. I can't quite make out their markings, but they've definitely been loved by somebody. Linda dukes our hazards around them, launching Boof into my lap.

"Move it or lose it," she hollers at the reptiles.

The next turn steadies us back to our respective sides of the car. Boof and I trade sheepish looks. I pray for shepherds.

FOR THE FIRST few miles the silence is thicker than a thigh on the Fourth of July. All we can hear is the intermittent sound of Easter Bonnet licking the ick out of Brawny's ear.

"You got a book on tape or something?" Linda finally asks.

I paw through the seat-back pockets to no avail. Where'd I use to keep the fun stuff? Oughta be an Etch A Sketch or a bingo card back here, something. One thing I cleared out completely was the trove of sexy magazines. I bought the Jeep off of Peep and Nina when I turned sixteen and the old horn dogs thought it would be a fun surprise to hide a few choice titles in the glove box. *In case you break down in the middle of nowhere,* Peep had told me. *Might as well have some entertainment while you wait for the tow.* It was all hee hee and ha ha until I drove my share of Girl Scout Troop 27 to their field trip at the Quarterflute Zoo and wound up with Deedoo asking if the busty lady's swimsuit top fell off when she jumped off the diving board or if she was up to no good. Lee Ray and I donated the rest of the magazines to the Boy Scouts and that was that.

"Well?"

"Come to think of it, I think I got the CD set of *Because of Winn-Dixie* in the glove box."

"Not gonna lie," Linda says, "I loved the hell out of that movie. You put a dog in a movie and I'mo watch it."

"Book's even better."

Linda drives with her knee as she reaches over and pops in the first disk. Exhausted, I fall asleep. I miss the Jack Daniel's billboards and the little white crosses. The smushed porcupines and greasy white boxes of Krystal cheeseburgers. By the time I wake up, it's dark. Starry, even.

"I'm starving," I remark to no one in particular.

"Hush," Linda chastens. "I'm trying to hear the story."

She turns the volume up.

"I'm pretty hungry, too," Boof whispers, wiping the tee-tiniest spool of drool from the corner of her mouth. Damn, that girl is precious.

"Can we talk now?"

"Yeah, how about that pit stop? We could use a snack."

"Well, lucky for you lazy bums, we're almost to Nashville."

Thirty miles according to the road sign. My stomach grumbles, but I try to stay strong. All that fast food litter don't make it easy. Corn dog wrapper, taquito-stained bag. The stuff of dreams. Just when I think I can't wait another mile, a salty whiff of dog breath reaches my nose. Whew! I'm about to toss my cookies if we don't stop soon.

"We seriously need to eat."

Linda checks the clock on the dash.

"All right. The dogs'll be wanting their supper anyhow."

We yawn off the next exit, searching the little strip of gas stations and drive-thrus for something that's still open.

"Look." Boof points.

A Chickie Shak branch, asleep for the night. Its roof, snowflaked with streamers, indicates some sort of send-off party earlier today. Even if we could stop there, would we? The existence of another Chickie Shak is a stark reminder that, save for one lucky winner, we will never make it big. Sure know how to make it small, though. We've made it small hundreds of times. Each time somebody tastes our chicken for the first time, lets out that delighted hum, that unfettered *hot damn*. Each family reunion that pitches tents in the backyard and stays all week, feasting and fighting and making up under our watch. These little victories sustain us.

We approach a baby-blue, fifties-style trailer stop. Loretta's Half Moon Diner. Out back we can see a sleeping smattering of cows lathered in light. Moonbathing, if you will. Linda doesn't even have to ask, just pulls right in.

I wonder if Brawny, who snuck onto my lap while I was sleeping, will be joining us inside or if this restaurant bans the kind of critters that are easily confused with clogged YMCA shower drains.

"Giddy up," Linda instructs us, pooches and all.

She spoons a jumbo can of Little Debbie Dog Slop into three bowls and sets them on the ground next to a beach towel.

"Stay put, you hear?"

I have no doubt they will. You don't leave a mamma who keeps you heavy in the Debbie.

The cowbell tolls as we walk in. It's tumbleweed hour, just us and a little lady called Elma who wakes up from her nap in time to direct us to our booth. Her bob looks straight out of a 1974 sewing pattern, set firm with hairspray and concrete.

"Hey, I recognize y'all," she says. "Chickie Shak Pennywhistle, right?"

I elbow Boof.

"Lookee here. We're famous."

"My niece, Doozy, she's representing Fort Champ. You might have seen her in the talent portion."

We smile politely but unconvincingly. Elma wrestles a school picture from her wallet.

"This here's what she looked like before she broke her nose." Elma prods. "I told her not to ask for one of them ski slope replacement noses. So much pressure on girls with pretty noses like that. Did you see her on TV? Real sweet. Does the birdcalls."

Boof touches the picture and smiles.

"She takes after you."

"Oh, you're too nice. I think she looks like my sister, Learline—"

"Do you serve booze?" Linda interrupts.

Elma giggles.

"Not officially."

"Got anything we can borrow for a twenty?"

Elma returns with a coffee pitcher full of whiskey.

"I could go for some waffles," I say.

"Me too."

"Y'all do a Reuben?"

"Best one in the county," Elma brags.

"Hit me."

We stack our menus and pass them over.

"If you don't mind me saying so, you ladies remind me a whole lot of my *Bachelorette* Bible Study group," she says and, sensing the need for a little elaboration, adds, "We study the teachings of Christ and then we make bets on which fella the lady on the show will end up with."

"Trust me, we ain't as glamorous as all that," I say.

"You made it this far. You must be something."

By Elma's missing tooth, we just might be.

LINDA POURS EACH of us a coffee mug of whiskey.

"Who's gonna drive?" I ask, thinking of my car's beautifully un-dented hood, its adorably unbloodied windshield.

"Hotel's across the street, stupid. We'll walk."

Cherries ain't this waitress's only secret, apparently. The way Linda doles out the golden liquid speaks to a lifetime's worth of sneaking.

Perhaps she's more cowgirl than cowpat after all.

"Girls, I consulted my psychic, and she said there's only one way to fix a situation like this."

"Years of therapy?" I try.

"It's called Spill Your Guts or Suck My Butt."

"Is there a *neither* option?"

"We go round in a circle. Ask any question you want and that person's either gotta answer or drink."

"Sounds like a recipe for a hangover," I say.

"Not if you're honest," Boof dares.

I once caught my braces on a rope swing and hung there for an hour before the orthodontist and the paramedics arrived. Spill Your Guts or Suck My Butt feels slightly more precarious.

"Who wants to go first?" Linda asks.

"Me," Boof says.

She turns on her elbow to look me in the eye. A lone curl shakes above her ear like a question mark.

"What does *PJ* really stand for?"

"Ughhh." I groan.

"Pamela Jo? Peggy Jessica?"

"No."

"Spill your guts or suck my butt," Linda reminds me.

"It stands for Pennywhistle's Jewel."

"Your legal name is Pennywhistle's Jewel Spoon?"

"It was the centennial! And my daddy loved history!"

"Well, that explains it."

Their laughter both drenches and embarrasses me. I need a towel or a new identity before I can show my face again. Then again . . .

"With a name like Boof I'd cool it on the judgment."

"It's not my real name."

"Well, then, spill your butt, missy."

"My real name's Ruth. I couldn't pronounce it for the longest time, so everybody just called me what I could say, which was Boof."

"Or, if you're Mr. Puddin," I correct, "*beuf.*"

We go at it like this for a while. Hemming. Hawing. Spilling syrup on our jorts. It strikes me that for three people who deal with food all damn day, this is the first time we've ever shared a meal. Linda salts her Reuben. I pool my syrup in the corner so it doesn't flood my waffles. Boof, on the other hand, drenches hers to saturation. Hell, sitting together in the glare of the window we almost look like a family. And, just like a family, we can sense when awkward's en route. Can feel it in the way the conversation swings to a stop like a newly vacant hammock. Finally Boof clears her throat.

"Why'd you give us up?"

Linda pours herself a little more whiskey but doesn't drink. The diner lights seem sad all a sudden, cheap. Like they'll never be all the way on, just flickering. I notice a crack in the booth, a rip that over time will become a canyon.

"Figured that was coming," Linda says, raking her hand through her bangs. "Elma, can I smoke in here?"

"Sure, honey."

"Bless you and your birdcalling niece."

She lights up and takes a long drag.

"Y'all ever heard of Knee? Way up in the Smokies?"

We shake our heads.

"Smaller than shit and I really mean it. Hell, Knee makes Pennywhistle look like Paris. I was all set to get out of there and go to beauty school down in Knoxville. Had my classes lined up. Mamma and Daddy even gave me a pink blow-dryer for high school graduation. Can you imagine? Pink? What I wanted was a red one."

She scoffs, sips, smokes.

"Well, a few weeks after that, my period stopped showing up. Mamma and Daddy took that blow-dryer right back to JCPenney. *Guess you won't be needing it now.*"

We can't help but frown over the lost pink blow-dryer. Because, really, it's so much more than that. It's the fact that you can be counted out for a single decision. For three minutes in the back of a pickup truck, or, on the sunnier end, forty-five in a seedy motel. After that, somebody decides if you're worth a pink blow-dryer or not. No matter how successful you get, that lost blow-dryer's mighty hard to shake off.

"Linda, I'm so sorry," Boof says quietly.

Linda shakes her head.

"Makes sense you're so good at braiding," I muse.

"Could have been better if I'd gone to school, but I figured it out. Your mamma bought me one of those training mannequin heads when I turned twenty-one."

She turns back to Boof.

"But, you probably wanna know about your daddy, don'tcha? Shoo-ee! Had the voice of a goddamn angel. Used to go watch him play at the Rusty Tambourine every Friday night. That's how I knew you were you when you started singing. You'da sang at work and I'd have recognized you on day one."

"Whatever happened to him?" Boof asks.

"He's probably still playing at the Rusty Tambourine. His mamma was a sweet old widow. When she found out I was pregnant she said she knew a place I could go. That poor woman gave me twenty dollars and a bag full of clothes. Fixed me up a basket of food and sent me off on the next Greyhound to Pennywhistle. Little knocked-up Red Riding Hood."

"What were the sisters like?"

"Oh, they were all right. They had some money from the church so they'd take you to the doctor and fix you dinner, which is more than I can say for my folks. I can remember looking at the ultrasound with one of them, the sweet one, Sister Jill with all the moles, and she said, 'Look! Twins!' I made the nurse swish the wand around to make sure."

"So, they were kind of . . . nice?" Boof asks.

"They were smart. When you first got there they made you think you had options. I told them, I says, all I need's a job and a place to stay and I'll be just fine with my babies. They said oh, sure, sure. But let's just look at some of the couples who want a little family and see which one you'd pick if you had to. Just for giggles. Nothing much else to do when you're pregnant and there ain't no air-conditioning or TV. I picked your mamma and daddy because your mamma had curly hair. I'd always wanted curly hair. Ever since I saw Shirley Temple at the drive-in. I thought it made your mamma look glamorous. Is she?"

"She's lovely."

"And your daddy?"

"Him too."

"Well, good. Figured you can't be too messed up if you've still got all your fingers and toes. You do got all your fingers and toes, right?"

"We do," Boof assures her.

"Good. Anyhow, on Sundays, while the other girls were sleeping in, I'd look in the newspaper for the help-wanted ads. Even found one at the salon. Just sweeping up hair, but I figured it was a start. I cut it out and put it under my pillow. Next thing you know, I went into labor. It was one of those freak snowstorms we get out here. Used to get 'em more but now they're practically extinct. It was all snow and wind and you two were coming out fast. They put me under something. By the time I woke up you were long gone."

"That's awful."

"How's your brother, by the way?"

"Beans? He's great. Lives in Memphis."

"Lordy, Beans and Boof? The least they could do is name you better." Linda laughs. "No offense."

"Technically he's Andrew. What'd you have in mind?"

Linda scratches her head, squints. Like the past is some kind of equation she could solve if she only knew the formula.

"I don't remember anymore, to tell you the truth. Spent most of my life since trying to go on with things. Met Buck. Got married. Won a few dog shows."

Boof scratches at the syrup with her fork. This part's the hardest.

"And did you ever think about us?"

"Course I did." She reaches across the table and takes Boof's hand, a little awkward, a little unsure. "I don't guess it ever stops hurting."

Maybe this is my cue to fake diarrhea, hide out in the bathroom for an hour so they can have some privacy. But under the table Boof searches for my hand. I hold on tight. Outside Brawny, Easter Bonnet, and Gator taunt the sleeping cows. Maybe it'll all turn out.

We startle when Elma places the check on the table.

"Well, ladies, I'd love to stay up all night shooting the booty with you, but I gotta close up."

There's still so much left to say. Whole books. Libraries. At least as much as can fit on an episode of *Judge Judy*.

"That hotel any good?" Linda points across the street.

"Oh, it's great if you like bedbugs. They're fumigating at the moment."

"You don't happen to have a spare couch or two, do you?"

Elma beams. Claps her hands in a way that says *former cheerleader*.

"Why didn't you say so? I'll call Carl and tell him to start pumping up the inner tube in the guest room for you."

"How about these lovebirds?"

Elma nods at me and Boof knowingly, like she used to hold hands with her Carl under this very table.

"Well, you two can stay in the lodge."

ELMA HANDS US a fat stack of blankets and nods up the trunk of an old maple. A tornado-kissed tree house awaits.

"Doozy and Debbie used to sleep out there on Christmas Eve. Thought they had a better chance of catching Santa if they could see the roof."

We hoist ourselves up the ladder, a rickety rope structure I pray to Jesus won't shrug to the ground the moment we reach the top. For a tree house, it's pretty well appointed. Old camp bed, stacks of *Nancy Drews*, just enough breeze to lull you to sleep. Once we're settled, I real-

ize Doozy and Debbie's Christmas Eve hideout has the very same am-
biance that Seven Minutes in Heaven used to. Everybody knows you'd
always spend the first two minutes in there mumbling *Aw shucks, we
don't gotta do nothing, it's just a stupid game.* Then all a sudden that little
closet would go quieter than a mouse trapped in a cheese soufflé and
someone would lean forward, cautious but daring, and seize the last
five minutes of heaven.

Boof clears her throat. Did she hear me thinking all that? I wonder.
And does she remember the feeling? Thinking about closets reminds
me we haven't even told each other our coming-out stories yet. Was
she unabashedly smooching Suzies at a young age or did it take a little
longer to dawn on her? I've learned that for some people the story is an
epic, for others a Post-it. Most folks will tell you eventually. They'll get
a wistful look, like the kid standing before the kitchen table, trembling,
was not them, but a younger sibling, someone they loved deeply but
who had a little growing up to do. No matter how easy or hard that
moment was, I think we all have a soft spot for who we were back then.
A person on the precipice of authenticity, of life itself. Even if she's still
steamed at me, Boof's presence reminds me that we are not alone in
this journey.

We spread our blankets over the bed gingerly. Gingham life rafts,
flannel floats. Bless Denny's and Jesus, there's only enough room to
sleep side by side tonight.

"Is it terrible if I say I'm still hungry after all that?" I ask.

"Oh, my God, I'm starving."

We root around in the stack of board games and cigar boxes for a
clandestine candy bar, a rogue Ritz, anything.

"Come on, Doozy." I curse at an empty Mickey Mouse cookie jar.

"Check the first aid kit."

The box is as rusty as a wrestler with a wrist ache. I rub the hinges,
knock it with my foot. Either Band-Aids used to be a heck of a lot
heavier, or this thing's chock-full of goodies. I look around for something to pry with. Mamma's good at that sort of thing, both physically

and emotionally. She can wedge open a locked car door and get you to reveal your herpes status in one fell swoop. I swipe the bobby pin right out of Boof's bun and sneak it under the lip of the box.

"Hey!"

Finally, it cracks open.

"Jackpot."

With her hair all splayed up in the heat, Boof looks downright wild. Good. A wild Boof is exactly what I need, the kind of ruffian who's apt to take chances and accept dares. I hold my breath, keep my eyes on her. How much distance can there be between two blankets and four knees? I pray the road of crisscross applesauce is a short one.

"I haven't had a Goo Goo in years," she says, smiling.

For those nestled anywhere north of the Carolinas, a Goo Goo Cluster is—and I could not make this up—a butt-ugly, chocolate-marshmallow-caramel-peanut glob of glory we Tennesseans call a delicacy.

"But I do sort of wonder when these expired."

"Don't look!" I swat the wrappings away. "That'll spoil it."

"Okay, okay."

I don't care if they were made before color television. These are the best darn things I've ever put in my mouth. Salty. Sweet. Just melted enough to be magic. They pull memories from places I thought didn't exist anymore.

"What?" Boof asks of my secret smile.

"I'm thinking about how Daddy used to take me and Lee Ray to the Goo Goo factory on the way to Dollywood."

"Oh?"

"He was the best advertising they could have asked for. We'd sit on the bench outside and he'd just hoot and holler with every bite. Drew people in like crazy."

"That's amazing."

"Mr. Goo Goo, or whatever his real name was, came out one day and told him he could be an ambassador. Said, *Fella where'd you come from?* Pennywhistle, Daddy said. *They like my candy in Pennywhistle?* Hadn't made it there yet. That man sent us back with more Goo Goos than you can shake a stick at. Sure enough, by the next summer Daddy had spread Goo Goos into every little holler and hick town in West Tennessee. We handed them out at his funeral, actually."

"When did he die?"

I wipe my mouth on my sleeve.

"Few months back."

"And that's why you left school?"

"Who told you that?"

"I'm a waitress. Superior hearing comes with the territory and folks talk."

"Right."

All run out of words, I scarf down another cluster.

"These are the kinds of things I want to hear about," Boof says softly.

"Really?"

"Of course."

"I'm sorry, Boof. I shouldn't have lied to you."

"So, why did you?"

"After Daddy died I felt . . . smaller. Or I made myself small. I pruned. Well, that's not exactly it."

Boof plays with my ponytail and nods for me to go on. I lean into her warm hand.

"When I was little, Daddy and I would go out in the snow together. I always wanted to wear gloves, but he told me to wear mittens. He said that when your fingers are apart, there's more space for the cold to touch. When somebody dies, it's like you find all the places on your body the cold can touch. Places you didn't even know existed. So, I thought, okay, I'll just get smaller and the cold won't be able to get in. Like school. School was something Daddy and I did together. So, I couldn't have that exposed anymore. I got so huddled into myself it almost started to feel normal and then you came along and all those places the cold had found suddenly got filled with warm things. It's like I wanted to throw off all my sweaters and sunbathe in it. When I found out about Linda being your birth mom, I realized how naked I was. The cold could get in just as easy as the warm. So, I started huddling back up again."

I pause.

"Does that make me nuts?"

In the dark, Boof's freckles disappear. The moon only allows for the tip of her nose, the bridge of her eyebrows. I can only guess what she's thinking, that it's a bunch of excuses, that lying's not a symptom of grief, that this tree house ain't big enough for the both of us.

"You should know by now," she says as she takes another bite, "I'm into nuts."

"Can't hear you with your mouth full."

"I said I'm into nuts!"

The warm creeps back in. Maybe because, terrifying as it is, I believe her. It takes an eternity for Boof to finish the caramel center of the Goo Goo, but when she does, I lean across the blankets and kiss her. There's a chance she'll pull back and slap me. Retreat from the tree house to parts unknown. But she stays. Oh, she stays! Her hands find my waist and she tastes like marshmallows and chocolate, like summer and second chances. Below us the cicadas sing. I'm so happy I could die.

"You were right, by the way," I whisper in her ear.

"About what?"

Digging through my duffel, I unearth the red notebook.

"That I oughta let people read this thing. Here. But only if you want to."

"Oh, PJ," she says, laying a gentle hand on its marred cover. "What's that old poem? Take your shoes off when you're walking on me?"

"You mean, 'tread softly because you tread on my dreams'?"

"Right. I'll be sure to tread softly."

I wonder if Linda plans to join us up here, poke her head in with a tender smile and a family-size tub of Marshmallow Fluff, but the clink of light beers below tells me otherwise. She and Elma are the kind of friends that come easy and fast, buds light if you will. One of them cracks a joke. The other hee-haws. Their laughter races the campfire smoke to the top branches of this old maple. Suddenly, I feel a twinge of guilt as I remember all the mean things I've thought about Linda these last few months. Childless Christmases, heat-up burritos. It was easier to imagine her alone than as a fully formed person with triumphs, joys, and the kind of husband who knows how to airbrush.

I tuck a curl behind Boof's ear.

"What are you singing for tomorrow?"

"Depends," she says. "How fast can you learn a new song?"

"Faster if you'd told me on Monday."

"I was still mad on Monday."

"Tuesday?"

"Livid," she stage-whispers.

"Wednesday?"

"Simmering."

"Thursday?"

"Boiling again."

"And what about today?"

"Today I ran into your mamma."

"Can't imagine where."

"She showed up at my doorstep half naked and riding a pony."

"Fridays, right."

Mamma and the Hog Club have been riding to the courthouse in tube tops every third Friday morning to protest the tampon tax.

"Gushing blood and burning bridges every full moon ain't no god-damn luxury," she likes to say. So, the ladies ride in on whatever they can find—horses, tractors, brooms—and give the bigwigs a reason to shut their windows. The courthouse doesn't have air-conditioning, so they know they'll eventually steam the legislature into dropping the tax.

"Apparently she and Sticky Ricky go way back," Boof explains.

"My almost daddy," I say. "What was she doing at yours? Recruiting for the Hog Club?"

Boof rubs her thumb along my jawline.

"She told me not to give up on you."

"I'd sleep on that if I were you."

Inches away, a barn owl hoots.

"'Bout time we get to bed," she says, "now that you and that feathered thing mention it."

I check my Dollywood watch. It's close to midnight. Not much time for beauty sleep, so we'll have to manage on cute sleep, bless-her-heart sleep, good personality sleep. The sleep slept by runners-up and, possibly, by dark horses like us.

We settle into the blankets like squirrels do in an old boot. Noses and necks making a little heart shape. At least that's what the acrylic-on-velvet painting in my bedroom would have you believe about the sleeping habits of rodents. Maybe they prefer to cozy up in softball mitts or wigs. Who knows.

The owl settles down, but I can't seem to shake my thoughts tonight. What will tomorrow look like? What about a year from now? Minutes tick by as I pray my peepers will roost, but at 12:22 I'm still wide awake. I squeeze Boof.

"I need a little help falling asleep."

"I'm not sure I have the energy for knocking boots."

"No, not that. Can we do a one-word-at-a-time story? We used to do them at summer camp. Kind of soothing."

"Once," she begins. A natural already!

"There."

"Was."

"A."

"Coyote."

"Who."

"Talked."

"Fancy."

"And."

"Skinned."

"His."

"Knee."

"On."

"A."

"Nickel."

"So."

"He."

"Got."

"Stitches."

"And."

"Ate."

"A."

"Popsicle."

"The."

"End. Now go to bed," Boof says.

"Okay."

I settle back into her arms and slow my breathing. When I am one wheelbarrow away from sleep I hear Boof whisper against my neck.

"I love you, Pennywhistle's Jewel Spoon."

WELCOME TO NASHVILLE

The Hot Chicken Beauty Tour check-in table is so crowded with butts it might as well be an ashtray. There are forty-five contestants overall, due to the fact that some branches don't have any female employees.

"Your schedules, your goodies, your toothbrush," a fanny-packed brunette explains as she hands me a tote the size of a suitcase. "Be back here at six for first call. Six on the dot. We will not wait for you."

"Roger that"—I squint at her name tag—"Penny."

"Hey, like Pennywhistle. That's a good sign!" Boof says.

"You got a boyfriend named Whistle?" Linda inquires.

Penny frowns.

"No, his name's Jeep and he's all mine."

The line bustles behind us. As many miniskirts as there are overalls, mullets as there are blowouts. There's a rumor going around that the pageant's short on goody bags, so we best scoot if we don't want to be trampled. Penny, still locked in what she thinks is a heated exchange over her four-wheel-drive fella, clutches Linda's loot. Boof and I exchange looks as Linda tugs on the bag.

"Sweetheart"—she laughs—"I'm married and they's gayer than Ellen's undies. Jeep is all yours. Now hand it over."

Penny relaxes and releases the goody bag.

"Good luck, then."

Linda spits into a nearby trash can. Clucks her teeth.

"Don't need it. We're the ones to beat."

One of the contestants pushes past us with a double stroller. Two curly-haired cherubs with faces like spoiled oysters. Linda stops.

"I remember now."

"Remember what?" Boof asks.

"I was gonna call y'all Bertha and Ernest."

"Bert and Ernie?" I scoff.

They smile at each other, like there's a whole lot more archaeology to unearth between them. Like there's gold.

"You didn't want to go with Scooby and Shaggy?" I ask. "Tom and Jerry?"

"I ain't too sentimental to skewer you, PJ. These here are fresh."

She flashes her latest manicure, a look only a veterinarian could fashion.

"All right, all right."

The registration area spills into a lobby with bad coffee and a great gift shop. While a group of East Tennessee hopefuls rubs elbows with the glamorous Nashville contestant, Della Blue, the three of us pore over our schedules. Socials, hair-removal tutorials. This thing's chock-full. Much as I'd love to take Boof upstairs and watch reality TV as we spoon in big, white robes, I've got other plans that need attending to.

"Y'all mind if I slip out for an hour or so? Gotta take care of something."

"Toilet's right yonder." Linda points.

"Little bigger than a number two. I'll meet you back here for lunch?"

"Sounds good," Boof says. "I think I'll take the Ryman tour. Linda?"

She whistles for the dogs to stop snooping around the Chattanooga crew and return to their mamma. They hesitate—the Chattanoogans brought a steaming trunk of jerky with them—but eventually return, tails wagging.

"I'm taking the dogs to that big ole replica of the Parthenon. Don't wait up."

Brawny growls at a nearby blonde. I give Boof a quiet goodbye kiss and begin the trek into the unknown. Out of the corner of my eye I can see Della Blue approaching Linda, but for what I can only imagine. Cigarettes? Tanning advice? Linda's garnered quite a few autograph requests since her Pennywhistle victory but most of the pen-wielding ruffians sport rattails, not Louis Vuitton bags. Bamboozled, I scurry on.

For all her glamour, Della seems like exactly the kind of person Dean Jackson warned against me becoming. Well spoken, but snooty. Like she's never worn a yard of gingham or danced in the shape of a square. While we waited for our turn at the registration table I saw her getting snippy with Doozy, Elma's niece. Fresh-faced on account of her new nose, Doozy was only trying to offer her compliments of Della's rendition of "Mary, Did You Know?" when the soprano laughed her off.

"Tweet, tweet," she snickered. "Get lost."

Doozy's face drooped like her old nose. Poor thing. I'd have hugged her, but we got called up for our turn right then. Come to think of it, what the hell is Della doing working at the Chickie Shak anyway? Probably claims it's for shits and giggles when in reality that big ugly purse cost her two months' wages. Seems to me it's far too easy to become a villain in your own life.

THE MOMENT I'M past the hotel and on the street, I feel the shift in the air. Trouble weather. Tornado warning? Or maybe it's just the feeling that my world is changing fast. The river's getting wider, the waves stronger. I might just drift all the way to the Gulf if I'm not careful.

It reminds me of my first day on campus. Mamma and Daddy spent a couple nights at the Opryland hotel reliving their honeymoon while I gathered up my school supplies and looked for an apartment. On the one hand I wanted them to trail me like a poodle to all the new places, but on the other, it felt important to shuck a few cobs on my own. After spending twenty minutes looking at a campus map upside down, I finally made it to the student center to collect my ID. Much like Dollywood, Vandy had a gatekeeper. In this case it was a middle-aged woman at the front desk wearing pearl earrings like it was church or the Derby. Well I'll be, I thought, I'm gonna have to get my ears pierced. And there it was again, that feeling I'd shouldered since the moment I got in. That I'd somehow bamboozled my way onto a campus meant for giants. That I'd somehow lied.

The only person who could set me straight when I got to thinking these ugly thoughts was Daddy. After his mamma passed, he started seeing a therapist out in Dimehorn. Mind you, to the town of Pennywhistle a big strapping guy like Daddy taking the time to sort out his feelings with a shrink seemed about as cuckoo as a beauty queen changing her tires with a fresh manicure. What on earth was he thinking? Oh, they had some big laughs, the boys down at the motor pool. Snickering at the Mountain Dew watering hole, they'd taunt Daddy every time he stopped by. Day after day, joke after joke, until he finally shut them down.

"Hey Earl," said Texaco Dunny, "I'm a shrink. Tell me how it feels to have such a tiny wiener."

Now, Daddy could have paid for his motor oil and gone on his merry way. He also could have shoved old Texaco Dunny into a pile of hubcaps. Instead, he used his trademark Earl Spoon generosity to part the sea of ne'er-do-wells.

"Texaco, when you saw a doctor about your skin cancer I never questioned the size of your pecker. I prayed for you is what I did. Carl, when you showed up at my door with gallstones I took you straight to the ER, no questions asked. Why's it so different when I tell you I need a little help with my heart?"

Chastened, the fellas grew quiet. Daddy continued.

"I ain't afraid to say I miss my mamma. I miss her like crazy. And I'm not gonna spend the rest of my life feeling like somebody washed my insides out with a power hose just because I might be called a sissy by the likes of you."

I don't guess anybody had ever spoken to the boys like that before. At least not since they were little, but like Mamma always says, you're never too grown-up for a good old-fashioned talking-to. Texaco stepped forward and held his baseball cap in his hands. Bashful, like you do when Carrie Underwood sings the national anthem.

"My apologies, Earl. Seems like I got a few heart problems to sort out m'self."

"His name's George Hawk," Daddy said, handing over the therapist's business card. "Anybody else?"

By five o'clock George Hawk had more clients than you could shake a stick at.

All this to say, when I told Daddy how making it big could sometimes make me feel small, he knew exactly what to say. He patted the adjacent beanbag and set me straight.

"Young, old, rich, poor. Everybody gets scared when they's starting something new. First time I rode a horse I hurled all over your uncle Sal. Thing is, I really, really wanted to ride in the rodeo when I grew up. That's how I learned you can be brave and scared at the same time."

That whole summer before I left we went over it again and again. Daddy treated my fears like honored guests and, when they'd outstayed their welcome, he helped me kick their keisters to the curb.

As the woman at the student center looked up from her computer I tried to remember the whole brave and scared thing.

"Name?"

"PJ Spoon."

The way she looked at me made me wish my last name were a little more ordinary like Brown or a little more sophisticated like Croissant. She probably had my whole transcript laid out in front of her on that little screen, every accomplishment and stumble in one tidy document. My summa cum laude degree from U of M, my junior year suspension from Pennywhistle High for sneaking out of class with Lee Ray to catch the *Raccoon King of Raisin Lagoon* premier in Memphis. Hell, it probably listed my weight and my credit score.

"Stand with your feet on the X and look straight at the camera."

I shuffled over.

"A little to the left."

"Okay."

"Miss Spoon."

"Yes?"

"You made it this far. You can relax now."

HOW ABOUT NOW? I think, walking the same paths, smelling the same magnolias. The squirrels still leap from the trash cans with reckless abandon and the monkey grass still sways, steadfast, in the summer wind. Things are familiar, but foggy. Like my life's been cling-wrapped in the fridge since I left it. All it would take to lift the film is one person I know waving across the trees to ask which classes I'm taking. Or maybe if I spotted Frank, my favorite custodian, who knits beanies for his grandchildren, I could pretend I never left.

But I did leave. I gave up my spot on the sidewalk, my wave, my squirrels. It feels important to let that information sink in.

I take my time on the stairs.

"Can I help you?"

Dean Jackson's receptionist has clearly never seen a Reba for Dillard's ensemble by the looks of her drab blazer and dry expression. Not a rhinestone in sight.

"It's PJ Spoon. I'm here to see the dean."

"You've got about twenty minutes before he heads to his tailgate," she says, checking her watch. "Preseason. They all go a little crazy."

"Right."

"I'll let him know you're here. You can have a seat."

I make my way to a black-and-gold armchair and glance around to see if any of my classmates are similarly situated, stray dogs come home and hoping for forgiveness. That's when I notice a skinny old lady with Reba-red hair.

"Mamma?"

"That's my name. Don't wear it out."

She fans herself with a campus map. Kirkland Hall grazes her ear, Dudley Field, her neck.

"How long you been here?"

A jaunty wave to the receptionist.

"Been sitting here just about all morning."

"Is that right?"

"Finished a whole crossword," she says, flashing the *New York Times.* "Couldn't make it through the sudoku, though. Never can tell what the numbers mean."

"Where'd you tie up the horse?"

She gestures to a nice-looking fella studying the vending machine offerings.

"My boyfriend, Eddie, drove me."

"Boyfriend, right," I say quietly. "He knows how to park without hitting the gnomes."

She holds my hand, squeezes tight.

"You are just like your daddy, you know that? Never miss a damn thing unless it's right under your sniffer."

Boyfriend Eddie looks like he might play the postman on a children's show. Curly hair that's more salt than pepper. Soft brown eyes that match his skin. He's taller than Daddy, skinnier, too, and while he's never brought me mail, he has a quality about him that feels familiar.

"Ain't you gonna grill me?" Mamma asks. "You'd be more than welcome to."

"Hold on. I'm struggling to find the male equivalent of 'rack or can.'"

Mamma smiles and looks back at Eddie, who's still doing battle with the vending machine.

"'Can' works."

I pause. Nice as he looks, there's still a tightness in my chest. Be supportive! Be supportive! Best I can muster is a half smile. If Mamma starts sharing a toothbrush with Eddie, it means Daddy will never meet her at the sink again. When people die, you know this kind of thing on the surface—of course Daddy's done with his brushing days—but they still manage to up and surprise you. Mamma letting herself be loved again seems impossible. Then again, here I am, sharing eggs with Boof, singing her songs, falling asleep in her arms like my heart's never been broken.

"I know this ain't easy to take in, sugar," Mamma says, "but it's a good thing. I promise."

"Where, um, where did you meet?"

"Grief support group. He lost his wife a few years back. Apparently, she was just as big of a pain in the ass as me, hence the attraction."

"Just don't forget about Daddy, okay?"

"Oh, honey, how could I?" she says, pulling his ashes from her purse. "He's good luck."

"That he is."

"Thought maybe after the pageant we could sneak him into the Goo Goo factory."

"Mamma, that is downright unsanitary," I say, shaking the little white potato hand.

A sad smile, a plastic hand. I reckon both of us are remembering the way we shook the Ziploc remains of Daddy into the potato one night when we couldn't bear to see him through the plastic anymore. A few scoops got lost in the carpet and I'm pretty sure a speck or two ended up in our oatmeal the next day, but at least it felt like he had a home. Mamma even bought herself a Mrs. Potato Head, "for when the time comes."

I returned it, loath to believe I could lose two parents in a lifetime.

"Never did thank you for coming back for me," Mamma says.

"Well, I never thanked you for coaching the Bee Stings. Or sewing my clothes. Or doing all the other things you did."

She tuts.

"That's what mammas are for."

"I'm glad I came back."

She cups my face.

"I am, too, sugar. But I think it's about time for you to take this little staycation back on the road."

If I squint hard enough, I can see my old apartment from this window. The would-be singers upstairs cook vats of pasta and practice their scales. The lady across the hall picks up a tambourine in revenge. Even the little birds that flit around the hallways boast a fine melody. Back when it was my everyday, I neglected to take an ear to the orchestra tuning up all around me. My red suede jacket, with its happy tassels, shrugged, unknowing, across my shoulders as I took that life for granted. Just now it occurs to me how much I might want it back. And here's Mamma holding out her hands saying, *Take it, why don't you?*

"Now don't you cry or you'll start me crying. You know this mascara ain't water-park approved."

She wipes my chin with her thumb.

"There we go. There's my purty girl."

I let her linger there. They say at some point your mamma sets you down and never does pick you up again, but I reckon the same thing could be said in reverse. One day I stopped letting Mamma brush my hair and button my shirts. Hell, I even scorned her PB&Js after the sixth grade. Seems awfully foolish now.

"I've got something for you," I say, reaching for my bag. "I've only been working on it for a few days, so it's not all the way done, but I think it's pretty . . . well, see for yourself."

Mamma thumbs through the binder.

"This looks real nice, sugar, but ain't you a little too old for book reports?"

"No, no. These are all the counties that have gotten their tampon taxes repealed. See the tabs? They each used different strategies, but I think there's enough here for us to work with."

"Where did you . . . ?" she tries.

"Mrs. Heller."

"That old coot." She smiles. "Always had a soft spot for historians."

"I really want to help. I think we can take what's in here and build a case. That is, if the Hog Club will have me."

Mamma considers this.

"Well, you'll have to pass the initiation ceremony. How many gallons of butter do you reckon you can drink in a minute?"

"No gallons. Not a one."

"Alrighty, then. Bacon grease it is."

Before I can protest, the receptionist calls my name and says the big man's ready for me. I'm old enough to know she doesn't mean Santa but desperate enough to hope. Mamma squeezes me a little tighter.

"Go on. We'll see you tonight."

"Will you be in the front row?"

"Never left."

As I stand, more tears well up in my eyes like broken toilets. I mop them as best I can. I'm no Doodle Barnum.

"Eddie, she made it," Mamma yells. "We can go to the museum now."

His pork rinds finally make it to the bottom of the vending machine.

"Somebody's got a type." I wink.

"Oh, hush."

She shoos me toward the door.

And just like that I'm on my own.

IT STRIKES ME as I walk in that I've never actually been to Dean Jackson's office. We've sampled all of Nashville's finest breakfast eateries—Noshville, Le Peep, the Loveless Cafe—but never so much as mentioned the little cave where he writes reports and sends his weekly newsletter. I'm not sure what I expected. A fern? Some bookends? Instead, the wood-paneled nook boasts not one, not two, not even three taxidermied raccoons, but a whole football team. Really. Fitted with miniature jerseys, they await passes, score touchdowns. I'm not sure whether this is a good omen or a terrible disregard for my beloved woodland rascal.

"What a fantastic collection." I smile.

Been so long since I've seen him I almost forgot what he looks like. Trim in the legs and hefty in the middle. His khakis wrinkle around his knees like a paper bag does a Slim Jim, meanwhile his football jersey holds on to his gut for dear life. If it weren't for the racoons, you might pin him as the kind of fella with a money clip and a secret family. Somehow, I doubt someone with his taxidermy prowess would bother with a mistress.

"A man's got to have hobbies, PJ," he explains. "So many gentlemen my age think sitting around watching the golf channel counts as a raison d'être. Pains me."

I find what appears to be the raccoon quarterback. And, poking out from a collection of romantic novels, his lipsticked raccoon sweetheart. Letterman jacket and all.

"They're beautiful."

"Thank you kindly." He beams.

"The raccoon is the Tennessee state animal."

"Bingo! Not a lot of people know that. Then again, that's exactly why you're in this department. Or are you? Have a seat."

Suddenly I'd rather be a stuffed quarterback with mismatched glass eyes.

"How are you, PJ? I must admit I've missed our brunches enormously."

"Me too."

"There's a new spot on Twelve South that everyone in the department has been raving about. A full eggs Benedict menu. Can you imagine?"

"I love a good eggs Benny."

"I know you do."

Guilt soaks me straight through from my scalp to my socks. And yet, Dean Jackson smiles like I've never done him wrong.

"Sir, I really appreciate everything you've done for me," I say. "The waiting. Holding my spot. I reckon I don't even deserve another chance, but I thought maybe if I came here and went to the hearing I could try to explain what's been going on."

He cuts me off.

"If you're looking for a stern talking-to, you're not going to find it in this office."

"Sir?"

"Register for your classes. Check in with your advisor. Turn things in on time."

"I don't understand. What about the hearing?"

Dean Jackson pets the raccoon wide receiver. One of the critter's eyes pops out. He shrugs like his beloveds lose sight all the time and snaps the eyeball back in without looking. It takes a certain level of comfort not to fuss at that sort of thing.

"You'll excuse me for pulling the wool over your eyes just this once," he says gently.

Realization sets in like a cat in a lap.

"There's no hearing, is there?"

"No."

"Then why . . ."

"It started as a little white lie, a last resort. When you cut me off the other day I thought we'd lost you for good. So, I called your emergency contact. Your mother is an absolute delight. She told me all about the pageant."

"Jesus Christ."

"Hot chicken! What a bizarre and delightful ritual. You, my dear, are part of a living history. I'm fascinated with the whole thing. We probably talked for an hour."

"I'll have you know my participation was mandatory."

"The best challenges always are."

He checks his watch and closes his laptop.

"Tailgate," he explains.

I wonder where those raccoons are, the ones with little red Solo cups and chests painted to spell out *Go, Vandy!*

"To be clear, you're letting me off the hook because you talked with my mamma and now you think I can win the pageant?"

"Of course not. Frankly, I'm rooting for Linda."

"Everybody is."

"I'm not 'letting you off the hook,' as you say. On the contrary, I have been led to believe over the course of our many wonderful brunches and through your mother's stories that you have vast potential to succeed here."

He rubs the nose of the tight end and makes for the door.

"Now get that banjo, slap on some sequins, and make the university proud."

"Wait!"

He pauses. Once again, I marvel at everyone's ability to be patient with me. Feels like the time to pay them all back.

"I had a whole speech written out for the hearing, you know. If you don't mind, I'd like to share it."

"Of course." He turns the light back on. "We'll call it the interview portion. Esteemed colleagues, Miss PJ Spoon."

The raccoons await my confession. The raccoons seal my fate.

I clear my throat.

"First of all, I would like to thank you for bearing with me as I took the time to honor my father's death. As anyone who studies history knows, honor is a powerful motivator. It inspires great rulers, gruesome battles, and ordinary people, too. Seems pretty lofty when you put it like that, though. Right?"

Dean Jackson nods.

"I think I like what Socrates wrote best. 'The greatest way to live with honor in this world is to be what we pretend to be.' Basically, he means honor is about showing up even when you're scared shitless, if you'll pardon my French. I may be a little nobody from a little nobody town, but moving forward with my degree is the best way I know how to honor the legacy of my father. To fake it until I make it. And maybe in doing so I can bestow a little honor on my hometown, too. Pennywhistle's just a tiny corner of Tennessee famous for its nuclear water and its haunted post office. But, as all the world now knows, it's famous for its hot chickens, too. If you'll do me the honor of letting me stay, I will try to push past my fears and make everyone from here to Critter County proud. Thank you."

I scribbled the speech down on the back of our Loretta's Half Moon Diner receipt this morning in the murky dawn before Boof woke up. Part of me wishes I'd come to the words sooner, not spent so long shaking in my boots. But then I never would have met Boof. Or Mr. Puddin. Or even Linda. I would have remained an old version of myself, perhaps one who didn't quite believe she deserved to be at school at all.

Dean Jackson shakes my hand and pulls me in for a hug.

"I think I speak for the entire committee when I say welcome back."

As he ushers me out, hell-bent on making it to his tailgate on time, I swear I catch a whiff of pork rinds. And is it just me, or did one of those raccoons just wink?

RELIEVED, I START walking. Past the Smoothie King and the flower shop, the funeral home and the Parthenon. By the time I realize where I am, the key's already in my hand. It's not the same as it was—the girl who rented out my place mailed back my red tasseled coat and covered the apartment with the kind of plants that beget beetles—but I'm not here for my apartment. No, my destination lies one floor up.

A woman with a toddler on her hip answers the door.

"Can I help you?"

"I'm sorry, I was looking for Carlos and Rick."

"They moved out in March."

"Oh."

I'm strangely sad to find this vestige of my old life gone, like driving past your old church come to find it's a Quiznos. Did they give up? I wonder. Go back to Wisconsin and shovel snow for their parents? Before I can wonder too hard, the door behind us creaks open to reveal a woman in a long purple muumuu. Something about the nightgown screams cough drops, crime novels. The cockatiel on her shoulder's just gravy.

"Those noisy idiots"—she groans—"finally wrote a song that doesn't irritate my birds and then poof, they're gone. Signed a deal with Big Machine."

"They did?"

She nods.

"That's great! What's the song called?"

"I can't remember."

"Who sings it?"

"James Dean Mustache, something like that."

"Kacey Musgraves?"

The cockatiel pecks at her ears as she shrugs. Meanwhile, the little girl on her mother's hip begins to wiggle.

"Excuse us. Somebody's learning to use the big-girl potty."

The toddler shakes her head vigorously. No siree bob.

"You can do it," I tell her.

"Hey, aren't you in the Chickie Shak pageant?" the old woman asks.

The bird bobs in recognition.

"Yes. Yes, I am."

"Good luck. If Carlos and Rick can make it, anybody can."

Waving goodbye, I feel, for the first time in a while, a little more hot than chicken.

JUST BEFORE I reach the hotel, Lee Ray's number lights up my phone. I plug one ear so I can hear him over the buskers. Between the honky-tonks and the actual honks, they have to play pretty damn loud to make a dent. Feathers in their hair, jeans painted on tight. Some are so talented you wanna take a picture with them before they get famous. Others really ought to head back to Pasquo.

"Where are you? I thought you said you'd have no service."

"We made it to New Orlee!"

I spit out my Goo Goo.

"You made it all the way to New Orleans? In a canoe?"

"No, no. New *Orlee*. It's about a hundred miles south. But it has the biggest Bass Pro Shop I've ever seen. And an Olive Garden. The EFPs are delighted."

I can just see him now, leaning up against a taxidermied fish while a gaggle of geriatric rascals tear through the aisles in search of bait and booty.

"We met the New Orlee fishing group. We're going to start an alliance. A network of Elderly Fisherpeople from here to the gulf. Big things are happening, PJ. I've already emailed a few grant applications for a permanent structure in Pennywhistle. We're going to be the hub of culture!"

"That's fantastic."

"Promise me you'll come back and visit?"

"Oh, Lee Ray."

My voice cracks just like Meemaw's stage makeup used to, a few small rifts and then one big canyon down the middle. Lee Ray will be the hardest to leave behind. When we were kids I wouldn't even go to the dentist without him. He'd stand on the other side of the chair and narrate everything. Made it funny, too. *PJ, I swear if Dr. Jessica taps on your left back molar one more time she's gonna break it. Bite her if she does it again.*

"I'm so proud to know you," I say.

It's not enough. Nothing could be enough.

"Nobody's dying here," he says gently. "Just coming alive is all. Listen, we'll be watching from the lobby of the Holiday Inn tonight, so please remember what I told you."

"Kitten heels are the devil's toothpicks?"

"Have fun. Give 'em hell. And check the trunk."

"You didn't."

"Of course I did."

In the background I can hear the Loosahatchie River lapping at the canoes. The sound recalls Lee Ray's tenth-grade rendition of *The Odyssey*. No stage, just a river. The talent bobbed between the waves, waiting, as the mammas lined up on the shore to unfold their beach chairs. It was already sticky hot by then. Late May or early June. They fanned themselves with the programs we'd stayed up all night folding and watched as, clad in tankinis and swim trunks, we performed an epic. How on earth did Lee Ray imagine such a staging? And why did we agree to it? I will never stop admiring the way whole worlds spring up around that boy.

"You're the one who should be onstage, Lee Ray."

"PJ."

"Really, you could speed up here and play my banjo."

"I would," he says, his voice warm with sun, "but I think we both know you're not an understudy anymore."

DOGGONE TROUBLE

The lobby is empty when I arrive, save for a few employees doing their best to gussy it back up after the carnival of contestants. Half-eaten cinnamon rolls sugar the seating area. Traces of lipstick smooch empty coffee mugs. And Boof sits on a love seat rubbing Linda's back.

"What's wrong?"

"That damn Nashville girl took my dogs."

"Della Blue? The one with the fancy purse?"

"She was asking me about them. Kissing my shitter, you know. I got to talking about my routine and next thing you know she called over the damn bellhop."

"So?"

"So apparently this ain't no dog-friendly hotel."

"I thought the 'no dogs or Yankees' sign was a joke. Like the ones in Cracker Barrel and Senator First's office."

Linda shakes her head.

"Della turned 'em loose," Boof explains.

"It's not safe out there," I gasp. "There are bachelorette parties every damn block. They'll slap a bandanna on Easter Bonnet and take her to Bonnaroo the first chance they get."

"Not helping," Boof whispers.

"I'm sure they wouldn't bother taking Brawny. So, that's something."

They share a look of scorn so genetic it might as well be left-handedness or buckteeth. It's kind of nice to see them bond. This morning I asked Boof how things were going and she said pretty peachy. She and Linda are planning on having dinner with Beans over Labor Day. Boof and Beans's parents, too. A regular family reunion, minus the paternity reveal and the greased watermelon, of course. I reckon all that would be slightly spoiled by an empty doghouse and a pile of leashes with nobody attached. Hell, I'm bummed when my strays don't show up for Sunday dinner. Can't imagine the emotional pull of dogs who actually sleep inside.

"What am I supposed to tell Buck? He already started working on their Christmas present."

What in God's pockets do you give a dog for Christmas? I wonder. Boof's as puzzled as me. She wrinkles her nose and continues rubbing Linda's back.

"There, there."

"Let me call Mamma," I say. "She and her boyfriend—that's right, *boyfriend*—are here to see the show. Maybe she can help us look."

I give Mamma the rundown. We don't have much time for a miracle, I tell her. Just five hours till dress rehearsal. She says she might can pull it off.

"Are they microchipped?" I ask hopefully.

Linda scoffs through her weepy drool.

"So's the government can find 'em and steal all their information? I don't think so, honey."

"Dammit, Linda. What information does a dog have?"

Glancing across the mustard-brown carpet, my eyes catch on a vending machine. Little hotel of Ding Dongs and Frito-Lays. Bethlehem of Baby Ruths. Cream filling won't get the job done, but suddenly I know what will. I whistle for the ratty junior manager in flip-flops. Cody?

Corky? His braces glitter with possibility as he looks up, scratches his crotch, and says, "What?"

"Where's the nearest Piggly Wiggly?"

I SHAKE MY can of I-Believe-It's-Not-Cheese with gusto. Haven't practiced my cursive since before my rack came in, but I figure it's time to dust off the old curly q's, if only in the name of a bona fide pooch rescue. The first hour of this was fun. The second, okay. Now it's just bleak, the three of us squatted down next to my car in the hotel parking lot dribbling nonsense. We're at the end of our supply, only a few ounces of orange left.

Pennywhistle was here, I write in not-cheese.

Babies, come home, Linda adds.

Boof attempts a smiley face that looks more like a colon. Thank goodness she can sing.

"Y'all go on," Linda says. "No reason for all of us to forfeit."

I can feel her hussy upper sag with the weight of defeat and double D's. Breaks my heart.

"We could always come back after dress rehearsal and see if they found their way back."

"I'm not taking that chance," Linda says quietly. "Why do you think I never moved out of Pennywhistle?"

A few blocks over, a busker strums the first few notes of Patsy Cline's "Crazy." Say what you will about country music, but, I tell you what, country's got songs for moments like this: when hot, fake cheese is melting "I love you" onto the pavement and your babies are God knows where and your fake eyelashes are all the way down to your chin. I clear my throat and start to sing.

Boof grins. I remember the way she looked that first day we walked to the bus stop together—cuter than a piglet in jorts—and how possible everything felt. Now she takes my hand and starts to sing. It's a song about loving somebody in spite of the fear, in spite of the fact that they could up and leave. I think we can all relate.

I nudge Linda. She's still the woman who stabbed me with a bubblegum-pink nail not too long ago. Also, a mamma. As she joins in, a teardrop brings what's left of her false eyelashes all the way down to the pavement. Maybe we're crazy for loving one another, but what else can we do?

We sing the last line in three-part harmony.

Six, if you count the dogs.

HOT CHICKEN

Brawny, Easter Bonnet, and Gator bound up to us followed by Mamma, her new boyfriend, and half the town of Pennywhistle. She's wearing her Saturday-night bingo ensemble—skinny jeans and a Wild Birds Unlimited sweatshirt casinoed with gems from the Kirstie Alley Sparkle 'n' Shine 3,000.

"What in the world?"

Bewildered, I pull Mamma in for a hug.

"Tell me you didn't hold up the Greyhound bus," I whisper.

"I'm starting to think I let you watch too many Westerns as a youngin."

"Just enough, ma'am," Boof interjects.

Mamma whistles through her gap. Lassos Boof in for a hug.

"Shoo-ee, if it ain't the future Mrs. PJ Spoon! Nice to see you again, sugar."

"MAMMA!"

"I'm not saying you's the man, PJ. It's just we already got the best last name in town so Boof might as well take it."

"Really nice to see you, too."

"She's so purty up close," Mamma remarks to me like I don't already know, then, warmly, "And her can is even bigger than I expected."

"Don't worry, Boof. We're euthanizing her soon."

"Are not."

"Lee Ray's got the Horse Creek Mortuary College on speed-dial."

"Then you'll just have to wait until he gets back from New Orlee to do me in. Anyhow, as I was saying, once I got the Bat Signal from you I made a few calls. Next thing you know, Peep and Nina got Senator First on the phone and asked him to charter a bus for sixty of your biggest fans."

"To which he said, 'Who the hell are you and how'd you get this number?'"

"Hardly. Let's just say he's one of their best customers. Might even be Peep's daddy, but that's a whole 'nother dachshund of worms."

The dogs lick Linda's makeup off until she's all jowls and no eyebrows.

"How'd you find them?" she asks.

"We split up the downtown area. A regular Scooby-Doo situation," Mamma explains. "Found the little critters trying to board a catfish boat."

"They go fishing with Buck every Sunday. Must have recognized the smell."

"Is he an EFP?" I ask.

"My husband ain't no E."

"Neither is Lee Ray."

"Point took."

We've accumulated quite a crowd at this point. Horse Wilson, Tommy Robertson, and Jesse Dupree adjust their newly acquired souvenirs, god-awful parrot T-shirts from the Margaritaville store on Lower Broad. Closest they've ever come to Jimmy Buffett is Sponge Cake Saturday at the Piggly Wiggly. Must be nice soaking in the real thing.

"This place takes me right back to your daddy's bachelor party." Horse chuckles. "I betcha you ain't never heard that story."

"And she ain't never gonna did," Mamma chastens. "You girls better go on and get or pretty soon that dog snatcher gon' start writing her victory speech."

"Yes, ma'am," Boof agrees.

Mamma gives her a jovial slap on the back.

"We can talk about the wedding details later."

"Writing your obituary," I respond.

"She always did have a way with words," Mamma tells Eddie, who gives a soft laugh and a crinkled smile.

"We didn't get a chance to meet properly. Eddie Davidson. Big fan of your mamma."

He offers his hand. I could go all in and wrap him in a bear hug, but he seems to understand I'm not quite ready for that. Instead, he gestures to the hotel, where a HOT CHICKEN banner flaps in the summer breeze.

"This pageant thing, it's been kinda fun to see. My late wife was always trying to get me to watch *Miss America* with her. She'd be glued to it every year. Popcorn and everything. I watched one or two here and there. Always thought the competition was a little mumbo jumbo, if you know what I mean. Is it corny to say I'm a devoted viewer now?"

"Not at all."

Somewhere in Horse Creek, Eddie has his own Horse Wilson, his own Peep and Nina, his own well of grief. I appreciate the way he offers it up, gentle-like. I ask if he's ever visited the Chickie Shak.

"Can't say that I have. Never spent much time in Pennywhistle outside your mamma's screened-in porch."

"Who in the hell's your dentist, then?" Jesse Dupree asks.

"Uh, Jean Crafton?"

"No, no, no," Jesse protests, lofting an arm around Eddie's shoulders. "You gotta switch to our Bobby Jennifer. She can fix that gray-lookin' canine lickety-split. Be like you never smoked at all."

"I didn't smoke."

"That's what I'm saying."

It's early yet for Eddie. He's just getting his footing when it comes to our extended Pennywhistle family, but like a toddler does a Rubik's Cube, he'll figure it out eventually.

TWO CANS OF hairspray and one pep talk later, we find ourselves backstage. We're supposed to stay in the holding pen and watch the show on a TV the size of a toenail, but the three of us sneak out and peer out through the wings anyway. A stagehand approaches. Not as pimply and dimpled as the ones from our Pennywhistle shows but still wearing that all-black uniform and snooty little headset that says *I'm in charge.* I nudge Linda, our resident shit talker, to fire up for a standoff, but turns out the lady only wants to wish us luck. Come up a cloud! Notorious EFP Asberry Judd is her great-uncle. She asks if he's still up to no good.

"The best no good there is, fishing with Lee Ray."

Oh, she's heard all about him. The lifeblood of Pennywhistle's elderly community and, apparently, the only one willing to slip condoms under the doors of their rooms. Leave it to Lee Ray to plug boats as well as he rows them.

The stagehand perks her head up and bids us adieu. As they say, it's showtime.

Mr. Puddin melts onstage in one hot bounce. He's sporting his usual purple. And is it just me or is that a new chin? For a man who's mostly pig cadaver at this point, he sure seems alive, prancing this way and that with a big, white smile. I wonder what he was doing all this time. Maybe he was waiting, like all of us, for something new to come along. And then, one day, he up and decided to make it.

"Ladies and gentlemen," he caws, "cupcakes and stud muffins, ruffles and rifles, welcome to the first annual Chickie Shak Hot Chicken Beauty Tour Finals!"

The auditorium roars with applause, silver spurs. I swear somebody's even got a tambourine. Mr. Puddin sways across the stage, ensuring every sequin on his tuxedo catches the light. He kicks one white boot up all the way to his can, a technicolor cheerleader with a taut rubber chin. Somebody whistles.

"What began as a nightmare I had in my hot tub has grown into a fabulous competition, an event exceeding all my wildest dreams. We have with us here tonight forty-five contestants from all across the South. And two from New Jersey." He waves to the cautious Northerners in the fifth row. "Bless your hearts. Each little lady will have but two minutes to impress the judges with her talent tonight. Let's meet the folks with the hardest job in the world aside from mine: our judges!"

Reese Witherspoon and Emmens Clementine take to the stage. A veritable who's-who of Southern culture. Reese, Nashville sweetheart and Hollywood star, and Emmens, greatest living Southern YA fantasy novelist. After so many years of devouring his books, seeing him in real life makes a Jell-O mold of me. Emmens Clementine! Here! Within spittin' distance! Despite the heat, he wears his famous turtleneck. It makes a mockery of every other turtleneck, every other author. Every piece of magic that isn't performed by a raccoon. My knees begin to buckle.

"Hey," Boof says, steadying me, "it's your buddy."

"You recognize him?"

"Duh. His picture's on the back cover."

I turn, delighted. She grins.

"What do you think I've been up to this past week, PJ? Missing you and reading about that damn Raccoon King. I'm on book three."

Emmens and Reese wave politely and take their seats. Hard to imagine the judge recruiting process. Was Reese walking to an important meeting downtown when Mr. Puddin descended on her like a webbed foot? Was Emmens en route to the monocle store when a hundred-dollar bill on a string crossed his path? Nevertheless, they sit poised for what radio stations across the country are calling "a hell of a dog show."

Mr. Puddin taps the mic.

"For one million dollars and free Chickie Shak for life, let the competition begin!"

ONE GIRL WRESTLES weasels. Another threads eyebrows. A seventy-five-year-old plays "Rocky Top" on a pan flute made of Coors Light bottles. Then there's a string of tap dancers and ventriloquists I could have lived without. A magician pulls an armadillo from Reese Witherspoon's ear. General confusion ensues when it runs offstage toward the exit. Needless to say, the competition's hot.

"Good luck out there, ladies," Della Blue coos as she walks offstage. "I know it must be so overwhelming to be so far from your little shoebox. If you embarrass yourself out there, just remember: they'll probably only show the rerun a few times."

"Eat balls, you twig-pussied, no-good, inbred, spoiled brat wig," Linda spits.

Now this is the Linda we know and love. Gator lifts a leg on Della's purse.

"Vermin! Absolute vermin!"

"That's not what the American Kennel Club called him."

Della storms off. Truth be told, her rendition of "Ave Maria" was only just all right.

BOOF AND I watch as Linda and the dogs take the stage. The crowd glitters with applause at the very sight of her. They are, as the shirts say, unabashedly horny for Linda. I can just make out Buck in the front row. Daddy too.

What do we think of Eddie? I ask.

The potato stares back.

Daddy?

Daddy, quit playing. I know you're here.

Did he make it to heaven? Or at least to Dollywood? We should have put a lock on that potato, dammit.

Daddy, come back. I'll wear my Easter dress more often. I'll catch up on your World War II documentaries. I'll even drive Mamma to Memphis so she can get that skin tag looked at.

Still nothing, just Mamma cheering and Boof holding my waist and Linda throwing dogs through flaming Hula-Hoops and the whole town cheering their lungs out across the auditorium. Which, I suppose, is quite a lot of good things in one room. Hell, even Emmens Clementine is here. Tipped his hat to me after our song.

I'm not ready.

He doesn't say, *Come on, sugar.* Or, *Yes, you are.*

But there, leaning against the backstage exit, is my bike.

EPILOGUE

Pennywhistle Psst:
Hot Chicken Queen Serves Up Surprises

Pennywhistle's very own Linda Carter Creel reigns victorious as the first ever Chickie Shak Hot Chicken Queen. Mrs. Creel won the hearts and votes of America with her show-stoppin', dog-spangled rendition of "9 to 5." As for how she plans to spend her million-dollar prize, Mrs. Creel says, "I got big plans." While she was tight-lipped and, in her words, "My ass is tight, too. Write that down!" about the details, word on the street is that she intends to build Pennywhistle's first Karaoke Bar/Teen Pregnancy Resource Center.

The last such establishment, the Blessing House, was condemned in August 1999 for its unorthodox adoption policies and, as Creel puts it, "ass-backward morals." The new facility will feature a GED program, a job center, and all of Alan Jackson's best tracks.

Moonshine Records Weekly:
Kidston Ain't Kidding When It Comes to Hits

We're delighted to welcome staff songwriter Boof Kidston to the Moonshine family. Kidston has already received critical acclaim for penning Miranda Lambert's latest single, "Mamma's Two Left Feet." Five weeks on *Billboard's* top ten country charts ain't too shabby. Look out for

Kidston's latest credits, "Treehouse Midnights" and "The Real Lonestar Lindsey," coming out later this month. And if you see her in the break room, be sure to say hello!

Hog Herald:
Snipping the String on Pennywhistle's Tampon Tax

Shoo-ee and praise the Lord! After last weekend's coup, the tampon tax will finally be lifted for good. Take that, you good ole boys! It's just like the Founding Mothers said, "There can be no taxation on our menstruation." Big thanks to Dottie Spoon for her megaphone and to her daughter, PJ, for bringing in all that fancy research to back us up. From now on we bleed tax-free!

Asberry's EFP Newsletter:
Please Bring a Shovel or a Big Stick

Lee Ray says I have to run this by him before I get my niece to print it out at the library but she's busy, so here goes. Saturday is a dandy day to be an Elderly Fisherperson. We're finally breaking ground on Trout Tower and we need your help. Bring a shovel or a big stick to 21 Rufus Street and get ready to dig. If you got a bad back, bring a snack to share with the folks who's actually helping. WL5 Memphis News says they might come out and do a story on us but only if nobody takes their clothes off this time. So keep your damn britches on and join us this Saturday for a digging extravaganza. Bones and coins are finders keepers, losers weepers.

A SPECIAL INVITATION FROM
THE PENNYWHISTLE PUBLIC LIBRARY

You are cordially invited to celebrate the graduation of
Pennywhistle's Jewel Spoon, PhD
Attire: Fancy
Rhinestones: Recommended
RSVP to Mrs. Joan Heller, 211 Harpeth Way
Copies of PJ's dissertation will be available upon request
If you're real nice, she might even sign 'em

The Raccoon King of Lake Tomorrow (**Page 552**)

*High in the sycamore tree, the Raccoon King and Lady Mink watched
the sun set over the lake. They passed a banana back and forth until
there was nothing left to do but slurp down the peel. Below, the Chef
Boyardee cans in the landfill glowed, a glorious kingdom of scraps.
The Raccoon King felt a sense of calm wash over him the way spaghetti
water used to when he was just a boy. For now, everything was right in
the world.*

*"But won't we get bored of all this happiness after a while?" Lady Mink
asked. "What will we do tomorrow?"*

"Tomorrow we will swim," he said.

"And after that?"

"We'll canoe."

"And after that?"

The Raccoon King pulled Lady Mink close.

"We don't have to worry about that."

"Why not?"

*"Because, my dear, I have a feeling Mr. Clementine will write us a
sequel."*

ACKNOWLEDGMENTS

Thank you to my mom, who has always said, "Somebody becomes a published author! Why not you?" Thank you for running fourteen marathons and showing me what hard work looks like. Thank you for every absurd and delightful Southern phrase in this book. Shoo-ee, I love you, Mom! All my lanyards are for you.

Thank you to my dad, with his trampoline-jumping glee, for showing me how to embrace my weird side. You never missed a game, a tuck-in, or a garage sale. Storyteller, fun spreader, I love you from here all the way to Omeletteville.

Thank you to my sister Corinne, who has always loved me without judgment, who said, "I don't want to miss a thing," and who read the very first draft of this book while on bed rest. Thanks for calling me every thirty minutes to tell me which parts made you laugh.

Thank you to my sister Graham, who both fiercely teases me and fiercely protects me. I look up to you more than you realize. When you like my work, I know it must be good.

Thank you to Bridget for sharing in my joy, for loving me wholly, and for agreeing to be written about for the rest of our lives. You are more than a Dust Buster. You're my favorite redhead and my very best friend.

Thank you to my stepfather, Charles, for the motivation and the math help. Thanks for writing the Quiet Family charter, too.

Thank you to Uncle Robin for teaching me to sparkle. I learned all my best jokes from you.

Thank you to my stepmother, Val, for loving Dad (and all of us hyper Hartongs).

Thank you to Gramma Liz for making the writing life possible and for occasionally answering my letters.

Thank you to my friends, the readers of drafts and comforters of tears. To Casual Thursday and Judge 3 and Team Best Life Plan and Wonder Women and Babes Palace and Wine Group and Aftercare.

Thank you to Jennifer Weinblatt, who said, "You are a writer!" to eleven-year-old me and continues to tell me every year at Starbucks.

Thank you to Janna Bonikowski for believing in this book in its zany, raw state and helping me shape it into something better.

Thank you to Rachel Kahan for always being a delight and a cheerleader. And for using exclamation points in your emails!

Thank you to the Knight Agency and William Morrow for taking a chance on me.

Thank you to Harding Academy, Harpeth Hall, Dartmouth, Fulbright, and UCC for the excellent education. Thanks to Harpeth Hall in particular for challenging me to raise my hand, work as hard as I could, and stand on the shoulders of the women who came before me.

Thank you to my Harpeth Hall Aftercare kiddos for all the fun (and fashion intel) you provide daily. As you would say, "It's giving . . . supportive."

Last but not least, thank you to all the queer people who have worked and are working to make this world a kinder place. When I came out—joyfully, and also with great fear—I recall people saying, "I don't want your life to be harder." I remember thinking, Maybe I'll be part of making it easier. Maybe I'll be part of making it better. My ardent hope is that reading this book will help someone feel a little less lonely. I hope someone comes out to their Southern mamma and uses this book to help her understand. I hope this book proves that queer people are not inherently sad, scared, or doomed. With a hefty helping of self-love and the security of communities that cherish us, we will thrive.

ABOUT THE AUTHOR

Mary Liza Hartong lives and writes in her hometown of Nashville, Tennessee. She graduated from Dartmouth College with a BA in English and women's, gender, and sexuality studies. She also holds an MA from Dartmouth in creative writing and an MA from the University College Cork in British and American Literature via the Fulbright Scholar Program. Mary Liza is the aunt of five boisterous nieces and a proud member of the queer community. When she's not writing, you can find her combing yard sales for treasures with her fiancée, Bridget. *Love and Hot Chicken* is her first novel.